"You are [ ] happy."

The look Rebekah gave him made his pulse quicken. Was this what being in love felt like? If it was, he wanted to feel more of it.

"Now tell me," Henry said, "what else are you fond of? And don't give me an answer you *think* I want to hear."

"I should like to learn more of your work with the council," she said.

"What else?"

"And I would like to learn more about this trial. Did you know that one of the accused conspirators is a woman?"

His heart slammed into his ribs. "Yes."

Of all the things he and his new bride could discuss, she had chosen the one topic he so wished to avoid.

"Oh, listen to me," Rebekah then said. "I'm prattling away… You'll be sorry you ever asked of my interests."

"No, I won't," he said. It was the truth. He wanted to learn her, win her, love her. What he didn't want was for Rebekah to open the paper one morning and find the names of Mary Surratt and John Wilkes Booth listed beside his own.

Shannon Farrington and her husband have been married for over twenty years, have two children, and are active members in their local church and community. When she isn't researching or writing, you can find her visiting national parks and historical sites or at home herding her small flock of chickens through the backyard. She and her family live in Maryland.

Books by Shannon Farrington

Love Inspired Historical

Her Rebel Heart
An Unlikely Union
Second Chance Love
The Reluctant Bridegroom

SHANNON
FARRINGTON

The Reluctant Bridegroom

H HARLEQUIN® LOVE INSPIRED® HISTORICAL
TM

Recycling programs
for this product may
not exist in your area.

LOVE INSPIRED BOOKS

ISBN-13: 978-0-373-28360-6

The Reluctant Bridegroom

www.Harlequin.com

Printed in U.S.A.

There is therefore no condemnation to them which are in Christ Jesus, who walk not after the flesh, but after the Spirit.
—*Romans* 8:1

In memory of Jessica Kathleen

Eye hath not seen, nor ear heard, neither have entered into the heart of man, the things which God hath prepared for them that love Him.
—*1 Corinthians* 2:9

And in honor of my wonderful editor Elizabeth Mazer Without whose patient guidance this story would not have been possible.

Chapter One

❧

Baltimore, Maryland
1865

What is he doing here? He has never visited our home before.

Rebekah Van der Geld watched from her position behind the large oak tree as her father's chief political rival, State Delegate Harold Nash, stepped from the porch and came down the front walk. The graying widower looked quite pleased with himself, as though he had just secured some grand victory.

Few men ever smiled after leaving her father's presence, and yet this particular legislator was whistling happily as he stepped through the front gate and headed up the street. He had just passed her next-door neighbor's home when Fiona, Rebekah's maid, spied her behind the tree.

"There you are, miss," she said. "I've been looking for you! You must hurry! Your father wants ya!"

Rebekah's stomach immediately knotted. She brushed her clothing. "Am I presentable?"

Fiona twirled her about. "There's mud along your back hemline," she said, "but I daresay you haven't time to change. Perhaps he won't notice."

He will notice, Rebekah thought, *and he will be angry*. She knew, though, there was nothing she could do to remedy that now. Her father would be even angrier if she didn't come straightaway.

Resigning herself to the inevitable, Rebekah hurried inside. The door to the study was ajar, but she knocked upon it just the same. She had been told more than once never to step into the room without her father's permission.

"Enter," he commanded.

Drawing a quick breath, Rebekah did so. Her father was standing at the window, hands clasped behind his back. Theodore Van der Geld was not a particularly large man, but his stern voice and iron hand were enough to intimidate most everyone with whom he came in contact, especially his daughter.

Rebekah positioned herself near his desk just so, hoping he would not noticed her soiled dress. "You wished to see me, sir?"

"Indeed," he said without turning around. "The time has come for you to wed."

Wed? The air rushed from Rebekah's lungs. Had she heard him correctly? If she had, then just *whom* was she supposed to marry? She had no suitors, at least none of whom she was aware. No young man had dared come calling for fear of facing her father.

And yet as shocking as this announcement was, deep down she had always known her father would orchestrate her marriage. He had arranged everything else in her life, and every decision he made was filtered through the lens of his own political benefit. Having become a successful state legislator, he now wanted to be governor.

Apparently he is going to hand me over to some well-connected gentleman in order to support his campaign. But whom?

Then she remembered Harold Nash's unprecedented visit, and the smile on his face as he walked away. A sickening feeling swept over her. *Oh no! Surely not!*

The man was more than twice her age, and up until today, her father had despised him. Harold Nash had voted against President Lincoln, had vehemently defended slave owners' rights all throughout last year's constitutional convention and had worked to delay outlawing the detestable practice of slavery for months.

And to be given to such a man! Rebekah feared her knees were going to buckle.

"You will marry Henry Nash," her father announced, turning to judge her reaction.

Henry Nash? Rebekah struggled to process this news. *So I am to be handed over to the delegate's son?* While the man was closer to her age, she felt little relief at the prospect. To marry him was to become not only a wife but immediately a mother, as well. The man had recently taken charge of his two orphaned nieces. Word was their father had fallen in battle while serving the *rebel* army, and their mother had died in childbirth.

None of this makes any sense! Rebekah thought. Why was her father so insistent on this match? Henry Nash had strong ties to the Confederacy, and her father had once called him a *self-serving coward* because he had not held office in the United States Army.

"Father, I don't understand…"

She should have known better than to question him, for the moment she did, Theodore Van der Geld stormed out from behind his desk. His eyes were wide. The veins in his neck were bulging.

"I do not expect you to understand," he shouted. "I expect you to obey! I expect you to do your duty!"

Rebekah immediately lowered her chin, stared at the floor. She dared not raise her eyes. She knew what would happen if she did.

When he spoke again, his voice had softened slightly. It was the same tone he used when addressing a crowd of potential voters. "Your marriage to Henry Nash will take place within the next few weeks," he said. "The ceremony will coincide quite nicely with our nation's victory celebrations."

The long, desperate war between the states was finally drawing to a close. The nation had been preserved, but all Rebekah could think of now was her own impending union. Terror overwhelmed her. Yes, she wished to marry someday. She also wished for children, but most important, she wished for love. How was she to love a man she barely knew?

Please don't make me do this! I don't want to do this! But she knew her father would not listen to her pleas, let alone grant them. He waved her away like a simple servant. "Go to your room."

Rebekah went obediently, knowing that in his mind, the marriage had been firmly decided, and she was powerless to alter his decision. Her only hope was that Henry Nash would somehow change *his* mind.

"You agreed to *what*?" Henry's jaw literally dropped when he heard the news. "You told Theodore Van der

Geld I would marry his daughter? Why on earth would you do such a thing? Why on earth would *he* even suggest it?"

Harold Nash, a shrewd man at best and conniving at worst, simply smiled. "The man wants to be the next governor, and he knows he can't win the office without our help."

"*Our* help?"

"Yes, by gaining the confidence of those who supported me in the past and those who will support you in the future."

Henry groaned. Now he saw the truth of the matter. His father wasn't running for reelection, but that didn't mean he was finished with his political scheming. Ever since Henry had expressed *a possible interest* in campaigning for his father's seat in the state legislature, Harold Nash had taken it upon himself to become his political advisor. "So you orchestrated all of this?"

The veteran politician laughed. "Of course not. Van der Geld did, but I am smart enough to recognize an opportunity for your advancement when it is presented."

"By mortgaging my future?"

"You want to have a say in what goes on in this state, don't you?"

Of course Henry did, but this was not at all how he wanted to go about it. Deal making and deal breaking, flattery and false alliances had led to war. After four years of killing, peace was finally within reach. Richmond had fallen. Lee and his army had surrendered. The nation, however, had to be reconstructed carefully, and so did his own state.

Although Maryland had not declared secession, there were many in the state who had chosen to fight for the

Confederacy. As a Baltimore city councilman, Henry had dealt with his share of people, both prounion and sympathetic to the South, who were hot for revenge. Loved ones had been lost, property damaged, dreams destroyed.

There is still a lot of healing to be done.

Henry had worked hard to ensure that his reputation as a councilman was that he was fair and trustworthy. He held his office honestly and kept it that way by maintaining an open, forthright dialogue with the mayor, his fellow council members and the people of his city. His yes was always a yes and his no a no. He was determined to go about matters the same way should he win the bid for state delegate.

If I decide to run for higher office, I don't need to form an alliance to do so, especially not with my father's chief political rival. Henry told his father so.

Harold shook his head. "You are too young to realize what is at stake here," he said. "Too young to comprehend fully the advantages of securing such power. Theodore Van der Geld is an Unconditional and you could have considerable influence over him."

The Unconditionals were the members of the National Union Party, and they had been a thorn in his father's flesh since ever since they managed to gain control of the statehouse. While Henry's father had been in favor of preserving the Union, he had not thought Washington should use any means necessary to do so.

Like his father, Henry had opposed many of the tactics employed to keep Maryland in line the past four years. He had been against the closing of newspaper presses critical of Washington, against voters being denied the right to vote simply because they were *suspected* of having Southern sympathy.

Henry wished to correct such wrongs, *but marrying Rebekah Van der Geld and trying to use my position as his son-in-law to sweet-talk her father toward my side of the aisle is not the way to go about it.* "I want no part of this," Henry said adamantly. "I earned my seat on the city council by honesty and hard work. *If* I decide to run for the state legislature, I will get to Annapolis the same way."

And it was a big *if.* He wasn't so certain he even wanted to run for the state legislature, at least not now. Henry had much more pressing matters on his mind. His sister Marianne's death had hit him hard, and now he had the task of caring for her children. Henry knew almost nothing of being a father, and that which he had witnessed from his own, he did not wish to repeat.

The older man's face lined with disappointment. "You won't get to the state capital by shaking hands and talking about your war record. You can't tell all those grieving fathers that while their sons were bleeding on the battlefield, you were floating well above it."

Henry resented the inference. He was no coward. He had done his duty with his military service. He had served as honorably as any other veteran. While it was true he'd never made a valiant charge, his service as an aeronaut in the balloon corps, scouting the positions of the rebel army, was just as valuable—and within artillery range, just like any other man.

"You didn't want me serving in the first place," Henry said, "and now you think I wasn't brave enough?"

"It isn't a matter of what I think. It's what the voters will think."

Henry was just about to respond to the mocking comment when footsteps in the hall caught his attention. The door to the study suddenly burst open. In flew his four-year-old niece, Kathleen. Her face was red and tear streaked. Henry was fairly certain of the cause of her distress. Since coming into his home, she had cried repeatedly for her departed mother.

Kathleen froze upon sight of her grandfather, instantly sensing she was unwelcome. Henry went to her immediately. True, his life had been turned upside down with the arrival of her and her sister, but the last thing he wanted was for his niece to feel unwanted. "What's wrong, pretty girl?" he asked as he bent to her level.

Kathleen's chin quivered. "I want Mama."

Henry's heart broke for her. "I know you do." He pulled her close, gently patted her back. As he did so, he could feel his father's disapproving gaze.

Henry wasn't certain if it was because the man thought such displays of affection were improper or if, deep down, he resented the fact that Marianne had chosen Henry to be her children's guardian and not her own father.

Hannah—his cook, and now temporary governess—came into the room. In her arms was a tiny blanketed bundle, Kathleen's little sister, eight-week-old baby Grace.

"I'm sorry, Mr. Henry," Hannah said. "She got away from me while I was feeding the baby."

"It's all right, Hannah. Tell me, have you any spice cake left?"

"I do."

"Then I believe this young lady would benefit from a slice." His niece looked up at him, eyes still cloudy with tears. "Go with Hannah, pretty girl. I'll be by directly to see that you are settled."

Kathleen slowly took Hannah's hand and turned from the room. Henry watched them go. He was thankful the ploy of sweets had worked. He wasn't certain what he would have done if it hadn't. *But such measures will work for only so long.*

"And there's another reason," his father said when the little girl had left the room.

"Another reason for what?"

"To wed Van der Geld's daughter."

Henry sighed. "Father, if I want help with my nieces, I'll hire a suitable governess."

"A governess isn't going to get you to the statehouse."

Henry shook his head, his patience wearing thin. "I'm not going to discuss this any further. I will speak to Van der Geld myself, tell him I want nothing to do with this."

This time his father grinned, but Henry knew full well it was not an expression of joy. "You go right ahead, son," the man said. "Do it your way. I'll be here when you change your mind."

Henry wanted to give a snappish reply, but he held his tongue. *He is my father. He deserves my respect if for no other reason than that.*

Leaving the study, Henry went to the kitchen. Kathleen was pale, but at least the tears had dried. Hannah had her at the table, a slice of spice cake in front of her. His cook kneaded bread dough for the evening meal.

How the woman managed, Henry was not certain. Surely she must be exhausted. He was, after all. It had taken him only forty-eight hours trying to manage glass feeding bottles and complicated rubber tubes before becoming so. To make matters worse, Grace cried incessantly and refused to take milk from the contraption.

Wise in the ways of motherhood, Hannah had abandoned the tube and metal mouthpiece for a soft rag. Grace sucked milk out of the bottle from that. It was messy and still somewhat cumbersome, but at least it worked. The goat's milk temporarily soothed the baby's stomach, but her heart was another matter. Hannah's fifteen-year-old daughter, Sadie, sat at the table beside Kathleen. She was steadily rocking Grace, trying to quiet her tears.

Henry sighed. Hannah must have heard him. "Don't you fret, Mr. Henry," she said with an expression akin to pity. "It won't always be this way."

How I hope she is right. For all our sakes. "We'll think of something," he promised her. "I'll find us help."

"The good Lord will see to all our needs," Hannah said. "We just gotta trust Him." She punched down her dough. "You goin' out on business today?"

"I'm afraid I must. There is a matter to attend."

"You gonna visit folks, too?"

She meant his constituents. From time to time he called on returning veterans, local merchants and others to see how they were faring. Most citizens welcomed him, and even those who were wary of public servants usually warmed once he heard their complaints.

"Yes, but I won't be gone long." He cast another glance at Kathleen. She was poking her cake with her fork.

"Like I said," Hannah replied, "don't you fret. We're gonna be just fine. You go on and do what you planned."

Henry drew in a breath. How appreciative he was of the woman, of her assistance and understanding. "Thank you, Hannah."

"You're welcome, Mr. Henry."

Leaving the house, Henry headed off to put the matter with Theodore Van der Geld and his daughter to rest. While traveling to the stately home, he went over in his mind what he would say. Henry didn't know whether or not Miss Van der Geld had been told of the arrangement. He certainly hoped she hadn't.

If she had, he seriously doubted she would be heartbroken by the change of plans. Still, Henry wanted to be gentle. *She may not like the idea of a union with a virtual stranger any more than I, but I am still refusing her, and no one likes to feel unwanted...*

Henry knew firsthand the misery such feelings could bring. While his mother, Eleanor, had married his father for love, believing he felt the same, it soon became apparent that Harold Nash had been interested only in her social standing and family fortune. When Henry's mother realized this, the life drained out of her. She had died on Henry's fifteenth birthday. Marianne had been twelve.

Were it not for his interest in public service, Henry doubted he'd have much of a relationship with his father, if any. He did his best to honor the man as Scripture commanded, but he refused to be like him, especially when it came to selecting a wife.

Henry believed in love. For him, marriage was a lifelong commitment of mutual respect and affection, not an opportunity to advance one's political career. He wasn't going to court a woman until he was certain he was prepared to give her his heart.

Arriving at the Van der Geld house, he knocked upon the front door. An Irish maidservant answered, only to inform him that the state delegate was not home.

For a moment, Henry was tempted to ask for the daughter but decided that would be unwise. If she *did* know of the marriage proposal, requesting to speak with her without her father's presence would paint him as a much too eager suitor.

And if she does not yet know, there is no reason to trouble her.

He handed the maid his calling card. Henry didn't like leaving matters like this. Miss Van der Geld was liable to get hurt.

But there is nothing I can do for the moment.

So he left the house, determined to return at a more opportune time.

Rebekah had heard the man's voice coming from the foyer. Terrified by the thought that Henry Nash had actually come to pay a call on her, she crept to her room and closed the door behind her.

If I stay hidden, she told herself, *I won't have to face him.*

From her sanctuary, she could no longer hear the conversation on the floor below, but she could make out the sound of Fiona shutting the door. Knowing Councilman Nash had gone, Rebekah moved to the window and watched him walk toward the street.

At least he has the decency not to insist upon seeing me while Father is out, she thought.

She tried to take comfort in that fact, but his sense of social propriety did little to quell her anxious spirit. She might not have had to face him *today*, but the moment was surely going to come.

Reason told her that things could be much worse. At least Councilman Nash was a churchgoing man. In fact, they attended the *same* church, and from what she'd observed of him there, he appeared to have a pleasant disposition.

But then so does Father when he is in public. In private it is an altogether different matter.

Her stomach began to roll. Her breath quickened. *I can't do this! I won't do this!*

It wasn't as though she was against marriage itself. Three of Rebekah's closest friends had been recently married. Julia Stanton, the daughter of a prominent local physician, had married her beloved Samuel Ward, a history teacher who was somewhat below her station.

Emily Davis had been raised as a supporter of states' rights, and yet her parents had offered no arguments when she'd married Dr. Evan Mackay, the Union army surgeon she had once despised.

Elizabeth Martin had gone to work as a newspaper sketch artist after the death of her fiancé, Jeremiah Wainwright, then fell in love with his brother, David.

Rebekah's father claimed that all three were foolish matches and her friends would soon regret their decisions. Yet she knew how happy they each were. She could see it on their faces. They basked in the glow of men who truly loved and respected them. Rebekah longed for the same.

Yet I am to be given to a man who scarcely knows me. One who most likely is more interested in an alliance with my father than with me. He seeks to further his own political career, and I will be expected to further his legacy. I do not love him, yet I will be expected to raise his sister's children and bear him more.

She paced the floor. *There must be some way out of this...somehow...*

The clock ticked on, yet Rebekah found no solution. Hopelessness pressing upon her, she sank to her bed. She was still there when her mother came to see her later that afternoon. Susan Van der Geld floated into the room in a cloud of gray silk and claimed the chair across from Rebekah.

"I understand that Councilman Nash came by the house today," her mother said.

Rebekah pulled herself into a proper sitting position, smoothed out her skirt and wiped her eyes. "He did."

"And you did not see him?"

"He did not ask to see me."

"Of course not," her mother said. "A proper gentleman would seek to speak only with your father, but you should have been gracious enough to greet him. Your father is very disappointed that you did not."

Disappointed. How often Rebekah heard that word? He was always disappointed with her in some way, and he always let it be known. What punishment would she receive this time?

"I am sorry, Mother. Truly I am. I am just so—" Dare she say it? What good would it do to admit she was afraid?

Her mother gave her a knowing look. "You do not wish to marry him, do you?"

Hope sparked inside Rebekah. *She understands! Perhaps there is a way out of this after all! Perhaps she will speak up on my behalf!* "No," Rebekah said. "I don't. I don't love him!"

"Of course you don't," her mother said expressionlessly. "You must learn to do so."

The spark died. *I must learn?* "Mother, how can I—"

Susan stopped her with an upturned hand. "This is

the way it is done, Rebekah. This is the way it was for me, for your grandmother and for her mother before her."

And you are miserable, Rebekah desperately wanted to say. *Just once, won't you intervene?*

Her mother stood and brushed imaginary dust from her skirt. "Things will go much easier if you simply accept this," she said. "Your father has firmly decided the matter. He will not change his mind. Now wash your face and come downstairs. You know how he dislikes tears."

Yes, I know. They only make him angrier. Resignation washed over Rebekah in suffocating waves. *So this is to be my lot in life: a politician's wife. I must mind my tongue, create an appropriate home and play the gracious hostess at all gatherings, just like you. And as for the children, his nieces and however many more may come in the future... I must manage them accordingly, for the voters will be watching.*

Anger roiled inside her, and so did hurt—two emotions she realized she must master. Rebekah had seen what those same feelings had done to her mother. For twenty-four years, Susan Van der Geld had pined for the affection of a hard-hearted man. Continual disappointment had withered her, and as a result, she'd grown cold and aloof to her own children.

Rebekah steeled her resolve. *I will not do so. I will not let him change me. I may be forced to give Henry Nash my life and my youth, but I will never give him my heart.*

Henry did his best to forget all about Rebekah Van der Geld as he rolled toward the Baltimore Harbor. Long before her father and his had stirred up such trouble, Henry had intended to spend the day visiting his constituents.

He hoped sticking to his original plan would take his mind off the unfinished business with the Van der Gelds. He made his rounds along the wharf. Then, upon reaching Eutaw Street, he stopped at the Branson Boarding House. Two Federal soldiers stood idly by the front steps. Henry acknowledged them, then knocked on the door. The proprietor's daughter, Maggie, a young woman of about twenty or so, answered. Henry had spoken with her once before.

"Good afternoon, Miss Maggie. Is your father home?"

"I'm afraid he is not," she said, "but may I help you?"

Henry explained why he had come. When Miss Branson learned he was willing to listen to her complaints, she invited him inside. A boarder had taken up residence in the formal parlor, so she offered Henry the dining room. Once they were seated, she wasted no time.

"Can you do anything about those soldiers?" she asked.

"Which soldiers, miss?"

"The ones outside. There are always two or three roaming about. Martial law hasn't been good for business, you know."

Miss Branson's family, as well as many others, had been forced to contend with the presence of scrutinizing Federal troops since the beginning of the war. Most of the soldiers Henry had encountered were honorable peacekeepers. There were always a few bad apples in every barrel, though, and knowing that, he was concerned for Miss Branson.

"Have the soldiers been harassing you?" he asked.

"Indeed so!"

He listened as she recounted a host of irritants, none of which, however, crossed the bounds of illegality or impropriety. Thankfully, it seemed the men were simply an unwanted nuisance, a sentiment shared by many in the city.

"Their presence drives away potential boarders," she said. "They make it appear as though something treasonous is going on in this house. The war is over. They should move on now."

"I should think a great many changes will be occurring in the future," Henry said, "although I wouldn't expect the troops to vacate anytime soon. I will speak to my fellow council members about your concerns, however."

"Thank you," she said. "I would appreciate that. I will let my father know you called."

"Please do, and tell him that if he has any other concerns, he should contact me." He handed her his card.

Miss Branson smiled. "Thank you, Councilman Nash. My father will be pleased to know you stopped by. He voted for you for city council. He hopes you will run for state legislature."

Henry appreciated the compliment. Wishing Miss Branson a good day, he stepped outside. The soldiers she had complained about were nowhere to be found. Satisfied, Henry continued on.

He visited several other citizens that day. Some were cheering General Grant's victory. Others were anxiously awaiting the return of sons who had joined the

Confederate army and were currently being held as prisoners of war. All, however, seemed eager to put the war behind them.

As he returned to his carriage, he caught sight of a familiar face. Henry was fond of the theater, and one of his favorite actors, John Wilkes Booth, was just about to cross his path. He'd had the privilege of meeting the man early on in the war at a social gathering.

"Mr. Booth," Henry called out, "How good to see you again."

It took the actor a second, but when he recognized Henry, he smiled. "And you, sir. Are you managing to keep the local leadership in line?"

Henry only laughed. "Are you in Baltimore for a performance?" He wasn't aware of any such productions, but perhaps as busy as he'd been with his nieces, he had simply failed to notice the advertisements.

"No," Booth said. "I only came for a visit."

"Oh, that's right," Henry said, remembering. "You are from Maryland, aren't you? Harford County, is it?"

Booth nodded as if pleased he knew such a detail. He reached up and shook Henry's hand. Two women made eyes at the debonair, mustached man as they passed. Booth noticed them, smiled somewhat flirtatiously, then returned his attention to Henry. "As of now, I am on my way back to Washington."

"Oh? Then may I offer you a ride to the train station?"

"Yes, sir. Thank you."

He climbed inside the carriage, and Henry urged his horse forward. They chatted about the theater. Booth had taken time off due to illness but was planning to return to the spotlight very soon.

"I am very pleased to hear that," Henry said. "I have enjoyed your performances, especially *Julius Caesar*."

"Ah, yes," Booth laughed theatrically. *"Beware the Ides…"*

The traffic grew heavier as they neared the Camden Street station. Family members waiting for loved ones clogged the road, and those who would soon be passengers were hurrying for the ticket windows. Henry pulled up as close as he could to the station so Booth could disembark.

The actor smiled. "Thank you, Councilman Nash."

"It was my pleasure, sir." As Booth started for the train, he couldn't resist calling after him. "Your next performance, sir…what role will you play?"

Booth looked back and offered a proud smile. "You'll soon find out," he said. "Rest assured, my name will make *all* the papers."

Henry couldn't help but laugh at the man's answer. He *would* look forward to reading the reviews.

But for now, I have more pressing matters…

He needed to get home. Hannah would have supper on the table soon, and he didn't want Kathleen eating alone. Henry hoped his niece would sleep well tonight, for his sake and hers. More than once since her arrival, she'd woken crying for her mother.

As he made the turn on to Charles Street, he thought again of Rebekah Van der Geld. Tomorrow was Good Friday. Henry planned to approach her father following the church service and request a private meeting with him. He did not wish to prolong this matter.

He wanted to observe a quiet Easter Sunday with his nieces—prayer and perhaps an egg hunt with little

Kathleen. A restful, peaceful day with no unfinished business hanging over his head—that was exactly what he needed.

On Friday morning, silent and somber, Rebekah filed into the church pew just as she had done every other time the sanctuary doors were open. Immediately following her were her younger brothers, Joseph, Austin, Gilbert and Teddy. Their mother then claimed her place. Last, Rebekah's father took up residence beside the aisle. As usual, they had arrived a good fifteen minutes before the service was scheduled to begin.

As a child, Rebekah used to think they did so simply because her father was eager to attend worship. When she grew older, however, she realized the truth. He came early because he wanted to be *seen* by his fellow parishioners as *they* arrived. He wanted the voters to take notice.

Inwardly she sighed. *For as long as I can remember, I've been on display. I've been told what to wear, where to stand, what to think and what to say.* Once again, here she sat, polished, pristine, every bit the exemplary charge of a would-be governor. Inside she cried out for freedom.

What would happen if I suddenly caused a scene? What if I had the audacity to bolt to my feet and declare to my father that I most definitely will not marry Henry Nash or anyone else he thinks will be of advantage to him? What if I then run for the door and keep running until I leave the city long behind?

Rebekah again sighed, knowing full well that no matter how much she wanted to flee, she would not do so. She would not dare disrespect her father. She knew the consequences such behavior would bring.

Her mother's words echoed in her ears. *"This is the way it is done, Rebekah... Things will go much easier if you simply accept this."*

Behind her, the congregants were arriving. Rebekah wondered if Councilman Nash was one of them. She did not turn to see. The last thing she wanted was for him to think she was *eager* for his attention.

Her father had not spoken to her about the impending marriage since he had first called her into his study, although she knew he was well aware that Councilman Nash had tried to speak with *him*. Her mother's disclosure that Rebekah had disappointed him by not greeting Mr. Nash was evidence of that. Rebekah wondered if her father would speak with the man after the service today. Would he require her to speak to him, as well? Her stomach knotted at the thought. It was troubling enough to deal with such matters in private, but here, in front of everyone?

At precisely noon, Reverend Perry, her minister since infancy, stepped to the pulpit and began the service. Rebekah wished to focus her attention on the hymns and prayers, but she couldn't seem to concentrate. Even the agonizing details of Christ's trial and crucifixion failed to pierce her thoughts. Her mind was just too full.

Just as she feared, the moment the service dismissed, Councilman Nash came to her father. Rebekah dared not look in their direction, but she strained to hear their conversation. She knew they were discussing her. Even at the far end of the pew, she could catch words in snatches.

"Out on business...my apologies...time to discuss... Saturday morning..."

Beside her, six-year-old Joseph, fidgety as always, had taken to tapping his fingers on the pew railing in front of him. Rebekah stilled his hands at once, hoping both to save him from a stern parental rebuke and to hear what else she could.

It was to no avail. Her father had concluded the conversation. Councilman Nash stepped back, allowing her father to lead his family from their pew. Heart pounding, Rebekah chanced a glance in the man's direction as she moved into the aisle. He nodded to her. The expression on his face was hardly cold or disapproving, but the look was still a far cry from loving.

Rebekah did her best to maintain her composure, although inside her emotions were swirling. She could tell herself that she'd protect her heart from hurt, that she'd accept her lot, but the pain of imagining a loveless union still stung.

She followed her family to the foyer, down the steps and then outside. While Teddy and Gilbert mounted their horses, Rebekah climbed into the barouche alongside Austin and Joseph. Her mother and father claimed the seat facing opposite them. The open-air carriage offered a good view of their surroundings. It also allowed *them* to be seen.

At her father's command, their coachman, Brooks, urged the horses forward. The carriage began to roll. The family traveled the length of two blocks in silence. Then her father spoke.

"Councilman Nash plans to pay a call tomorrow morning at eleven o'clock," he said, leveling his stern gaze on Rebekah. "I expect you to conduct yourself accordingly."

You mean you expect me to accept his formal proposal, she thought, *and do so eagerly.*

Her eyes drifted to her mother, silently appealing once more for her intervention. Susan simply looked aside.

"Is that clear?" her father asked.

"Y-yes, sir," she said, giving him the answer he expected. "I will do so."

He nodded curtly to her, then commenced smiling and waving at the potential voters passing by on the street.

Rebekah swallowed back her tears. *I must face facts. There is no changing the circumstances. Tomorrow I will become engaged to a man I do not love. I will go from one prison to another, and I must bear it with endurance, strength and fortitude.*

Much to her surprise, however, the encounter with Mr. Nash was delayed, but in a way she never would have imagined. When Rebekah woke the following morning, she learned the man himself had postponed the meeting due to urgent official business with the city council. The nation was in mourning and accordingly, Rebekah's father immediately ordered his entire household to put on black.

President Abraham Lincoln was dead.

Chapter Two

Henry still could not believe the news.

The president has been assassinated! How can this be? And shot during a performance at Ford's Theatre? His wife seated just beside him?

He didn't know what sickened him more—the thought of the slain leader or the fact that less than forty-eight hours ago, he had shaken hands with the perpetrator of the crime. The ride to the train station with John Wilkes Booth replayed through his mind over and over again.

"Rest assured, my name will make all the papers."

Indeed it had, for now every press was churning out the details.

"He leapt from the president's box…"

"…from the stage he shouted to the crowd…"

"Wielding a blood-smeared dagger, he then fled…"

A Federal manhunt was now underway. Those suspected of aiding Booth were quickly being rounded up. Henry nervously wondered if the provost marshal would soon come calling for him.

I drove him to the train station… I shook his hand…

Fellow councilman George Meriwether nudged Henry, jolting him back to the business at hand. "Your vote, Nash," George whispered.

Fearing bloody reprisal in the wake of the president's death, the mayor had suggested that saloons be closed and the entire city police force be put on alert. Henry agreed.

"Aye," he cast.

The measure passed. With business concluded, the council then dismissed. In a daze, Henry slowly made his way home. *Is it really true? Is the president really dead, or is this some horrible nightmare from which I will awake?*

But every step he took toward home dripped with reality. Already the church bells were beginning to toll. They would continue to ring until noon. The patriotic bunting that had draped the government buildings all week in celebration of victory was now being replaced by black crepe. Flags were lowered to half-mast. Nearly every person he passed on the street wore a grief-stricken or confused expression.

Henry didn't know whether to weep or clench his fists in anger at the enormity of the country's loss. While he hadn't voted for Lincoln, or agreed with all of his policies, he had believed the president truly wanted what was best for the nation. In the end, Lincoln had wanted peace, and had died just as it was achieved. What a cruel and senseless conclusion to the man's life.

What will this mean for our country now? he wondered.

Upon reaching home, James, his manservant, met Henry at the door. Already he wore a black mourning band on his upper left arm. Taking Henry's greatcoat and hat, he said, "You had a visitor earlier. I told him you weren't here."

"Who was it?"

Before James could answer, Henry's father stepped from the parlor. "That'll be all, James."

Henry shot his father a disdainful glare as James exited. He didn't like how Harold ordered his servants about.

"You could have let him answer," Henry said.

"You'd better be grateful that James didn't ask your visitor to stay."

"Why is that?"

"Because Detective J. E. Smith is the one who paid the call." His father offered the calling card for proof.

Fear slowly snaked its way up Henry's neck. He'd had dealings with this particular provost marshal detective before. Last year, a city council member had been investigated on accusations of bribery and extortion. The man was not guilty, and eventually his name was cleared, but not before his entire life had been turned upside down by Smith and his men.

Does Smith know of my encounter with Booth? Henry wondered. *Is that why he came to see me?*

Harold was well aware of the interaction with the detective, and he knew the fear it stoked. He added fuel to the fire. "You've another matter with which to be concerned."

"What do you mean?"

He encouraged Henry toward the study. On his desk was a copy of the day's paper. Picking it up, his father explained, "A man by the name of Lewis Paine is now under arrest for the attempted murder of Secretary of

State William Seward. They say he spent time here in Baltimore."

"I never shook his hand," Henry said, more for the easement of his own mind than that of his father.

"No," the older man conceded, "but you did grasp the hand of his hostess."

"His hostess?"

"Apparently this man was a boarder at the house on Eutaw Street as recently as last month."

"You mean the *Branson* Boarding House?"

"I do."

Harold tossed him the publication. Henry quickly read. According to the *Free American,* twenty-two men and women from the Branson Boarding House had been taken into custody by the provost marshal and were presently being questioned for possible involvement in Lincoln's death and the conspiracy to murder Secretary Seward.

The paper also noted that this was not the first time the boardinghouse had been under scrutiny. As Henry read the next paragraph aloud, a chill spread through him. "Miss Branson, a former volunteer nurse, was questioned in September 1863 by the provost marshal. She was suspected of helping a rebel prisoner, Lewis Thornton Powell, also known as Lewis Paine, escape from the US General Hospital here in Baltimore. No charges were filed then."

"And you visited that same boardinghouse," his father reminded him, "listening to that same woman complain about Federal soldiers prowling about her door."

Henry raked back his hair. His mind was racing. *Those soldiers saw me enter. The boarder in the par-*

*lor saw me, as well. He probably heard our very con-
versation.*

He told himself he hadn't done anything wrong—
certainly not anything illegal—but he knew that didn't
matter now. The nation had just endured four years of
war. Suspicion still ran high. Henry had entered the
home of a Southern sympathizer. That was all the proof
some men would need to declare him guilty.

*I'll be linked to the scoundrels who conspired to kill
the president and his men. God help me*, he thought.
What do I do now?

"You need to keep your wits," his father reminded
him. "You need to protect yourself."

Anxiety pulsing through him, Henry made the mis-
take of asking how.

"Van der Geld's daughter. The man has the army
in his pocket, you know. You can use that to your advantage."

Henry immediately dismissed the idea. He'd already
made the mistakes of listening to the complaints of rebel
sympathizer and shaking hands with a murderer. He
wouldn't make another by marrying a woman he did
not love, even if her father did hold considerable sway
over the authorities of this state.

"No," he said flatly. "I told you, I don't want any
part of that."

His father scowled. "When are you going to learn
that this is the way it is done? Crowns are won or lost
this way."

Henry had no desire for a crown. He never had. He
told his father so. "I only want to do what is right."

"Right or wrong has nothing to do with it. It's about

power…about how much of it you have over your enemies."

"I don't have any enemies."

At that, his father laughed. "I wouldn't tell Detective Smith that next time he comes calling. You had *better* claim a few enemies—namely John Wilkes Booth and the rebel army."

Again Henry raked his fingers through his hair. Of course he wanted Booth brought to justice, but Lee and his army had surrendered. The men in gray were no longer his enemies. Some, in fact, like his brother-in-law, John, never had been. Henry grieved the loss of life their war of rebellion had brought, but he didn't want retribution. He wanted restoration. He wanted to be part of the reconstruction efforts, to see his nation, his state, his city healed.

His father eyed him shrewdly. "Detective Smith will return. Just what exactly are you planning to tell him?"

"I will tell him the truth."

"The truth will earn you a jail cell." Harold reached for the paper and quickly flipped to another article. "The actors from Ford's Theatre are already there."

"What? Why? What did *they* do?"

"They were *there* that night, and *Booth* was there. Son, *the president has been assassinated*. Mark my words, this nation won't rest until every last person connected to Lincoln's death, no matter how trivial the role, is brought to justice."

All Henry could offer in response to that was silence. He knew his father was right, and although he believed the truth would eventually prevail, he wondered just how long it would take.

How long must I sit in a jail cell before Detective

Smith believes my encounters with Booth and Maggie Branson were purely coincidental?

He had seen what prison could do to a man. He'd visited returning veterans who had been held captive in rebel prisons. Many were starved, sick, withered.

Would a Federal prison have the same effect on me? Could I endure it?

And more important, what would happen to *Kathleen and Grace* if he were imprisoned?

They'll end up in the care of the man standing before me. The man my sister rejected as a guardian. And he will not offer them any affection or comfort. Henry was certain his father would ship Kathleen and Grace off to a home for foundlings at the first opportunity.

James came to the door. "'Scuse me, sir, but Delegate Van der Geld and his daughter are here to see you."

Henry sighed heavily and once more raked his fingers through his hair. *Not this...not now...*

"An opportunity presents itself, son," his father said. "If I were you, I'd make the most of it."

I'm not you, Henry thought. *I'll never be you.*

Despite his anxiety, he was determined to stand on the truth. As his father exited the room, Henry looked at James. He was still waiting for an answer. The delicate business of rejecting Miss Van der Geld was now the least of his concerns, but the matter had to be settled.

"Tell Delegate Van der Geld that I'll see him."

James nodded.

"And please tell Sadie to serve Miss Van der Geld some refreshments in the parlor."

James nodded again. He turned, only to have Henry call after him. "And James…"

"Yes, sir?"

"I wish to see Delegate Van der Geld alone. Please see to it that my father is occupied elsewhere."

"Yes, sir."

James had barely left the room before the elder statesman made his entrance. The man's very stance commanded authority. His hawkish look and confident voice could wither a weaker, inexperienced man, especially a man with something to hide.

But I've done nothing wrong, Henry reminded himself. Lifting his chin, he stared Van der Geld square in the face.

The men exchanged formal pleasantries before Van der Geld said, "Sir, I would presume you are as distressed by today's developments as I."

"Indeed," Henry said. He noted the small framed portrait of Lincoln pinned to the man's frock coat. "It is a black day for our nation."

Van der Geld nodded. "One that makes your proposal all the more pertinent."

My proposal? Henry stopped him there. "Sir, I must tell you here and now, whatever my father may have said to you—"

Accustomed to keeping the floor, Van der Geld did not allow him to finish. "Unity is necessary to maintain the peace. With such perilous times upon us, surely you see as well as I the necessity of proceeding with the wedding in haste. Our city needs uplifting news. It is no secret that your father and I take different views. The joining of our families, a uniting of opposite parties for the good of the land, will show the people of Maryland our willingness to work together...compromise... goodwill..."

Henry would have been tempted to roll his eyes at

the obvious stump speech had Van der Geld's tone not suddenly changed. All evidence of goodwill vanished when he then spoke of John Wilkes Booth.

"And that traitorous rebel scum! As for him and his coconspirators, I agree with what Vice President Johnson said concerning rebels—'arrest them as traitors, try them as traitors, hang them as traitors.' Rest assured, Councilman Nash, I will do everything in my power to bring such men and women to justice. The provost marshal is already dragging them in. I daresay the jails of this city will soon be bursting at the seams."

A rock lodged in the back of Henry's throat so tightly he could not breathe. Van der Geld had never proceeded cautiously when it came to suspicions of disloyalty, and it was obvious he would not tread lightly now. In the past, the man had been in full support of citizens being dragged from their beds simply because they had spoken against such tactics or knew someone who had served in the rebel army.

And what would he advocate for the man who not only had a brother-in-law who served the Confederacy but also had shaken hands with the president's murderer? "Arrest them as traitors, try them as traitors, hang them as traitors"?

Henry felt sick to his stomach. Van der Geld continued on, now promising that he personally would not rest until Booth and all those connected with him got what they deserved.

"They will suffer for their actions! Indeed they shall!" Suddenly he stopped. His hawk-like expression softened. "But I digress," he said. "We are here to discuss matters of life…"

Henry swallowed. *Life… My life is now devoted to*

raising those two little girls. They are dependent on me. Marianne depended on me. I can't let her down.

"This marriage will serve as a positive example," Van der Geld insisted. "The future of our state depends upon such goodwill…"

Future… What future will Grace and Kathleen have if their uncle is convicted as an accomplice to the murder of the president?

Henry couldn't stand the thought of them being shunned or scorned, unable to be placed in a proper home. He might not be the father they deserved, and he might not know how to care for them as wisely as he should, but Henry was determined those little girls would be protected.

"We've had our disagreements, for certain," Van der Geld said, "but I know you to be a man of your word. I know you will take good care of my daughter."

His daughter… Surely this man is as concerned for her security and happiness as I am for Grace's and Kathleen's. He wouldn't wish to see her husband carted off to jail.

"I have it on good authority that the president's funeral train will pass through our city in a few days. Thousands will attend. I think that would be the perfect opportunity for you and Rebekah to be seen together in public. Then, when our beloved president is finally laid to rest, we will conduct the marriage ceremony." The man stuck out his hand. "What say you?"

Images of moldy holding cells and interrogation rooms at Fort McHenry flashed through Henry's mind. Marriage to a woman he did not love would be a prison all to itself but surely more bearable than the former, especially when he thought of Kathleen's and Grace's tear-stained faces. His heart told him not to give in to such fears. He was a man of faith, and up until now, he had done nothing wrong. Shouldn't he trust that God would work all of this out? Shouldn't he believe Kathleen and Grace would be all right?

But Henry found he had not the courage to pray. Before he even realized what he was doing, he was shaking Theodore Van der Geld's hand.

Rebekah waited nervously in Councilman Nash's parlor while her father visited with the man. The news of President Lincoln's death had barely had a chance to register before her father summoned her to his own study and told her to make herself ready. In light of the national tragedy, *they* would pay a call on Henry Nash. Her father was apparently convinced her marriage to the man would ensure the continuation of the Union.

How that was, she could not say. Henry Nash was no great supporter of the president. He was no war hero. Rebekah had no respect for men who had shirked their responsibility to the nation. The only men she despised more were those who had owned slaves.

And remnants of such a loathsome past remain in this house!

A Negro manservant had taken her coat and bonnet when she had arrived. A young maid then followed, bringing tea and scones. Rebekah couldn't help but feel for them. *What must they have endured?*

But her thoughts then quickly turned to herself. *What must I now endure?*

Unable to swallow any refreshment, Rebekah left her tea and walked to the window. Beyond the glass lay a world of green, lush vegetation kissed by the April dew.

As she stared out at the garden, the idea of escape again crossed her mind. *If I could find the back gate, I could run away...away from my father, away from Councilman Nash...away from everything...*

But she wasn't given the opportunity to flee. At that moment, the two men stepped into the room. Rebekah turned to see the familiar look of smug confidence on her father's face. Obviously he had secured another political victory. She dared look then into the face of her father's newest ally.

He looked scared.

For one irrational second, she flattered herself with the idea that he was frightened of her. In reality, however, she knew it was probably more that he feared she would reject his proposal, and then whatever contract he had secured with her father would be null and void. Anger welled up inside her. Rebekah wanted to tell the councilman she was not a commodity to be bought and sold, but indeed, she knew she was exactly that.

She remembered her father's instructions. She was to accept this man's proposal with eagerness. *Or else.*

He nodded to her in a most formal matter. "Good day, Miss Van der Geld," he said.

She responded in kind. "Good day, Councilman Nash. Thank you for the tea."

He nodded again, cleared his throat. He was definitely unsettled, but whether that had to do with the proposal he was about to make or the fact that her father obviously intended to listen to it, she was not certain. Theodore stood guard, ready to offer Rebekah a disapproving glare or stern rebuke should the opportunity warrant one.

She swallowed hard, stole one more glance at the beckoning garden. Evidently her suitor noticed.

"The garden belonged to my mother," he said. "Would you care to take a turn in it?"

Would she? While escape might not be possible, she could at least flee her father's demanding presence for a few moments. "Yes," she said, "I would enjoy seeing the garden. Thank you."

Out of the corner of her eye, she saw her father nod. It was the closest thing to affirmation she had ever received from him, yet she felt no joy. Councilman Nash offered his arm. Rebekah dutifully accepted. Together they stepped outside.

The garden was a good size, with gravel paths and wrought iron benches. English ivy covered stately brick walls. They were beautiful, but they were walls nonetheless, meant to contain. *From one prison to another*, she thought again. Immediately she let go of her soon-to-be fiancé's arm.

The man took to pointing out the various flowers. "There is forsythia, and here are several varieties of daffodil, I believe."

When he made reference to the jonquils, Rebekah nervously blurted out, "They need dividing. Without room to grow, they will not bloom."

The moment the words were out of her mouth, she cringed. *What made me say such a thing? He did not ask for my opinion. How will he respond to such impertinence?*

"You are right," he said. "In fact, the entire plot needs tending, but I am afraid I haven't the time or the skill to make it what it once was. Have you much interest in horticulture?"

The question as well as the conciliatory tone shocked her. They also intrigued her. The councilman appeared genuinely interested in her answer. "Yes," she said guardedly. "I do."

He offered her just the hint of a smile. While Rebekah would not call him exactly handsome, he was at least pleasant in appearance. Nut-brown hair framed an angular face. His eyes were sky blue. "Then no doubt you could tell me to which class and order each plant belongs," he said.

"Only a few of them," she admitted. "Though I have wished to know more, I have not had much time to study such." *Father won't allow it. He thinks the pursuit frivolous.*

He nodded as if he understood. "There are many things that we may wish to do but that our present duties won't allow."

Rebekah immediately took offense. *Surely your duties are not as constrictive as my own. You are free to come and go as you please... You are not being pawned off at another's whim.*

"I have a copy of *The Florist's Manual* somewhere about this house," he said. "If you like, I shall ask James to find it for you. He knows this house better than I."

Though the offer was again intriguing, she couldn't help but stiffen at the mention of *James*. Noticing, the man asked,

"Have I offended you?"

"It is not the offer of the floral guide that I find offensive," she said. "It is the idea of continued slavery."

Councilman Nash's eyes narrowed. He immediately frowned. "James was *never* my slave. I retained his services when I took possession of this home, when my father first moved to his new home in Annapolis."

Retained his services? Rebekah blinked. "Then he… *didn't* belong to your father?"

"I don't like to think of him as *belonging* to anyone, but to answer your question simply, no. He did not."

Oh. Feeling foolish and fearing what might come next, she hurried to explain. "I assumed that since your father voted to keep slavery legal in Maryland—"

"I am not my father, Miss Van der Geld."

Rebekah lowered her eyes. While his voice had not the same bite as her father's, she plainly heard the firmness in it. "No, of course not. Forgive me. That was wrong of me to—"

"There is no need for forgiveness."

No need? She dared reclaim his gaze. His look was charitable, his tone soft.

"But since we are dealing with assumptions," he said, his tone softening further, "is there anything else about me that you question?"

Anything else? There were a thousand things, but Rebekah didn't know where to begin.

"You've probably been told by someone along the way that I never served in the army," he said.

"I have."

He nodded as if he had expected such an answer. "The truth is, I did serve, but I was never given a commission. I was part of the balloon corps. In the army's eyes, I was still considered a civilian."

"Balloon corps? As in hot-air balloons?"

He nodded again. "Yes. Although ours were filled with hydrogen. They were used for reconnaissance. We provided tactical information to the commanders on the ground."

"You mean the position of the rebel army?"

"Yes."

"But didn't your brother-in-law serve—?"

"In the Confederate army? Yes, he did. He did what he believed was his duty. I did mine."

He was not the first man from Maryland to be pitted against his own family. Rebekah couldn't help but feel a measure of pity toward him. "That must have been very difficult for your sister."

"It was."

"And yet she named you the guardian of her children?"

"John was killed at Monocacy Junction, a battle in which I had no bearing. Marianne also knew I was not *personally* at war with her husband, any more than John was with me."

They had reached one of the benches. He invited her to sit. A shiver ran through her as she claimed a place as close to the edge as possible. He claimed the opposite side. An awkward silence now prevailed. She and Councilman Nash were not here to discuss the war, or even his extended family. There was another matter to be resolved.

"Miss Van der Geld," he said. "I won't trouble you any longer. I'm certain your father has spoken to you. While he may consider this matter concluded, this moment only a formality… I do not. I should very much like to know what you think of all of this."

Rebekah was stunned. *What I think of all of this?* Was Henry Nash giving her the opportunity to refuse?

"Your father has given his consent, but all that means nothing if I have not yours."

"My consent?" she asked.

"Of course. It is your future you are deciding...not that of your father."

My future? Yes! Yes, it is my future! Suddenly she felt as though she'd found that elusive back gate, and freedom stood just beyond it. *The councilman is granting me leave to escape!* Like a butterfly in flight, she could go anywhere she wished!

As exhilarating as the feeling of freedom was, however, she realized it was not truly within her reach. Whatever flight she might take would be very short-lived. Her father would recapture her. *And then to whom will I be assigned?*

"You seem at a loss for words," Mr. Nash observed.

"I am afraid I am." What else *could* she say? What could she *do*? She was trapped.

Suddenly the door to the house opened. A little girl, four or five at the most, came charging down the path. *This must be one of his nieces*, Rebekah thought.

The child froze the moment she saw a stranger in the garden. Rebekah's heart immediately went out to her as she recognized the look on the child's face. Rebekah knew it all too well. It was a look of loneliness, of fear.

Apparently the councilman recognized it, also, for he spoke to his niece with a tender voice, welcomed her forward. "It's all right, Kathleen. Come and meet my friend, Miss Van der Geld."

Friend, *not* fiancée. Again Rebekah noted the choice he was granting her.

The man held out his hand toward the child. She crept closer. Rebekah couldn't help but notice the family resemblance. She had the same blue eyes, but whereas her uncle's hair was slightly curly, hers was completely straight.

Rebekah offered her what she hoped was a disarming smile. The little girl gripped the leg of the councilman's trousers.

"It's all right," he assured once again as he slid his arm around her protectively. Watching, Rebekah's throat tightened.

"There's a man in the parlor," Kathleen whispered, although the tone was loud enough for Rebekah to overhear.

A man, she thought. *My father.* Had the child had some sort of encounter with him? That would certainly explain her fear.

"Yes, I know about that man," the councilman said. "He hasn't come to take you away. You need not be afraid."

Rebekah heard the unspoken promise. *I'm here. I will protect you.* What was it like to receive such an assurance? *What is it like to be nurtured? Loved?*

Henry Nash then turned to her. "Kathleen has only very recently come to live with me."

"I see," Rebekah said, hoping he hadn't noticed the hitch in her voice. "And I understand you have a sister."

The girl stared at her.

"Her name is Grace," her uncle offered.

"Grace," Rebekah repeated with a smile. "What a beautiful name, as is Kathleen."

The girl didn't return the smile, but her grip on her uncle's trousers loosened slightly. Rebekah took that as an encouraging sign.

The back door opened again. This time the young

maidservant appeared. She hurried down the gravel
path, stones crunching beneath her feet. "I'm sorry, Mr.
Henry. I was puttin' the baby down to sleep, and when
I turned 'round, Miss Kathleen was gone."

"It's all right, Sadie," he said, and the expression on
his face told Rebekah he truly meant that. It was a far
different reaction than her father would have given.

Councilman Nash looked again at Kathleen. "Go inside with Sadie, pretty girl. I'll be in to join you after a
while. When I come, I will read you a story."

He calls her pretty, Rebekah thought. *He promises
to spend time with her.* Such declarations were unheard
of in her home. *This is the man my father insists I must
marry?*

Kathleen slowly moved away from her uncle and
took the maidservant's hand. After they had returned
to the house, the councilman said, "She doesn't remember much of her father—he had very little leave during
the war. But she misses her mother terribly."

"I imagine she must," Rebekah said. "How old is
Grace?"

"Eight weeks."

Eight weeks? Then she is an infant. A helpless infant.
Rebekah wondered how he was managing the feedings.
Had he employed a wet nurse or did the baby drink
from a glass bottle?

"Marianne died giving birth to Grace," he said. "The
children were then shuffled from one neighbor to the
next until one of them finally contacted me."

Rebekah's heart squeezed. *Poor little things.* "Did
you have to travel far to collect them?"

"Virginia."

In other words, to enemy territory. He had risked his

safety for them, yet acted as if the danger had been of no importance. "This has certainly been a difficult time for your family," was all Rebekah could think to say.

"Indeed."

After another long silence he said, "Miss Van der Geld, I know this is no ideal situation…"

No, it isn't, she thought, but she realized she could do a lot worse than Henry Nash. Granted, she did not know him well, but she sensed a humility, a gentleness about him. That was something her father had *never* possessed.

"I will make you this promise," the councilman continued. "Should you choose to become my wife, a surrogate mother to my nieces, I will care for you, provide for you and encourage your personal pursuits. I will do everything in my power to make your life a comfortable and happy existence, and I will never treat you with anything less than respect."

He did not use the word *love*, but few men she knew did. In twenty minutes' time, Henry Nash had bestowed upon her more kindness, more liberality than her father had in all her twenty-three years. While she certainly did not love this man, she could respect him.

On that basis, she accepted his proposal.

Chapter Three

Henry could not sleep that night. His conscience would not allow it. As he stared long and hard at the ceiling, the visit with Miss Van der Geld replayed over again in his mind. He had spent more time talking with her in one hour today than in all the years he had sat across the aisle from her in church.

She was quite a combination, a mixture of timidity, presumptiveness, austerity and elegance. Her dark blue eyes and the set of her mouth reflected suspicion, but they were also capable of displaying interest and affection. He had seen the latter when she'd spoken to Kathleen. *She was taken with the child at once. For that, shouldn't I be grateful?*

When his own father had learned of the proposal, he'd said he was proud. "You are finally using every advantage to further your own well-being. You won't regret it."

Won't I? He already did. Henry was intrigued by his betrothed, but he was not in love with her.

Wrestling with the bedsheets, he rolled to his side. *If I had any honor, I would tell her the truth. Then I'd march down to the provost marshal's office and tell Detective Smith what I know concerning John Wilkes Booth.*

But his father's warning echoed in his ears. *"This nation won't rest until every last person connected to Lincoln's death, no matter how trivial the role, is brought to justice."*

He remembered Van der Geld's words, as well, the ones that had ultimately caused him to shake the man's hand. *"They will suffer for their actions... 'Arrest them as traitors, try them as traitors, hang them as traitors!'"*

Henry's guilt consumed him. *I am hiding behind an innocent young woman, using her name to protect my own. I have become the very thing I swore I'd never become. I am no longer a public servant. I am a self-serving politician, just like my father.*

Kathleen's cry pulled him from his bed. Snatching his dressing robe, Henry hurried to the child's room. Hannah and Sadie were already there. Hannah was cradling a now whimpering Kathleen, while Sadie rocked and cooed her startled infant sister.

The young maid looked as spent as Henry felt. Going to her, he took charge of the baby.

"I'll go warm some milk for them both," she said.

"Thank you, Sadie."

It took only an hour or so to settle the children back to sleep, but you'd have thought the ordeal much more lengthy for the way they slept come morning. Though it was Resurrection Sunday, and Henry had hoped to take them both to church, he decided to let the children remain abed. Sadie, still sleepy herself, volunteered to keep watch over them.

Henry wasn't the only one operating in mind-numbing

confusion that morning. Although it was supposed to be the most joyous day of the Christian calendar, the mood of the service was somber. Men whispered newspaper details of Lincoln's murder among themselves. Even women, who typically paraded new bonnets and laces this day, remained in black.

When the preaching began, Reverend Perry did his best to remind everyone that Christ had risen and because of that, one need no longer fear the grave. It wasn't the grave that Henry feared. It was the path leading up to it. He believed because of Christ's sacrifice his eternity was secure, but for some reason he couldn't quite believe that same sacrifice capable of giving him protection, or provision for his nieces, this side of Heaven.

He prayed for forgiveness, for a cleansing of guilt, yet even amid his pleas his mind kept wandering. *Here I sit like a pious worshiper, while the US Army combs the countryside for John Wilkes Booth and the rest of his accomplices. Where will the investigation lead?*

The members of the Branson Boarding House were still detained. Henry was certain the army was giving the house quite a going over, looking for leads to other potential suspects. He hoped they would not find the calling card he had left there.

And if they do?

Loyalists everywhere were calling for swift execution of all those implicated in the president's assassination. *Is my own future to consist of a military tribunal and a hangman's noose?*

He glanced across the aisle. His soon-to-be father-in-law sat attentively in his pew, looking very much the self-proclaimed guardian of all that was noble and right. If Henry's indiscretion became public knowledge, would the man be willing to overlook such in his son-in-law, or would he seek justice, as well?

The service now ending, Henry stood for the closing hymn. Once more he glanced across the aisle, this time looking at Miss Van der Geld. Her black bonnet, however, hid her face from view.

When her family filed out of their pew, Theodore Van der Geld stopped to inquire of Henry and his father. *Miss* Van der Geld stood silently at the end of the family line.

"Are you gentlemen attending the veterans' ceremony tomorrow?" Van der Geld asked. It was to honor those returning from the war.

"I won't," Harold Nash said quickly, "but my son will."

Henry had already agreed to be the city council's representative at the event last week, but he had the impression that even if he hadn't been committed to going, his father would have wanted him there anyway.

It isn't a campaign stop, he thought, but he wouldn't argue the point here in the house of God.

Van der Geld looked pleased. "Rebekah will be there, as well," he said.

"Is that so?" Henry replied, gauging her response. There was that suspicious look again. Was it directed at her father or him?

Has she planned to attend the ceremony, or has she been told to do so? Was she told to accept me, as well?

He did not have time to ponder the thought further. Van der Geld closed the conversation and led his family away.

The following morning, Henry's fiancée was standing on the platform alongside her other family members while her father, Mayor Chapman and a representative from the provost marshal's office made their respective speeches to those on hand. Henry watched her from his position in the crowd.

He had brought Kathleen and Grace with him, wanting to give Hannah and Sadie a much-needed break and hoping the fresh air would do the children some good. Grace thankfully slept in his arms. Kathleen, recognizing Miss Van der Geld, tugged on Henry's sack coat. "The lady," she said.

He nodded but said nothing more. As speeches honoring fallen Union soldiers continued, Miss Van der Geld herself spied the children. The somber set of her jaw melted to an attractive smile. When she was freed from her position on the platform, she and several other women circulated the crowd. They presented the veterans' female relatives and sweethearts with fresh flowers, a token of gratitude, an acknowledgment of the sacrifices *they* had made while the men had been away at war.

Their paths soon crossed. Grace, now awake, wiggled fitfully in Henry's arms. Unable to lift his hat properly, he bid Miss Van der Geld good day.

She nodded formally to him but eyed Grace with a look of fondness. Then she smiled again at Kathleen. "She is just as pretty as her big sister."

Kathleen offered the barest hint of a smile. "Pretty flowers," she then said, having noticed the bouquet of jonquils in Miss Van der Geld's arms.

A look of uncertainty darkened the woman's face for the briefest of moments as she stole a glance in her father's direction. He was still on the platform, speaking privately with those gathered around him. Turning back to Kathleen, Miss Van der Geld's smile returned.

"These flowers are for ladies whose fathers or brothers or sons served in the army."

Kathleen's eyes immediately widened. "My daddy was in the army!"

"Yes, I know," Miss Van der Geld said as she presented Kathleen with a jonquil. "And here is another for your sister. Since she is so little, will you take care of it for her?"

Kathleen nodded solemnly as if she considered the act a sacred duty. Henry was touched. His niece, thrusting one hand into the crook of his elbow, pulled the flowers close with the other and sniffed.

"You are very kind," he said to Miss Van der Geld.

She lowered her eyes as if she were uncomfortable with the compliment. "It was only right," she said.

Movement behind her caught his attention. Her father had exited the platform and was now shaking hands with the veterans. A few feet behind him was a man in a charcoal-colored greatcoat. Henry recognized that flat nose and pensive glare from anywhere. It was Detective Smith.

The hair on the back of his neck stood up, for the man was maneuvering through the mass of former Union soldiers, coming in Henry's direction.

"...today, as well."

He realized then Miss Van der Geld had said something else to him. Shifting Grace from one arm to the other, he tried to refocus. "I'm sorry. What did you say?"

She offered him a shy smile, innocent and pretty. "I said, they should be honoring *you* today, as well."

Henry was again touched. Rebekah Van der Geld was a lovely Christian woman, *one who deserves the truth*. Once more the call to confession rang through him, but he quickly squelched it. He told himself that in this moment, the truth would do more harm than good. Detective Smith was drawing closer.

Henry forced himself to look only at Miss Van der Geld. "Again, you are very kind," he said.

"It saddens me, though, to think our soldiers' homecomings are held under such dreadful circumstances."

"Circumstances?"

"The president…"

That rock lodged again in his throat. "Ah, yes…"

Her father then approached. The moment he noticed Kathleen's flowers, he frowned. Thankfully Henry's niece was oblivious to the fact. Still captivated by the jonquils, she was humming to herself. It was the first time he had heard her do so. Henry wanted to take pleasure in this, but the situation would not allow him to do so. Detective Smith had stepped from his field of vision. Henry couldn't locate him anywhere. Would the state delegate's arrival be enough to keep the detective from approaching Henry and his nieces?

"It is a pleasure to see you again, Councilman Nash," Van der Geld said, his face now reflecting an expression of cordiality. "I know you will be attending President Lincoln's funeral procession. Will your father attend, as well, or will he be returning to Annapolis?"

"We will both attend," Henry said. "Like you, my father is waiting until after the procession to depart."

Pleased, Van der Geld nodded and smiled. "I hope your father and I may have a chance to speak with one another. Thousands are likely to attend the president's viewing."

Henry couldn't help but notice the look on Miss Van der Geld's face just then. Had she, like him, picked up on the unspoken meaning of her father's words? *Thousands* were likely to attend the president's viewing. Thousands of *potential voters*. Van der Geld wanted the public to see he was making nice with his chief rival.

That's the only reason he has any interest in me or my father, Henry thought.

Van der Geld was apparently eager to finish his rounds. "Come, Rebekah," he said. "I'm certain Councilman Nash has other matters to attend to. We mustn't keep him."

She nodded respectfully, then bid Henry and the children farewell.

Henry couldn't help but feel sympathy for her. It was becoming obvious to him that she had been groomed to be a sturdy, silent wife, one who would never even think of causing inconvenience to the man to whom she was bound or to the father who had arranged it. He despised himself for being part of such a plot. *How can I continue to go along with this?*

But he already knew the answer. There was an eight-week-old baby girl in his arms. Her four-year-old sister was standing beside him, and Detective Smith was still somewhere in the crowd.

Lincoln's funeral train arrived in Baltimore on Wednesday morning. The weather matched the somber occasion. A cold rain poured down, yet, just as Theodore Van der Geld had predicted, thousands turned out to view the elaborate procession. The president's coffin was removed from the train at Camden Station, placed in a rosewood hearse, then pulled by four horses through the city. Nearly every person who held a position of authority in Baltimore—military, political or clerical—followed the remains.

Henry and his fellow council members were no exception. They were placed just behind Governor Bradford and then the aspiring governor, Theodore Van der Geld. Henry drove alone in his carriage. The children were at home with Hannah and Sadie, while Harold and Miss Van der Geld were to meet him at the Merchant's Exchange Building. It was there that the late president's body would be available for public view.

It took nearly three hours to cover the short distance. Lining the cobblestone streets were grief-stricken faces. Sprinkled among them were those wearing various expressions of anger. Many were armless or legless Union veterans looking as though they would gladly sacrifice what remained of their bodies in order to capture those responsible for the death of their beloved commander-in-chief.

Henry shifted uncomfortably on the bench seat. He believed Booth and those complicit in his crime *should* be punished, but those who had nothing to do with the horrible deed should not be caught in the wake.

Yet am I not doing the very same to Miss Van der Geld? Sentencing her to a life of unhappiness, bound to a man who does not really love her?

Guilt surged through him and he decided right then and there to figure out some other way of protecting himself and his sister's children. To avoid embarrassing Miss Van der Geld, he would go through the charade her father expected at the Merchant's Exchange. He would not cause a scene, but before the day was through, he would end this matter once and for all.

I'll speak with Miss Van der Geld before I speak with her father. I'll tell her that it isn't right for me to expect her to become mother to my sister's children and that it appears to me that she may not have been given full choice. I will free her and face whatever consequences come.

His carriage crept forward. At the turn to Caroline Street, Henry spied that familiar charcoal greatcoat. His heart skipped a beat when he realized Detective Smith was waving him down.

God help me, he prayed as Smith commandeered the seat beside him.

"Dreadful rain," the man mumbled crossly.

"Have you been standing in it long?"

"You could say that."

A chill ran down Henry's spine, but it had little to do with the cold downpour. Smith's answer was vague. He knew exactly why. The detective had been *working* the funeral route.

"I appreciate you giving me a lift," Smith said.

I didn't, Henry thought. *You stopped me.* "Are you going to the Exchange?"

"Perhaps."

Neither man said anything more for several moments. Rain continued its thunderous barrage while the president's body continued its journey. Out of the corner of his eye, Henry could see Smith scouring the crowd.

He's still working, he thought.

Henry knew he needed to acknowledge the fact that Smith had attempted to pay him a call. If he didn't, it would bring further suspicion upon him. Swallowing hard, he hoped his voice remained steady.

"I understand you wished to see me the other day," he said. "I apologize for not being at home. I had—"

"—business with the city council. Yes. I know."

Henry swallowed once more. *What else do you know?* "Was there something particular you wished to see me about?"

"Not now," Smith said.

Not now?

As the carriage continued its plodding pace, Henry could feel the man's eyes upon him. The regimental band was playing a funeral dirge. Henry felt as though it was being played not for Lincoln but for himself.

The last thing Henry wanted to discuss was the manhunt for Booth, but he realized any normal, *loyal* man would be curious about the investigation.

"Are you looking for him?" Henry asked. He did not need to elaborate. Smith would know exactly to whom he was referring. "Do you think he's here in Baltimore?"

"He *was* here," Smith said, now eyeing the crowd. "That I do know. Just hours before the assassination, trying to recruit more conspirators."

Henry's grip on the reins tightened. His horse threw back its long golden mane in protest.

Smith turned from the crowd and looked directly at him once more. "But why should that be any business of yours right now, Mr. Councilman?" he said, voice devoid of any expression, any way to read his mood. "Haven't you other matters on your mind?"

"Have I?"

"Taking a bride? I should say so."

In spite of turn in the conversation, Henry felt no

relief. "How did you know of that?" he asked. "We've yet to announce the engagement publicly."

"I make it my business to know such things," Smith said, and he gestured toward an upcoming lamppost. "Let me off here."

Henry slowed to do so, and without further word, the detective disappeared into crowd. The man's words haunted him. *"I make it my business to know such things."*

Henry couldn't help but wonder just what else Detective Smith had uncovered.

He obviously suspects something. But what Henry couldn't figure out was why the detective didn't simply ask him what he wanted to know. *Is he waiting to see where else I might lead him?*

He told himself Smith would get nothing. He was no conspirator. He hadn't done anything wrong, at least not as far as it pertained to President Lincoln.

Rebekah stood silently in the place reserved for dignitaries and family members as President Lincoln's coffin was carried inside. A great sadness welled up inside her. She had never met the president, although she had always wanted to do so. Her younger brothers Teddy and Gilbert had been given the privilege once, when their father had traveled to Washington on business.

Rebekah had asked to go, as well, but her request had been denied.

"Politics is no place for you," her father had said, but what he'd meant was, it was no place for her unless it served *his* purpose. If he needed a lady to hand out flowers or nurse wounded soldiers so his family could be known for assisting the war effort, *then* she was called upon.

Otherwise I am expected to keep out of the way. Be seen but not heard, she thought.

The president's coffin was opened. The mourners began to file past, first the generals and military commanders and Governor Bradford, then her father and the rest of the state legislature. Each displayed a stone-like, somber face of dignity.

How ironic, she couldn't help but think. Some of those same men had despised the president. *Have they undergone a change of heart or are they simply seizing an opportunity to be present in front of voters?*

Rebekah then spied Councilman Nash. He had not voted for the late president, either, but the look in his eyes and the set of his mouth revealed he was clearly troubled by his death. He passed Lincoln's casket respectfully, then came to where her mother, her brothers and now her father stood. He greeted them formally, but with the same heartfelt expression still on his face.

She studied him. He was taller than her father, with a strong build. While she still would not call him handsome, there was something winsome about his face, something honest, tender.

He certainly cares for his two young charges, and he is kind to the servants employed in his household. The question, however, begged to be asked. *But is that simply what he wants me to think?*

Rebekah wanted to believe him a good, caring man, one who would always treat her and the children in his care with kindness, but she knew firsthand how deceiving appearances could be. Once more her promise to herself came back to her.

I will not give him my heart. I will share it with the children, but I will not allow him the opportunity to wound me.

The councilman approached. "It is a black day," he said.

"It is indeed." After a moment of awkward silence, she then asked. "How are the children?"

"Well, thank you. Or, rather, as well as they *can be*, given what they have just gone through."

She nodded in agreement. *At least he is attuned enough to realize such.* Little Grace had looked so fragile, so restless when she'd seen her. *Even a baby knows when something isn't right, and as for Kathleen, what emotions lie behind those vivid blue eyes? Does she know the circumstances surrounding her parents' deaths? Was she present in the house during her sister's birth?* Rebekah sighed. For all her upcoming marriage would be lacking in love between herself and her husband, she hoped she'd be able to bring a measure of peace, of happiness to the children.

Councilman Nash claimed the place beside her and offered his arm. Rebekah hesitated to take it at first, but knowing that her father was watching, she did so. She then returned her attention to those coming to pay their last respects.

State Delegate Nash entered the room. After making his way past the casket, he came to where Rebekah's father stood. The bitter rivals shook hands, exchanged words, then stood shoulder to shoulder so the rest of the room could witness their *unity*.

Sickened by what she considered a display of political grandstanding, Rebekah chanced a glance at the man beside her. Their eyes met only briefly, but he looked exactly as she felt.

He, too, knows what it is like to be the child of an ambitious man, she thought.

The councilman turned his attention back to the queue of mourners. So did she. The heartbroken public was now filing past the slain leader.

The hour passed in strained silence. Then the president's body was prepared for the northbound train. Citizens who had not made it inside in time for the viewing, or those who simply wished to continue the pilgrimage, would follow the horse-drawn hearse to Northern Central Station. Lincoln would lie in state in Harrisburg, Philadelphia, and a host of other stops before reaching his final resting place in Springfield, Illinois.

"Are you going to the train station?" her fiancé asked her.

She'd been told by her father that she was to go only if Councilman Nash did so. "Are you?" she asked.

"No."

"I see," she said. "Neither am I."

Both her father and his were remaining, as well, evidently to make certain the lingering citizens had opportunity to speak with their state representatives if they so chose. To Rebekah's surprise, many did. They came expressing their appreciation that in a time of national tragedy, the two rivals could put aside their differences for the good of the nation.

When the news began to circulate of their engagement, the councilman suddenly looked very uncomfortable. The news held no joy for *her*, but *he* had instigated this event. Why, then, was his jaw so tight? Why was he tugging at his tie?

"Are you unwell?" she asked.

"This day should be about President Lincoln," he muttered.

"Indeed."

He looked as if he were about to offer something more but hadn't the opportunity. Rebekah's friend Elizabeth Wainwright and her husband, David, came then to greet them.

Apparently the councilman was well acquainted with the couple, who both worked at a local newspaper— Elizabeth as a sketch artist and David as a journalist. He asked them about their recent time spent in Washington.

"We were there to cover General Grant's return from the war and Lincoln's celebratory speeches," David said. "We had no idea we'd be witnesses to his assassination."

Rebekah gasped. "You were at Ford's Theatre?"

Elizabeth nodded grimly. "We were seated in the second row. John Wilkes Booth landed on the stage right in front of us."

Rebekah felt her fiancé's arm tense. She wondered if he was imagining the horrific scene just as she was. "To come that close to such an evil man..." she said to her friends. "What did you do?"

Elizabeth exchanged a sad glance with her husband. "At first I thought it was part of the play," she said. "I had never seen *Our American Cousin* performed before."

"But I had," David said, "and I couldn't figure out why they had added gunfire and an additional character to the scene. I recognized Booth right away. I had seen him act."

"I could tell he had injured himself leaping from the presidential box," Elizabeth said. "He *limped* as he ran from the stage, but I still didn't recognize what had actually happened until someone shouted that the president had been shot."

"We realized then," David said, "that we were no longer witnessing a theatrical production, but an act of murder."

Rebekah drew in a shallow breath. She thought of her time spent serving as an army nurse. She'd seen the cruel damage a bullet could do to many a soldier, but she'd never witnessed a shooting actually take place. Cold chills ran down her spine. "What did you do?" she asked.

David told her how panic had erupted, and described the devastating scene that followed when the president was carried away. Elizabeth shuddered at the memory. Rebekah watched as David slid his arm protectively around Elizabeth, steadying her, offering unspoken encouragement. His wife drew strength from the action. The two of them seemed fashioned for each other, complete.

How Rebekah longed for the same. *Yet I stand beside a man I barely know and will have little opportunity to learn about before I am bound to him for life.* A shiver again ran through her.

The councilman must have felt it, for he laid his free hand atop hers. The gesture was not as intimate as the comfort Elizabeth had received, but the touch was gentle and conveyed compassion. Rebekah allowed herself to look into his face. Dare she think he would not *always* be a stranger?

The councilman turned back to David. "Will you return to Washington?" He asked.

"No. Our editor wishes us to remain here, to cover the effects the assassination is having on the city."

"I see."

"In fact," David said, "if I may be so bold, I'd like to interview you. It would be good to have a councilman's perspective."

"I don't know how much help I could be..."

Listening, Rebekah marveled. Her father would *never* turn down an opportunity to get his name in the paper, and yet Henry Nash humbly hesitated. She was so struck by the difference that she couldn't help but smile. When he gave her one in return, her heart quickened.

Elizabeth pulled her aside.

"I believe you have made a very wise match, Rebekah," she whispered.

"You do?"

"Indeed. Henry Nash is a respectable, honest man. David has told me so."

"He knows him well?"

"He's met with him several times. According to him, the councilman is a committed public servant. He has a true heart for the people of Baltimore."

A true heart... Rebekah couldn't explain the feeling that flittered through her own heart upon hearing those words. Yes, she was still nervous about becoming a bride, and she was still resolved to guard her heart carefully, but was it possible—might she indeed one day have the kind of marriage of which she had always dreamed, one grounded in love and mutual respect?

It seemed almost impossible...and yet she desperately hoped so.

The moment he saw her smile, Henry felt as though a dagger had been run through his chest. He knew he'd given Miss Van der Geld all the indications that tenderness lay at the root of this match on his part. He had held her hand. He had smiled at her. He was slowly convincing her that he wanted her, when in reality what he truly wanted was the protection her father and his connections could offer him and his sister's children.

And he was more and more certain he was going to need that assistance. Detective Smith had entered the room. After circumspectly navigating the lingering crowd, he once more singled out Henry. As soon as the reporter and sketch artist bid their farewells, Smith stepped forward.

"So this is the lovely bride," he said.

The detective was eyeing his fiancée in a way that any gentleman would not like. Henry protectively threaded her arm through his. Though disinclined, he introduced them.

"May I present Miss Rebekah Van der Geld…"

Smith nodded cordially. She very promptly thanked the man for his dedication to duty in locating John Wilkes Booth.

"Rest assured, miss," Smith said. "Booth and every other traitor who dared conspire against our beloved late president will soon be brought to justice."

Every traitor… Henry's collar felt even tighter than before. He dared not tug at it again, however, for fear Smith would read something into the gesture.

Theodore Van der Geld then came to them. Smith acknowledged him with a nod.

"Rebekah, I am leaving now," her father said. Then he turned to Henry. "Councilman, would you be so kind as to escort my daughter home?"

A blush immediately colored her cheeks. Henry wasn't certain if she appreciated the request or was disconcerted by it. *Likely the latter. A carriage ride un-chaperoned? So Van der Geld trusts my character, but she does not. Wise girl.* He drew in a shallow breath. *Tell her,* his mind insisted. *Tell her you're doing this to save your own skin. Tell her before she gets hurt.*

Detective Smith was watching the entire exchange with a look that made Henry even more uncomfortable. What should he do? If he spilled the entire story here and now, he'd embarrass Miss Van der Geld in front of everyone. *She deserves better than that.*

"Well," her father said. "Off you go."

Henry was not in the habit of taking orders from others, but not knowing what else to do in the present moment, he offered Rebekah his arm. "Shall we?"

The blush on her cheeks darkened, but she allowed him to lead her toward the building's exit. Outside the rain had stopped, but puddles covered the cobblestone.

"If you'll wait here, I'll fetch the carriage," he said.

"Oh, that isn't necessary. I don't mind walking."

So they started off. Henry had to resist the urge to look behind him, to see if Smith was following them.

"I cannot help but think of Mrs. Lincoln," Rebekah said. "Of the pain she must be suffering. Her entire world has been turned upside down."

Henry forced himself to focus. "I have heard she will remain in Washington for the next few weeks, until she is better able to make the journey back to Illinois."

"Her heart must be broken."

"Indeed."

"I wonder if she knew what she was getting herself into when she married him."

"I suppose not," he said. *And neither do you.*

She looked up at him. Henry saw a myriad of emotions reflected in her eyes. Uncertainty. Vulnerability. Hope. Fear. He couldn't take it any longer. Stopping in his tracks, he looked her square in the eye.

"Miss Van der Geld, there is something that I need to tell you—"

A passing news boy clipped his confession short. "Extra! Extra! New conspirator named! Right here in Baltimore!" A crowd rushed to devour the details of the latest suspect's fate. Most of them had already pronounced sentence.

"There's another one to hang…"

"…and it can't happen soon enough."

In his haste to grab the latest edition, a particularly bullish man was barreling down on Miss Van der Geld. Henry pulled her aside and shielded her from contact. Secure in his arms, she was close enough that he could smell the lavender water she had combed through her hair, close enough that he could feel her trembling. When she looked up at him, however, eyes wide with innocence and fear, Henry did not see her. He saw Kathleen.

Her future and that of her sister's is still so uncertain.

"You were saying?" Miss Van der Geld asked.

Henry drew in a breath, once more letting anxiety override his conviction. Steering her away from the burgeoning crowd, he said, "It isn't important right now. The streets aren't exactly safe. I'd best get you home."

Chapter Four

Five days later, alone in his study, Henry scoured the latest edition of *Harper's Weekly*. The front-page article, entitled "The Murder of the President," featured a full formal sketch of John Wilkes Booth. He looked poised and polished, much like he had the day Henry had offered him a ride.

Revulsion tempted him to toss the paper aside. Fearful curiosity, however, kept him reading. The article gave an overview of Booth's family, acting career and known associations. "His companions have been violent secessionists," the publication read, "and there are doubtless many others involved to a greater or less degree in his crime."

Henry's heart beat faster. The article went on to describe just how the assassin had carried out the murder, citing evidence of deliberate preparation. Details included everything from a small viewing hole bored through a door panel to the seats in the presidential box, which "had been arranged to suit his purpose," either by himself, or "by some coconspirator."

He read further. "The villain succeeded in making

his escape without arrest. In this he was probably assisted by accomplices…"

Henry laid the article aside and pinched the bridge of his nose. He knew full well what would happen to those accomplices if they were caught. The local papers were reporting on the vast number of believed conspirators currently incarcerated in the Washington city jails.

Next he picked up the *Free American*. "As the search for Booth and his fellow conspirators continues, authorities turn their eyes toward Baltimore." The paper for which David Wainwright and his wife worked spelled out what Detective Smith had hinted at during the funeral processional and what the paper boy had proclaimed loudly from the street corner. A man by the name of Michael O'Laughlen, a twenty-four-year-old Baltimore engraver and former Confederate soldier, had been arrested.

"According to authorities," the paper said, "O'Laughlen was visited by Booth here in the city the day before the assassination."

Breath quickening, Henry read on. "O'Laughlen insists in a statement that Booth did indeed come to Baltimore to convince him to join his plot, but he told the actor he wanted no part of any such activity. He then told Booth to leave…"

Henry was fully aware of what Booth had done then. *He climbed into my carriage, and I drove him to the train station. It is only a matter of time before Detective Smith realizes this.*

Or did the man already know? Was that why he'd boarded Henry's carriage the day of Lincoln's funeral procession? *Does Theodore Van der Geld know, as well?* Anxiety chilled his blood. It wasn't *only* the thought of his potential political protector turning against him that caused it. It was the memory of Rebekah Van der Geld's eyes the day he had sheltered her from the crowd.

What will Miss Van der Geld think if she learns her fiancé is a lying conspirator? Henry then wondered if his indiscretion could jeopardize *her* freedom. As the national outrage over Booth's actions continued to grow, everyone from the stable owner who'd sheltered the actor's horse to the widow who owned the boardinghouse where he had met with fellow traitors was now in custody of the authorities.

And they are determined to round up more. Would the authorities think her suspect because of her connection to me?

Reason again told him simply to come clean, that he could protect Miss Van der Geld, his nieces and himself much more effectively by going straight to Detective Smith and confessing. Yes, he had given Booth a ride to the train station. No, he had no idea what the actor was actually doing in Baltimore. He could tell Smith he had visited the Branson Boarding House as well that day, that he had listened to Miss Maggie's complaints of loitering soldiers without any knowledge of how sympathetic she and her family were to the Southern cause.

But Henry was certain how the scene would play out. Smith would wonder why he had waited so long. He would tell Henry a truly patriotic man would have come forward with the information the moment he learned of the president's death.

And then he will question my family's past actions. My brother-in-law's enlistment in the Confederate army. My journey to Virginia to collect his children.

The detective will also point out how, at the beginning of the war, my father was against sending troops to keep our sister states in the Union by force...how he later voted against measures that would strengthen the federal government's control in Maryland.

Surely Detective Smith would then remark how Harold Nash had openly criticized Lincoln's wartime policies and had voted against him in the presidential election not once but twice. Henry raked back his hair.

And I did the same. But just because I didn't agree with the president's policies doesn't mean I wished him dead! Yet he feared that was exactly the conclusion Detective Smith would draw.

Despite my service to the Union, I'll be painted a turncoat, one who saw an opportunity to strike back at the president for the "wrongs" inflicted upon my state.

Head now pounding, Henry closed his eyes. He wished he could see a clear way out of this, one that would not involve entangling an innocent woman in the process, or breaking her heart. His own heart told him to pray, but his shame would not allow it. *How dare I ask God for any help, now that I've made such a mess of things?*

The door to the study clicked open. Henry looked up to see his father entering. He was holding out a slip of paper.

"This just came for you," he said, handing it over. "The rider is still here, waiting for your reply."

Henry unfolded the message. It was a dinner invitation, of all things. Theodore Van der Geld was requesting his presence in his home. Henry quickly realized only *he* had been invited, not his father. He told him so.

The older man only laughed. "I am not surprised.

There won't be more than a handful of voters present this time."

Henry laid the invitation aside. "I'm not going."

"You had better. Now that they have placed Booth in Baltimore the day before the assassination, you don't want to run the risk of offending one of the most powerful men in this state."

"It's too late for that," Henry said.

"Too late for what?" His father asked.

"Why should Van der Geld assist me?"

"Because he wants the votes you will bring."

"And what will the voters think of me when they learn of my *association* with John Wilkes Booth?"

"There's no reason they have to know. Should the provost marshal uncover anything, Van der Geld would be able to keep it under wraps. Appearances will be maintained, and that is all that matters."

It was one of the most presumptuous statements Henry had ever heard, but before he could say so, his father reminded him, "You must remember your nieces."

My nieces. Your grandchildren. Did the man even know their names?

"Do you want them growing up openly shunned as wards of a coconspirator?"

Henry's stomach roiled. *No, of course not*, and he didn't want them growing up as wards of the state, either, which he was certain they would become if his father gained control over them.

"Forward," his father said. "Forward is the only way. I'll tell the messenger you will attend." And with that, the man left the room.

As the appointed hour approached, Henry shaved and put on his nicest vest and coat. He even went to the garden in search of a proper bouquet of flowers. Deciding, though, that his crop fell far below a lady's standard, he stopped at the florist before heading to the Van der Geld home. Knowing red roses would be insincere, he chose a pale pink bouquet. He hoped his fiancée would like it.

An anxiety far different than what he'd felt upon reading the recent newspapers washed over him as he rang the Van der Geld's bell. Henry had just enough time to give his collar a tug when a white-gloved butler opened the door. The man took Henry's topper, then ushered him into a formal parlor, where the state legislator, his family and several other male guests were waiting. Miss Van der Geld was in the corner opposite her father. She blushed the moment she saw Henry.

Something inside him stirred.

I will not allow her heart to be broken. I will make this work. This may not be the life I wished for, but I will never let her know that. She wants love. I will do my best to give it to her. I will do my best to make her happy. If she is happy, Grace and Kathleen will be, as well.

After acknowledging her parents' hospitality he walked toward her. "Good evening, *Rebekah.*"

Her blush darkened. Although apparently unsettled by the sudden familiarity, she followed suit. "And to you, *H-henry.*"

When he handed her the flowers, a look of surprise, of genuine pleasure, filled her face.

"Oh, how kind of you," she said with a smile. Snuggling the roses close, she breathed in their scent, just as Kathleen had done with her jonquils. "Pink is my favorite color."

He told himself to remember that piece of information, then offered what he hoped was a steady smile in return. "I'm pleased that you approve."

The brief act of courtship was quickly brushed aside, for her father then promptly steered Henry toward his other guests. What Henry had hoped would be a simple family supper appeared now to be anything but. Among Van der Geld's visitors was a reporter from the *Baltimore Sun*, an assistant state's attorney and Colonel John Woolley, chief marshal from the provost department.

The moment Henry recognized Detective Smith's superior officer, he couldn't help but think he had just stepped into a trap.

At her mother's insistence, Rebekah's pink roses were quickly whisked away, but not before she instructed her to pin one to her bodice.

"You'll want to show him you appreciate his gift," Susan whispered.

In truth, Rebekah *was* touched by the councilman's gesture. No man had ever brought her flowers before, and the joy she felt at being presented with such a lovely bouquet stirred her heart. Fear and a host of other emotions, however, kept those feelings in check. Henry Nash *appeared* to be a kind and considerate man, but she knew for a fact there was another side to him—a forceful one. She had seen it firsthand.

That day at the Merchant's Exchange, he had pulled her into his arms. It had been for her protection, yes, but his way of providing it was as frightening to her as the raucous crowd. Rebekah had never been so near a man before, except during her time as a nurse, and those men had been either feeble bodied or unsettled in the mind. Henry Nash had been close enough that she could smell the soap powder on his clothing, feel his labored breathing. His hands upon her arms were strong, overpowering.

Will he display further strength if I displease him?

Fear prickled her skin. For twenty-three years, she had been trying to please her father. The harder she tried to live up to his expectations, however, the less her father seemed to approve of her. More than once he had told her that she was inept and had no natural beauty. Rebekah told herself that physical beauty was not an attribute for which to strive, but she desperately wanted to be seen as lovely, to be dear enough to be beautiful to someone.

And my temperament is hopelessly flawed. She tried to be sweet, demure and obedient, but deep inside her, fiery opinions burned. They dared not flame in her father's presence, but they had elsewhere. Damaged relationships with her friends were only one example.

At the beginning of the war, Julia and the others in their sewing circle had all supported secession. Rebekah made it perfectly clear to them that she thought that position traitorous. It caused quite a rift in their relationship. It wasn't until Rebekah took time to understand their point of view that the friendships began to mend. The girls were sympathetic to the South not because they wished for disunion or the continuation of slavery but because their brothers had chosen to fight for that side in defense of states' rights.

Though she could never fully agree with their support, she could at least feel sympathy toward them. She witnessed the high cost of war when Sally's brother, Stephen, was killed in battle; Julia's brother, Edward, turned up in the hospital severely wounded and half out of his mind with grief; and Elizabeth's brother, George, was taken prisoner.

And Henry Nash lost his brother-in-law, his nieces their father...

She thought then of that day at the soldiers' memorial service. How proud little Kathleen had looked when Rebekah had given her those flowers. Henry had thanked her for doing so, as if he knew exactly how much it would mean to the little girl.

Any man who pays such attention to a child cannot be like my father... I must remember that.

He had been kind to Joseph tonight, as well. When Henry had greeted her youngest brother, he bent down to his level, shook the boy's hand in a most grown-up fashion and tousled his hair.

The greeting had made quite an impression on Joseph. Even now the child was watching him intently.

"I like that man," he whispered to Rebekah.

The conflict inside her intensified. She watched from across the room as Henry spoke with her father and the other gentlemen. As a city councilman, he was surely accustomed to making speeches and working with high-ranking officials of the state, yet Rebekah couldn't help but notice that tonight he seemed rather nervous. Why? He had already won her father's approval.

Does he seek mine? The thought brought a tingle to her cheeks.

When dinner was announced, Henry returned to escort her to the dining room. To Rebekah's surprise, they were seated together at the midsection of the table, which was a much higher position than she had ever claimed before. Her younger brothers, even Joseph, always outranked her in proximity to her father and the invited guests.

Rebekah now felt an excitement so strong it made her hands tremble. Half had to do with the favor her father had just bestowed upon her. The other was the gentle kindness with which her fiancé was attending her. Henry assisted her with her chair, then claimed his seat beside her. Colonel Woolley was across from them.

"I've just been telling Councilman Nash how fortunate he is in marrying a lady as lovely and as gracious as yourself," he said to her.

The compliment made her blush, and she thanked him for it. As appreciative as she was of the colonel's words, Rebekah couldn't help but wonder what the councilman had said to him in return. Did *he* think she was lovely and gracious? Would he ever tell her so?

Her father quickly commandeered the conversation. The subject was the national scene. "Pendergast," he said, addressing the newspaper man to his left, "are you as concerned over the ability to implement President Lincoln's peace policies as I?"

"Indeed," the man said, "I wonder now if there can even be a lasting peace. There are many who see the assassination as a call for the renewal of war."

"I can tell you," her father said, "President Johnson isn't happy about having to abide by Lincoln's plans for reconstruction."

"He promised he would honor the late president's wishes," Colonel Woolley said.

"Well, he had better keep his eyes open," Theodore insisted. "A country can be lulled by promises of peace, yet still be at war."

Rebekah listened quietly. She had her own opinions

on the subject but did not dare share them with this audience, even though for once she actually agreed with her father. While she did not believe the average rebel soldier sanctioned the president's murder, she'd overheard enough men in her own state say they would rather die by their swords than suffer defeat.

Will the Confederate leadership follow the terms of surrender, or will they now fight this war in a different, even more horrendous way? Is Lincoln's death only the first?

Apparently her fiancé thought differently. "Lee did surrender," he reminded them. "Once Booth is caught and tried, things will quiet down. No one wants a return to war."

At that, her father laughed. "Don't be so certain. The list of conspirators is growing longer every day. There are plenty of men who hated Lincoln enough to want him dead. The elections prove that."

Rebekah wouldn't go that far. There *were* plenty of people who had voted against Lincoln, but for *various* reasons.

"I grant you, sir," Henry said, "there were accomplices to Booth's crime, but I would caution our leadership to be careful. Not every man who voted against our late president wished him dead."

Well said, Rebekah thought. *That is one opinion we share.*

But her father, joined now by the state's attorney, only laughed.

"And that, Theodore," the lawyer said, "is why you are wise in claiming this man to be your son-in-law. You've got to keep the other side's opinions in mind if you want to win the governorship."

Rebekah's cheeks burned. The men were now chuckling, all except for her fiancé. Rebekah wondered what Henry would say or do now. Would he grow angry? Part of her wanted him to put her father in his place. The other part feared he would do just that. However, the man had no time to respond.

At that moment the butler stepped into the room. On his heels was a soldier. "Excuse me, sir," Stevens said to her father, "but this man has a message for the colonel."

The soldier stepped forward and delivered the missive.

After reading it, Colonel Woolley replied, "Very good," and he then dismissed the man. "Well, gentlemen," he said to those around the table. "We shall see if Councilman Nash's opinion of our future proves true."

"How is that?" Her father asked.

Woolley's chest seemed to swell with pride. "The United States Army cornered John Wilkes Booth in a barn in northern Virginia. One of the sergeants shot him. He is dead."

Rebekah saw a flicker of emotion pass over Henry's face, but she wasn't able to distinguish exactly which one it was. It didn't seem to be relief, which was what she felt. She was thankful the president's murderer had been stopped. Now he could harm no one else. It wasn't triumph, either, which was the look her father's face clearly bore.

"Was Booth alone when they took him?" Theodore asked.

"No," Colonel Woolley replied. "He had an accomplice, but at least the scoundrel had the sense to surrender."

"Then there is information to be had," said her father.

"Indeed," said Mr. Pendergast, "and likely more conspirators to be found."

Now Rebekah recognized the look on her fiancé's
face. It was one of fear, but why exactly it was there,
she could not say.

"More conspirators to be found..." Henry's chest
was so tight he could barely breathe. *John Wilkes Booth
is dead and President Lincoln is about to be laid to rest.
Will the nation's strife be buried with them, or is there
another storm on the horizon, one that will consume
not only my country but also my household?*

He could feel Rebekah's eyes upon him. He knew
his face was betraying his fears. Her father confirmed
it, though he seemed to misinterpret the cause.

"Cheer up, Councilman. Booth might have met his
judgment, but there are still plenty of others to be questioned. The extent of this web of evil will be exposed.
The truth will be revealed."

"I hope the rule of law will be upheld," Henry replied as neutrally as he could.

"Hear, hear," said the state's attorney, lifting his
glass.

"Of course it will," Van der Geld said. "I have every
faith in our national leadership."

The call to confess again beckoned, but Henry knew
here was not the place. Rebekah would be mortified.
Colonel Woolley, who had been so complimentary before, would surely arrest him on the spot—if not for
his conspiratorial associations, then for tarnishing her
reputation.

And what of Grace and Kathleen?

Dessert was served. Henry tried his best to swallow

it. Afterward, the party returned to the parlor. Henry chose a seat close to Rebekah and as far away from her father and the other men as possible. She clearly looked troubled.

Is that due to my reaction at the table or something else?

He saw tonight the way this particular household operated. Theodore Van der Geld placed low value on the presence of ladies. His own wife seemed little more than a shadow, never opening her mouth unless it was to offer refreshments to one of the guests or answer affirmatively when her husband issued some sort of command. Rebekah had been ignored practically altogether. Henry had wished to engage her, but her father's control over the conversation made it difficult for anyone to venture to a new subject.

Is she starved for attention, for affection?

His own mother had been that way, and Henry had watched her slowly wither away into silence. He believed that somewhere inside Rebekah lay a woman of strength, but how long would that strength remain?

"You weren't offered much opportunity to speak earlier," he said. "Is there a particular topic of interest you would like to discuss?"

She blinked in surprise, then stole a glance at her father. Henry followed her eyes. Van der Geld appeared to be watching them both. Rebekah looked back at Henry. Fear now flickered across her face.

"What topic would suit you?" she asked.

Henry leaned forward, his words meant only for the two of them. "Come now," he encouraged. "You must tell me something of your preferences, or how are we ever to hold a conversation?"

A flush crept into her cheeks, and a smile, one she seemed almost determined not to give, tugged at her mouth.

She is pretty, he thought.

"I am interested in the full citizenship of former slaves," she then said.

He blinked. He wasn't exactly expecting that, but the topic was of interest to him, as well. "Did you support giving them the right to vote?"

"Oh, yes, but I believe more is needed."

"Indeed? Such as?"

"Education. There is little opportunity for them to better themselves. Something must be done."

She spoke her mind firmly. He admired that. "I couldn't agree more. The council is looking to improve education opportunities for the local freedman, at the very least basic reading and writing skills, but so far there is a shortage of willing teachers."

"I see." Rebekah's boldness vanished the moment her father came toward them. She immediately looked down at her lap, as if she'd been caught in some sinful act.

"Rebekah, I hope you aren't boring the councilman with frivolous talk," he said.

"Not at all," Henry said in her defense. "We were just discussing the education of freedmen."

Van der Geld's eyes widened, as if he couldn't believe his daughter capable of sustaining an intelligent conversation. He looked back at her. "Well, you've had your amusement. Your mother needs your help serving the coffee."

She immediately rose. Her father then tried to assert his authority over Henry. "Come, Councilman. I'm certain you'll find the conversation on this side of the room much more to your liking."

He knew what kind of conversation it would be. Henry didn't wish to continue discussing the potential renewal of war, nor the conspirators who might still be roaming the Maryland countryside.

"I assure you, Delegate, I thoroughly enjoyed your daughter's conversation, but...now I must be going."

To his surprise, Van der Geld did not argue. Henry didn't know if that was a sign of respect or suspicion. Would the man be discussing him with the provost marshal once he was gone?

He cast a glance in Rebekah's direction. She was silently refilling the cups of her father's guests. He nodded to her, she to him. There was an understated elegance about her that he was only now beginning to notice. *And her long brown hair, curled and plaited tonight, is indeed lovely.*

But growing attraction aside, Henry knew their life together would be difficult. He could determine to care and provide for her, but if the fear of being named a coconspirator in treason remained a motivating factor, how effective a husband, a father to Kathleen and Grace, could he actually be?

Chapter Five

The week passed slowly and laboriously. Every morning, Henry attended city council meetings and listened to his fellow members debate how to handle the uncertain future. Every evening he returned home to assist Hannah and Sadie with the children. He was physically and mentally drained.

Grace cried incessantly unless held. Henry found himself often trying to balance her in one hand while poring over council minutes or business letters. Kathleen evidently followed Hannah or Sadie about the house sullenly by day. She took to shadowing Henry each evening.

Since she'd shown interest in his various books and atlases, Henry let her have the pick of anything in his study. She'd thumb silently through the pages, pretending to read or studying illustrations. One night, while examining a map of New England, she suddenly asked, "Is this where my mama and daddy live?"

Henry wasn't certain if she was erroneously using present tense, longing for her former home in Virginia or if she believed the map was of eternity. He chose to address the former. Laying aside his own reading, he shifted Grace a little higher on his shoulder, then beckoned Kathleen closer.

"No," he said. "That's Massachusetts. Your family lived here." He found the page for Virginia and showed her the location.

Kathleen's forehead furrowed slightly. "Will I ever live there again?"

Henry drew in a breath, wondering what to say. "Perhaps when you come of age, you may wish to return to your old home, but for now, it's best that you and your sister live here with me."

She didn't say anything to that. Henry then noticed a bedraggled jonquil fastened to her bodice. It instantly reminded him of what Rebekah had done with his pink roses. Did all young women do this with the flowers given to them? He had honestly never noticed before.

"That's very pretty," he said to Kathleen.

She fingered the fading yellow petals. "The flower lady gave it to me."

"Yes. I remember. Her name is Miss Van der Geld."

Henry had yet to tell Kathleen that "the flower lady" would soon be taking up residence in their home. Perhaps he feared the potential anxiety the thought of such change would bring Kathleen. Perhaps he still held out hope such a change might not be necessary. Perhaps tomorrow he'd wake up to find Detective Smith had concluded his investigation, and there were no more conspirators to be found.

But he knew the latter was highly unlikely.

And I could not break the engagement now anyway, he thought, *not after it has been publicly announced. I would not embarrass Rebekah like that... And given*

*what I've witnessed of her father's treatment of her,
how could I leave her in such a home?*

Henry wouldn't put it past Van der Geld to marry
her off to someone else to suit his political agenda.
While there were many good men in Maryland leadership, there were some who were not. Henry did not
wish to see Rebekah in the household of a drunkard or
a violent man—or even one who would be indifferent
to her happiness, as his own father had always been of
his mother's.

*I will care for her. I must make this work...for ev-
eryone involved.*

"She had flowers like my mama," Kathleen said.

Henry wasn't sure what to say to that, either. Would
Kathleen welcome a woman who reminded her in some
small way of her mother? He hoped so. "Miss Van der
Geld is going to come live with us soon," he explained.
"She has agreed to become my wife." He paused to
gauge Kathleen's reaction. All his niece did was blink.
Henry swallowed back a multitude of feelings, then
shifted Grace once again so he could draw the older
child up onto his lap.

"Miss Van der Geld will become your Aunt Rebekah.
Would you like that? Would you like having an aunt?"

He could see the uncertainty on her face. He felt
his own.

"Will we live here?" Kathleen asked. "In this house?"

"Yes," Henry said. "You and your sister."

"Will you be here with us?"

The question cut him to the core. "Yes, pretty girl.
I will be here. I will always take good care of you."

Kathleen laid her head against his chest. Henry's

heart was pounding. He had made a promise to her. He prayed he'd be able to keep it.

On the day before the wedding, Rebekah's dress arrived. She had hoped for white—which was all the fashion now—or at least something befitting the season of spring. No matter how nervous she was about the impending union, she still wanted to be a beautiful bride. However, she had not been given the opportunity to choose her fabric.

"Midnight blue is fitting in a time of national mourning," her father had insisted, and so the dress had been crafted to *his* liking.

At her mother's insistence, Rebekah stepped into the dark silk and turned about, watching herself in the looking glass. Although the color was not what she wished, it *was* a beautiful gown.

Even her mother seemed pleased. "Yes," she said, "it fits exactly as it should."

It was not quite a compliment, but Rebekah chose to take it as one. When her father then stepped into the room, she dared to ask for his praise, as well.

"Do you approve of the gown, Father?"

He scanned her up and down with little more emotion than one would show reading a grocery list. "It will do," he said.

It will do? Was that all he thought? Her heart sank. *What must I do to gain your affection? Have I not done everything you have asked of me?*

"The ceremony will take place tomorrow evening promptly at six," her father reminded her. He then turned to his wife. "Make certain Fiona has her trunks packed."

Susan nodded obediently.

"I have business to attend in the study," he said. "I do not wish to be disturbed." With that, he exited the room.

A profound sadness rolled through Rebekah. Here it was, the last night in her father's house, and although he had never shown her any affection, she had hoped tonight, perhaps just once, he would tell her that he loved her.

She glanced at her mother. For one quick moment, she saw a similar longing on her face. It quickly passed as Susan lifted her chin.

"You'd best take off that gown," she said. "You don't want to spoil it."

"Yes, Mother."

Rebekah exchanged her new blue dress for a cotton sacque and skirt. Fiona packed her trunk, and her mother made certain her father was not disturbed by their children. As usual, the day passed in order and silence. The only difference came when Joseph bounced into her room that evening. He had brought her a tulip from the garden.

"I thought you might want to take this with you tomorrow," he said. "Just in case Councilman Nash doesn't have a garden."

She scooped him up and sat down in the nearby chair. She would miss Joseph dearly. "He does have a garden, but I thank you just the same."

"Will I be able to visit you?" her brother asked.

Rebekah gave him a smile. "I should hope so, for if not, whom shall I conquer?" To demonstrate, she tickled his ribs. Joseph giggled until at last he was able to free himself from her grasp. He then turned serious once more.

"Does Councilman Nash like children?" he asked.

"I believe so. He is most kind to his nieces. And think of how he greeted you when he came to dinner."

Joseph grinned proudly. "He told me I was a fine boy."

"And you are indeed. I think you have no cause to worry."

A dark thought then pressed her mind. Joseph might have nothing to fret over, but she still did. She had told herself she would guard her heart, and only do her duty as a mother, as a wife, but Rebekah couldn't help herself. With each passing encounter, she found herself being drawn toward Henry Nash. The way he engaged her in conversation, that bashful smile… He *seemed* to care for her, but in believing this, was she setting herself up for disappointment?

What if he was marrying her simply because he needed a mother for his two nieces—or worse, because he wanted a *male* heir? *What if I am not able to deliver one?* She knew firsthand how dissatisfied her father was that his firstborn had not been a son.

Rebekah quickly shoved the thoughts aside, concentrating instead on her brother. "You must come and visit me in my new home every chance you get, or I shall be very lonely."

"You won't be lonely," he said. He hugged her tightly, then slid from her lap and skipped out the door.

Watching him go, Rebekah hoped his words would indeed come true.

Just before six o'clock the following day, Henry pulled his carriage in front of the church.

"Are you ready for this?" his father asked.

"No," he said honestly.

The older man laughed. "Son, if you want to make state delegate one day, you had better learn to give answers that are open to a little more interpretation."

Running for the state legislature was now the farthest thing from Henry's mind. He wasn't looking for advancement. He wanted only to keep the position he had and do it as honestly as he could.

But is that even possible anymore?

His father nudged him. "You'd best not keep your young bride or her father waiting."

Reluctantly Henry climbed from the carriage and went inside the church. Reverend Perry, Henry's minister since childhood, greeted him and his father warmly. He was a kindhearted man who, through four years of war and factions in his own congregation, still treated everyone with Christ-like compassion. Henry had always respected the minister and tried to emulate his example. Today he had difficulty looking the man in the eye.

Reverend Perry noticed right away. "Do I detect a hint of anxiety?" he asked with a jovial smile. "No need to worry, young man. While it's true a happy marriage does indeed require hard work and sacrifice, I've no doubt you're up for the task. You've never shied away from doing what is right."

Until now, Henry thought. Hadn't he once promised himself he'd never marry a woman he did not love?

His bride's expression seemed equally anxious when she arrived a few moments later and took her place beside him at the altar. There was no music, no march. There were no guests beyond his father and her parents. At Van der Geld's insistence, the ceremony was simple and to the point. Anything more than that, he said, would be unseemly in a time of national mourning.

President Lincoln might have entered his final rest and received his reward, but Henry felt his own trial was only beginning. Still, he made his vows before God and His witnesses, honestly promising he would give all his strength to keep them.

When Reverend Perry told him he could kiss his bride, Henry hesitated. He had wedded her, yes, *but what right do I have even to touch her?* He saw the fear in her eyes. Had she guessed what he had been trying so desperately to hide?

No. She couldn't possibly.

Feeling the Reverend's eyes upon him, he offered Rebekah what he hoped was a disarming smile. After nearly knocking noses with her, Henry lightly pressed his lips to hers. Reverend Perry seemed to find the awkwardness amusing. He chuckled. As for Rebekah, one would have thought she'd been kissed ardently from the blush that now colored her face.

My wife, Henry thought. *Innocent, trusting and obviously full of faith to bind herself to a stranger like me.*

The wedding certificate was signed. Following that, Harold offered congratulations and a charge to Rebekah. "I am leaving for Annapolis on tonight's train," he told her. "Take good care of my son."

She smiled humbly and nodded. A hint of color still darkened her cheeks. "I will do my best, sir."

No doubt she means it. Henry made the same promise to *her* father, but Van der Geld seemed more interested in moving on to his next matter of business than in making certain his son-in-law looked after his only daughter.

"Well, we must be off," he said to his own wife.

Mrs. Van der Geld nodded quietly. Even she hadn't wished Rebekah a proper goodbye. There were no fond words, no embraces. All Henry overheard whispered to her was, "Remember to hold your tongue."

And hold it she did, all too well. After Henry assisted Rebekah into what was now *their* carriage, they rode in silence for the distance of several blocks. Out of the corner of his eye, he watched her fiddle with her skirt and tug at her bell-shaped sleeves. He could only imagine what must be going through her mind.

"It must be difficult leaving your family," he said, trying his best to make conversation.

"Indeed," she said, "My life with them is…all I have ever known."

He wanted to promise her that her new life would be a happy one, but he couldn't bring himself to do so. Henry had no idea what the future would bring for either of them. He did, however, try to ease her pain. "Your family is welcome anytime in our home," he said. *Our home. Will I ever get used to saying that?*

She offered him an unsteady but appreciative smile. "Thank you. My brother Joseph will be happy to learn of that. He was wondering if you cared for children."

"I do," he said.

He had meant the statement in terms of children in general, but it singled out the obvious expectation for a man and woman beginning their wedding night. Rebekah realized it, as well. She tugged again at her sleeves.

Knowing he had to say something, Henry cleared his throat.

"Rebekah, I realize our courtship was brief…" *and*

my reason for uniting unconventional at best. "That being said, I don't expect—" He could feel the tips of his ears getting hot. He knew he was turning red. "What I mean is—I see my role as husband as providing for you, for Grace and Kathleen. And I see yours…well, as seeing to their day-to-day needs, running the home… Anything else can wait until our relationship…"

He stole a glance at her. She understood exactly what he was trying to say. Now *she* was the one turning red.

Henry quickly refocused his attention on the road before them. "I want to win your heart first," he said.

Rebekah offered no words in response to his declaration, but he clearly heard the sigh that escaped her lips. Was it one of relief? Disbelief? After all, what kind of man married a woman and then left her alone?

The horse click-clacked his way along.

"I think Joseph will get along nicely with Kathleen," Henry said when he could bear the silence no longer. "They are about the same age. Are they not?"

"He's a little older. He's six."

"I see."

They drove the final distance in silence. He'd been sincere in saying he wanted to win her, but now he had his doubts on whether he could actually do so. *Our marriage isn't based on honesty. Aren't we already at a disadvantage?* Pulling the carriage to a stop in front of the house, he climbed down. *There is no turning back now,* he told himself. *Forward is the only way.*

He is willing to build our relationship before building his family. As appreciative as Rebekah was of her new husband's comments, her stomach was still full of butterflies. Yet when Henry pulled the carriage to a stop and offered her his hand, she pasted a smile on her face, took hold and stepped to the sidewalk.

"Welcome home, Rebekah."

She stared at the lovely brick Georgian-style home in front of her. *Our home*, she thought. *Yours and mine.*

The butterflies collected now in the back of her throat. What kind of home would it be? He had spoken of roles, but with little detail. How exactly did he expect her to run his home, manage his children? How well would she fare with the task—and what consequences would she face if she did not measure up to his standards?

Hand still in his, she allowed Henry to escort her to the front door. James, who must have been watching for their arrival, opened it immediately. He offered Rebekah a dignified nod.

"Welcome home, Mrs. Nash."

The title was going to take some getting used to, but it was a hardship she would willingly bear. No longer did she carry her father's name. Never again would she be known as Miss Van der Geld, but who exactly Mrs. Henry Nash would be remained to be seen.

"Thank you, James," she said.

Henry let go of her hand so she could untie her ribbons. Rebekah handed James the bonnet. Then, while he saw to her trunks, she glanced about the foyer. A pleasant scent filled the space, and the sconces on the wall glowed welcomingly.

"I believe Sadie is settling Grace and Kathleen for bed," Henry said. "She hoped to have them asleep before we arrived."

Rebekah didn't know whether to feel relieved or disconcerted by that fact. She knew the longer she waited to assume the position of mother the more nervous she would become. *But perhaps this is best. I should learn his preferences for his household first, should I not?*

"Would you care to see the rest of the house?" Henry asked.

She offered him what she hoped was a steady smile. "Yes, thank you. I would like that very much."

In addition to the formal parlor on the lower level, there was an elegant dining room and a large kitchen. The latter was not nearly as grand as her mother's, but it was well stocked and maintained by a most pleasant cook. Her name was Hannah.

"She keeps me well fed," Henry said.

Hannah, however, disagreed. "Not well enough," she told Rebekah. "Always puttin' off meals to get more work done. I'm sure glad Mr. Henry has done found himself a bride. I's beginnin' to worry about him. He was fast becomin' married to that city council and that ain't good."

Rebekah was stunned by the cook's informality and good-natured scolding toward her employer, but when Henry laughed, a far different emotion washed over her. Joy. Apparently this was a home where each person cared for the other, regardless of bloodlines or station.

"Hannah has kept me and this household in order for years, and she's done exceptionally well looking after my girls."

My girls, Rebekah thought. So he had claimed them as his own.

"Are you hungry?" he then asked her.

"I'd be happy to serve you," Hannah added.

While Rebekah greatly appreciated the offer, she

politely declined. She couldn't have eaten a bite. The butterflies were still fluttering.

After they bade Hannah farewell, Henry showed Rebekah a door to a section of the house that belonged to his father. "This is where he stays when he is in town."

"Does he stay with you often?"

"Only when he comes to visit. He prefers his home in Annapolis."

Rebekah would be lying if she said she wasn't relieved to hear that. Granted, she did not know her new father-in-law very well, but so far she did not particularly care for him. There was an insincerity about Harold Nash, a quality she sincerely hoped had not been passed on to his son. Thankfully, she'd seen no evidence of it in Henry so far.

"The last room on this level is the study," Henry said.

As he opened the door, she gasped. The room smelled of cedar wood and overlooked the garden. Stately bookshelves lined the walls but there was a cozy aspect to the room, as well. Greenery lay just beyond the windowpane.

"How beautiful," she said, turning about. "Is this where you work?"

"When I am home."

She longed to ask him more about his work, but her father had told her repeatedly it was unseemly for a woman to ask questions concerning a public servant's duties.

It is enough to be granted entrance into such a place, she thought. "It is a lovely home."

"I am pleased that you approve, my dear."

My dear? Rebekah's heart flip-flopped. Did he really mean that? Was she dear to him?

Henry crossed the floor and picked up a small book from the table. "This is the book I told you about," he said. "Remember?"

It was the promised floral guide. She remembered their conversation about it, of course, but what astounded her was the fact that *he* had. "Thank you. I shall enjoy reading it."

A bell sounded, and James soon appeared at the study door. "There's a man here to see you," he told Henry.

A slight frown creased her husband's brow. At that moment Sadie, the young maid Rebekah had seen on her earlier visit, stepped to the threshold, announcing that both children were fast asleep. Henry nodded contemplatively. "Very good," he said. "Will you please show Mrs. Nash to her room?"

"Yes, sir."

"Will you excuse me?" he asked Rebekah.

She offered him a polite smile. "Certainly," she said, and she followed Sadie to the second floor.

The girl couldn't have been more than fifteen, but she was efficient and very well mannered. In addition to tucking in Grace and Kathleen, she had unpacked Rebekah's trunks and laid out her set of combs and brushes. Even Joseph's bedraggled tulip had been placed in a vase of water. It seemed odd to see her things put about so, in a strange room.

"Will you be wantin' to take down your hair, Mrs. Nash?" Sadie asked.

Did she? Rebekah didn't know, but she supposed she should. "Yes."

Sadie motioned to a seat in front of a dressing table, and as soon as Rebekah sat down, she began removing pins. Rebekah studied herself in the looking glass as her thick chocolate-colored hair fell about her shoulders. She had never considered herself pretty. Her features were too large, her jaw too sharp, but one thing she was proud of was her hair.

Is he pleased with it? With me?

Sadie brushed out the locks, then asked, "Which nightdress will you be a wantin'?"

Nightdress? Should she put one on just yet? Was the routine of this house "early to bed, early to rise"? Surely Henry would return to give her further instruction regarding the children. *Shouldn't I be ready to receive him properly? If I am not...*

Sadie was still waiting for an answer, but Rebekah wasn't entirely sure what the correct one was. "Thank you for your assistance, Sadie, but I'll see to the rest."

The maid smiled, nodded and then pointed to a bell pull near the mantle. "Just ring that if ya need me."

"I will. Thank you."

With that, Rebekah was alone, and as on that day in the garden, she suddenly had a strong urge to escape. Again she surveyed her surroundings. It felt wrong to be here. *This is Henry's home, not mine. What makes me think I am capable of being mistress of such a place, mother to his nieces, wife to him?*

His return only added to her fear. When Henry knocked upon the door a moment later, Rebekah knew right away that something was wrong. There was no longer any laughter in his voice, no smile on his face.

Is it my dress? My hair?

A variety of emotions filled his eyes, none of which were comforting. "I merely wanted to wish you good-night," he said. "It has been a long day. I'll leave you to settle into your new surroundings."

With that, he closed the door behind him. Rebekah sank to the bed. He'd given her no further instructions concerning the children, and his sudden change of behavior, his abrupt departure, left her little opportunity to mend whatever she had done wrong.

Just what would morning bring?

Chapter Six

Rebekah lay in the darkness for hours, listening to every creak, every groan the strange house made. It wasn't until the wee hours of the morning that sleep finally claimed her. When Sadie drew back the curtains and sunlight flooded the room, Rebekah woke with a jolt. The maid promptly set a breakfast tray on her lap.

"Mama said if you'd like something else, let her know. She'd be happy to oblige."

Rebekah looked the food over. There were eggs, tea, toast and jam. She wouldn't have been able to eat all of it even if she was hungry—which she wasn't. "Oh, this is plenty," she told Sadie. "Please tell your mother I am most appreciative."

The young maid nodded. "I'm about to bathe Miss Grace, and Mama said to tell you Miss Kathleen is downstairs having her breakfast. Mr. Henry's already had his, bein' as he left so early."

Rebekah's stomach lurched. *He's gone?*

She had thought surely he would speak to her this morning concerning the children. How was she to fulfill the role of mother if she wasn't sure what steps to take? Why had he left her on her own?

"Mama said the council sent for him," Sadie offered. "Said it was urgent business."

So was it work? Was something pressing happening in the city? "Did he say when we should expect his return?"

"No, ma'am. He didn't. At least not to Mama, but perhaps James might know."

Yes, Rebekah thought. *I shall ask him. Perhaps Henry left some sort of instructions with him.* At that, she drew in a breath. It was time to begin a new day. Her first day as a mother. She had no idea where to begin.

Not wanting to offend Hannah, Rebekah ate what she could of the tray, then sent it back downstairs with Sadie. After dressing, she went in search of James. However, he was nowhere to be found.

She went to the kitchen. A pot was steaming on the stove, and bread dough lay upon the table. One meal was finished, and Hannah was already hard at work preparing the next. She smiled when Rebekah approached.

"Well, good morning, Mrs. Nash."

"Good morning, Hannah."

Kathleen was sitting at a small table in the far corner of the room, nibbling on her own plate of eggs. She was already dressed, her dark locks plaited and bound. That eliminated any notion Rebekah had of passing the time with the child by brushing her hair and assisting with her clothing. She drew in a nervous breath, then smiled at the girl. When she failed to receive one in return, the butterflies in Rebekah's stomach once again took flight.

I can manage this, she told herself. *I spent over a year managing a ward full of wounded soldiers. I can surely manage a four-year-old child and a baby.* In the military hospital, however, she had been given detailed instructions, a strict schedule to keep. She turned back to Hannah. "I was looking for James. Do you know where he is?"

"Out on errands," the woman replied, hands deep in the bread dough. "Is there something I might help you with?"

And there went any hope that Henry might have left instructions for Rebekah with Hannah. If he had, she surely would have said so. "No. That's all right. Thank you for breakfast."

Again the woman smiled. "I asked Mr. Henry what kind of eggs you liked, but he said he didn't know."

No. Of course he wouldn't know, Rebekah thought. *How could he?*

"Mr. Henry always takes his poached. He suggested I make the same for you, and if you weren't pleased, I could make something else."

She could barely swallow the food, but that wasn't Hannah's fault. The truth was, on an ordinary day, she would have thoroughly enjoyed poached eggs. They were her favorite. *At least Henry and I have that in common.* "I was very pleased. Thank you."

"What time will you be s'pectin' supper?" Hannah then asked.

Rebekah balked. Dinner was always served in her father's home promptly at seven, with no exceptions, but she had no idea what time her husband normally dined. Rebekah didn't wish to run the risk of doing anything of which Henry might disapprove.

"At what time is Henry accustomed to dining?" she asked.

"'Round six, but he don't always mind his watch. If he's got business, sometimes he don't show until nigh eight."

"But when he *is* home he prefers to eat at six?"

"Yes."

"Then let's keep the same schedule."

Hannah then inquired what she would care to have served. It felt odd to be plied with such questions, for Rebekah had never been asked her preferences before. *But I was never the lady of the house before.*

While there were certain foods she liked and certain ones she disliked, again Rebekah was hesitant to put forth her opinions. She didn't wish to do anything contrary to Henry's preferences.

"Whatever meals Henry is used to having will be fine," she told Hannah.

Hannah nodded and then went back to her bread dough. Kathleen was silently watching Rebekah from across the room. Rebekah wondered for a moment if she should have asked whether the child had any meal preferences, but again, she did not wish to do anything without her husband's permission.

Standing there for a moment longer, she was tempted to ask the cook what she should do next. In her father's house, she had always been issued orders, told where to go and whom to see. Now she had no direction.

For some strange reason, Rebekah thought again of Mary Lincoln. What had life been like for her those first few days of her husband's presidency, trying to settle into a strange house, while he saw to the urgent business of the nation? *And what must it have been like for her children? Lonely, I suspect.*

Kathleen was still staring at her. Loneliness was an

emotion Rebekah never wanted this little girl or her sister to experience. Marshaling what she hoped was a cheery, confident face, Rebekah claimed the chair beside her.

"You are to be my Aunt Rebekah," Kathleen said.

Rebekah's heart was stirred by the title. "Yes," she said, "I am, and I would be very pleased to get to know you better. What would you like to do today?"

Kathleen blinked and shrugged her shoulders.

"Shall we find your sister and then decide?" Rebekah offered her hand. The child cautiously accepted. Giving her another smile, Rebekah led her to the foyer.

Sadie was just coming down the staircase with Grace in her arms. The baby wiggled, rooted and began to fuss. "I think she may be ready to eat again," Sadie said. "She woke earlier than usual this morning, begging for a bottle."

Rebekah was embarrassed that she hadn't been woken by the child herself. Had Henry? Had he been irritated by the fact that she hadn't come to feed the little one? Not that she would have known what to do, anyway. She'd never fed a child before.

But I must learn. And now is as good a time as any to start.

"If you'll fetch me the necessary items, I'll see to her," Rebekah said.

The maid seemed most eager to hand the baby over. "Yes, ma'am," she said before she flew off toward the kitchen.

A writhing babe now in her arms, Rebekah looked at Kathleen. "We'll give your sister her bottle, and then we'll find something amusing to do."

They moved to the parlor. Rebekah settled in a comfortable chair while Kathleen took up post beside the nearby tea table, eyeing her sister and her new aunt with silent curiosity. Grace's cry grew louder. Hannah came into the room.

"You sure you want to do this, Miss Rebekah?" she asked. "Sadie can feed her."

For one quick moment, Rebekah was tempted to relinquish the child. However, she hid her nervousness with a smile and a bit of reason. "You and Sadie have done so much already. Please let me help you."

Hannah grinned appreciatively, then showed Rebekah how to fix the rag inside the bottle and dab it on the baby's lips. Grace quickly began to suck.

"There, that's it," Hannah said encouragingly. "You'll want to give the bottle a slight turn every so often or it will leak. My, she *is* hungry."

"Then she is growing," Rebekah said, parroting what she'd heard her friend Julia say many times about her own child.

"Indeed," Hannah said. "I believe she likes you."

Rebekah's heart swelled. Grace stared up at her, dark blueberry eyes wide with interest. *So delicate, so helpless*, Rebekah thought, *and so easy to love*. Inadvertently she thought of the baby's uncle, wondering, *Will he prove the same?*

Shoving the thought aside, she gave Kathleen a smile and then returned her attention to the baby. Hannah, seeming confident the children were in good hands, left the room.

All went well for a few moments. Then milk began to dribble down Grace's chin. Rebekah turned the bottle as directed but apparently did so much too fast. Milk suddenly rushed out, choking the child.

Oh! Rebekah frantically tossed the bottle aside and heaved the baby upon her shoulder. Upset by the sudden change of position, Grace spewed a mouthful of milk, then let out a wail.

Rebekah quickly patted her back. Milk was running down her own back and bodice, soaking through her corset cover and everything else. The forgotten bottle was leaking all over the nearby tea table, dripping to the floor below. Kathleen was now staring at it wide-eyed.

Rebekah gasped as she noticed the spill. "Oh no!"

Of the same thought, she and Kathleen both reached to right the bottle. Their hands collided. Rebekah succeeded only in knocking the bottle into the poor girl. Now her dress was wet, as well.

Kathleen fanned out her skirt, looking as though she wanted to cry. Rebekah was very near tears herself. Her cheeks burned with shame. "Oh, love… I'm so sorry. Please forgive me."

How thankful she was that her new husband wasn't here to see this. He would think her an incompetent fool. Perhaps that's what she was. Grace, now beet red, was still screaming, and the milk meant to soothe her was everywhere but in the baby's mouth.

Hannah returned, her eyes wide at the sight that greeted her. Repressing a smile, she came to Rebekah's aid. "Here, miss—let me help you."

"Bless you, Hannah," was all Rebekah could think to say. The woman took the baby. "Oh, your dress," Hannah exclaimed.

"It's all right." *Kathleen is worse off than I.*

"This is my fault," Hannah said. "I shouldn't have left you. You just seemed so confident—" She stopped, obviously uncertain if she could speak as frankly with

Rebekah as she could with Henry. Rebekah, though, welcomed the friendly tone. In her father's home, all her mistakes had been criticized with harshness...and sometimes violence. Hannah's gentle reprimands were painless in comparison.

"No, Hannah. It is entirely *my* fault. And confident? I am anything but!"

Grace's was still wailing, but the older woman seemed to take it in stride. "Don't you worry, now. You'll master things soon enough," she assured Rebekah. "Why don't you go and take care of Miss Kathleen, then change your dress, as well. I'll finish with Miss Grace, and Sadie can see to the rest."

The rest, meaning the milk-coated tea table and the stained carpet. Rebekah winced. *If my father saw this, he would...* She shook off the thought, for it was this family she needed to concern herself with now. She looked again at poor Kathleen.

"Come, love, let's take care of that pretty dress of yours."

The child once more reluctantly put her hand in hers. Together they walked upstairs.

"Have you a favorite color you like to wear?" she asked her.

"My mama likes yellow."

Oh dear, Rebekah thought. Hence the yellow dress Kathleen now wore.

There were no other yellow dresses in the girl's wardrobe, so Rebekah did her best to encourage her into a cream-colored one. "It's *almost* yellow," Rebekah said.

"But it's not the same."

"No, it isn't," she conceded, "but if you put this one

on for now, I shall make certain your yellow dress is cleaned well so that you can wear it again very soon."

Kathleen reluctantly stepped into the dress. Sadie arrived the moment Rebekah finished fastening the last of the hooks and eyes.

"If you'll give me your dress, as well, I'll see to it now," she said to Rebekah.

Leaving Kathleen in her room, Rebekah went to change. When she returned, the little girl was at the window. In her hands was a tintype of a woman bearing her and Henry's likeness.

"Is that your mother?" Rebekah asked gently.

Kathleen nodded but said nothing. Rebekah could only wonder what was going through the poor child's mind.

"She is very pretty," Rebekah said. "You look like her."

The little girl stared down at the picture as if she were trying to decide if Rebekah's words were true or not. Rebekah's anxiety grew. She so desperately wanted to connect with Kathleen. She herself knew all too well what it was like to feel distant from those who were supposed to care for her.

As she glanced out the window, an idea came to her like a gift. *The garden!*

She remembered Kathleen's delight over the jonquils presented to her. She remembered the conversation she'd once had with Henry, as well.

"I am afraid I haven't the time or the skill to make this plot what it once was," he had said.

"Would you like to go outside and help me in the garden?" Rebekah asked Kathleen.

Finally a look of interest, even eagerness, crossed the girl's face. "Mama had a garden," she said.

Enormously relieved by the response, Rebekah released a pent-up breath. "What kind of flowers did she have?"

"Big ones, little ones, pink ones, yellow ones..."

"Then what say we go outside and see if we can find some of the same?"

Kathleen nodded quickly.

"Very good!" Rebekah said.

They returned to the first floor. Rebekah found a cradle basket in the foyer, which she imagined Hannah laid Grace in when she was busy. "We can put your sister in this," she told Kathleen. "She can look at the trees and the sky while we work with the flowers."

The feeding now finished, Grace and Hannah were in the kitchen. The cook was holding the child in one arm, stirring a pot on the stove with the other hand.

"Here, Hannah. I'll take her now," Rebekah said.

"Thank you, miss."

Rebekah told Hannah of her plan.

"That's a good idea," the woman said. "I sure would like to see that garden looked after, but I just don' have the time for it, myself."

Pleased, Rebekah was ready to move forward. However, the instant she laid the baby in the basket, Grace began to cry. Rebekah immediately tensed. What was she doing wrong? She patted the baby gently. "Shh, shh, little one. It's all right..."

"She doesn't like bein' in that basket," Kathleen informed her.

That was obvious by the wailing. Rebekah wondered how such a tiny child could produce such an earsplitting protest. She continued to pat the baby, tried to reassure her. Short of being held, however, Grace was inconsolable.

What do I do now? How am I to work with Kathleen if I must hold the baby?

"You might try tyin' her to your bosom," Hannah suggested. "That's what I sometimes do. That way she still feels close to you, but you can have your hands free."

It was worth a try, for clearly Grace did not wish to be on her own. Hannah brought a large piece of cloth and secured it around her. "There. Now we put Miss Grace in just like so…"

The added weight of a child against her chest was something Rebekah wasn't used to, but she would gladly adjust. Hannah had been right. Snuggled now against Rebekah's heart, Grace soon settled. Rebekah's nervousness did, as well.

"Well, then," she said. "I believe this will work. Thank you, Hannah." She offered a now free hand to Kathleen. "Shall we?"

Outside, the early May sunshine felt warm and comfortable. A rain shower the previous evening had freshened the air. Rebekah drew in a deep breath, filling her lungs with the scents around her and her heart with determination. She didn't bother to search for hand tools or gloves. The ground was soft, and she soon discovered that the weeds easily surrendered to a simple tug.

"We need to give the flowers room to grow," she explained to Kathleen.

Soon the child was knees-down beside her, hands deep in the moist earth and loving every minute of it. The mud did not bother her in the least. It had never bothered Rebekah, either. Only her mother and father were offended by it. Rebekah smiled to herself. She need not worry about appearing unladylike now.

If Henry isn't due to arrive until six, we can work until midafternoon and still have plenty of time to bathe and dress for dinner. Wouldn't her husband be surprised to see how much she had completed by then? *Won't he appreciate the effort it takes to restore his mother's garden to the beauty it surely once must have held?* But most important, she was certain he'd appreciate the fact that Kathleen was enjoying herself. The little girl's personality was beginning to blossom. She was asking questions about the flowers, pointing out butterflies. Grace was also content. From her pouch, she now cooed.

Rebekah's anxieties evaporated with the morning dew as she and Kathleen rescued tulips from strangling weeds and braided spent daffodil greenery so next month's flowers would have their turn on the stage.

Confidence bubbled up within her. Despite a disastrous beginning, she believed she could indeed be a good mother, even if she was still unsure how to be a good wife for Henry. Hopefully she could make her husband happy by making the children happy. The pile of weeds beside her was proof of her determination, and Kathleen's delight at discovering wild geraniums was Rebekah's reward.

"One of my mama's flowers!" she exclaimed.

Rebekah happily plucked her a cluster. "Don't they smell good?"

Kathleen buried her nose in the purple petals, then grinned.

"Here now," Rebekah said, "we'll put them in your hair. Then you'll be a fairy princess."

"And fly with the butterflies."

"Indeed." Rebekah grinned.

The sun climbed higher, as did the temperature, but Rebekah welcomed the warmth. Grace, well protected from the sun, now slept soundly against her chest. Kathleen flitted about the garden, discovering budding vines and grasshoppers in a mixture of play and curiosity.

"You have dirt on your face," she said to Rebekah with a giggle.

"So do you. Never fear. A little soap and water will have us presentable again soon enough."

"When Uncle Henry comes home, I'll show him all the pretty flowers."

"I'm certain he will be most pleased," Rebekah said. *I won't disappoint him this time.*

It was then that she heard the sound of the back door opening. Thinking it was probably Sadie coming to claim Grace, she looked up. Embarrassment flooded through her. It wasn't Sadie, and it was too late for soap and water now.

Henry was home early.

Henry paused the moment he saw his new bride. She was a sight for certain. The prim and proper daughter of the next would-be governor was in dirt up to her elbows, with a baby strapped to her chest like a common field laborer. Beside her, Kathleen looked much the same. Dirt caked her hands and stained her dress. Neither of them was wearing a sunbonnet. Hair had escaped the confines of their combs and buns. It was now flower bedecked and tangled. They were smiling and laughing, and Henry had never seen a more beautiful sight.

The moment Rebekah noticed him, however, the smile fled from her face. She immediately stood and tried to wipe the dirt from her dress and hands. It was to no avail. Henry would have laughed were it not for the look of fear on her face. Why did his appearance provoke such a reaction? Did it have anything to do with his behavior last night? The visitor who had paid him a call?

Did she somehow know that Detective Smith had asked to see *her*?

"Why?" Henry had immediately wished to know.

"To congratulate her on the wedding nuptials," the man had claimed. "I was not able to attend your wedding."

Henry hadn't known what to say to that. Had Theodore Van der Geld actually invited the man? If so, to what end? His father-in-law had come to *him* seeking this marital arrangement. What would he gain if Henry was publically humiliated? Or was it that Smith had simply invited himself—to the wedding, and now to their home? Was he about to finger a new conspirator? If he was, he didn't need Rebekah to do so.

"Mrs. Nash is not to be disturbed," he had told the man. "If you wish to call, you may do so at a more convenient time."

Smith had accepted the firm reply with contrite posture. "Of course. My apologies." And with that he had left.

Henry had gone to Rebekah directly after the disturbing encounter. He realized now that he shouldn't have done so. *Surely she recognized my distress.* Had she misinterpreted it as some deficiency of her own?

He tried his best to be jovial now as he approached her. "Well, you've been hard at work today," he said.

"Yes…" she stammered. "I…th-thought I'd…s-start on the garden…"

"So I see." Henry glanced about. There were plants now visible that he hadn't even known he possessed. "You've done a fine job." Inwardly he winced. *A fine job? I sound like I am complimenting Hannah or Sadie, not speaking to my wife.*

"We found flowers like Mama's!" Kathleen announced. "See?" She plucked a purple blossom and presented it to him.

"Beautiful," he said. "Thank you." The little girl grinned at him. Henry tried to encourage one from his wife. "Your dress." He chuckled. "If your father could see you now…"

His comment had not the effect he intended. Reddening, Rebekah looked down at the ground. "I apologize for my appearance… I d-did not expect you home so soon. If you will excuse me, I'll make certain Kathleen and I—"

He caught her arm before she could reach for the child. He felt terrible. "I didn't mean…the truth is, I think you look…beautiful."

Her eyes slowly met his. They were filled with incredulity.

He couldn't blame her for her disbelief. He knew he hadn't acted right last night. It had been her very first evening in a strange home, and he had done little to make her feel welcome. After saying good-night, he had walked to the room at the end of the hall and shut the door behind him. And today, he had left while she was still asleep—hadn't even thought to leave a message for her with Hannah. How could he win his wife's love if he didn't spend time with her? *How can I spend time with her without running the risk of her finding out why I married her in the first place?*

Henry tucked Kathleen's blossom in the pocket of his frock coat as she scampered to the far end of the garden. When she was out of earshot, Henry tried his best to explain. "I was distracted last night, and for that I am sorry. I was thinking politics...the assassination and all..." He didn't tell Rebekah any more than that, and thankfully, she did not ask.

"And the council is what took you away early this morning," she said. It was a statement, not a question, as if she completely accepted the intrusion of public service on one's private life.

The request to convene had come just after sunrise. The concern was over former rebel soldiers now making their way home. The provost marshal was worried they would stir up trouble. With much of the Federal army still involved in the investigation surrounding Lincoln's murder, the acting authorities wanted the Baltimore city police department to remain on full alert, and to have funding for additional deputies approved.

Henry told her all about it. Rebekah's eyes were wide with interest. "It's no wonder they are so concerned," she said. "I saw the newspaper on your desk. The trial of the conspirators begins today."

He felt the jolt of that last sentence. The emotion must have shown on his face, for Rebekah immediately looked contrite. "I'm sorry," she said.

Henry blinked. Why was *she* apologizing?

"I didn't disturb the paper," she explained. "I only glanced at the headline."

He blinked again. "Rebekah, why do you feel the need to assure me that you only *glanced* at the headline?"

She hesitated, then looked again at her mud-stained skirts. "Father didn't wish for his mail to be disturbed."

He tried to make sense of what she'd just said. There had to be more to it than a man wanting to keep his desk in order. "You mean, he didn't wish for *you* to disturb it?"

She nodded slowly. "Especially the newspapers."

"Why?"

She bit her lip before answering. "He said young ladies needn't concern themselves with such things. That we have no aptitude for understanding such matters."

Indignation swept through Henry. His proud father-in-law, Theodore Van der Geld, champion of liberty to the slaves—and at the same time, enslaver of women. The contradiction sickened him.

"He is wrong," Henry said firmly. "Rebekah, you may read the newspapers and anything else in this house that is of interest to you anytime you wish. You need not ask my permission or pardon."

Her face brightened. "Truly?"

"Indeed. You are my wife. I want you to be happy."

The look she gave him made his pulse quicken. Was this the beginning of love? Was this what it felt like? Henry didn't know, but if it was, he wanted to feel more of it.

"Now tell me," he said, "besides the garden and the newspapers, what else are you fond of? And don't give me an answer you *think* I want to hear. Hannah has already told me you've made absolutely no changes to the menu whatsoever."

Embarrassment once more colored her face, but this time the hint of a smile accompanied it. "I should like to learn more of your work with the council," she said. "What you do day in and day out."

"All right. What else?"

"I'd like to know more about your time in the balloon corps."

"I'd be happy to share such things with you," he said.

"And I would like to learn more about this trial. Did you know that one of the accused conspirators is a woman?"

His heart slammed into his ribs. "Yes." *Mary Surratt, the widow who ran the Washington boardinghouse where Booth supposedly plotted to kill the president.*

Of all the things he and his new bride could discuss, she had chosen the one topic he so wished to avoid. How was he to escape this conversation without discouraging her? Thankfully, he didn't have to come up with a solution.

"Oh, listen to me," Rebekah then said. "I'm prattling away… You'll be sorry you ever asked of my interests."

"No, I won't," he said. It was the truth. He wanted to learn her, win her, love her. What he didn't want was for Rebekah to open the paper one morning and find the names of Mary Surratt and John Wilkes Booth listed beside his own.

Chapter Seven

The dresses had been set to soaking, the dirt from their faces and hands completely washed away. While Sadie assisted Kathleen and looked after Grace, Rebekah donned a simple cotton wrapper and made her way down the back staircase to the kitchen.

"I admire your persistence, Miss Rebekah," Hannah said as she handed her a bottle of warm goat's milk.

"And I your patience," Rebekah replied. After claiming a seat at the table Hannah handed her a fidgety Grace. "Now, little one," Rebekah said in what she hoped was a calm, soothing tone, "let's try this again, shall we?"

The baby hungrily began to suck. Hannah stood guard over Rebekah's right shoulder. If she had been stern, eager to find fault, then it would have been intimidating. But her intentions were so clearly helpful and supportive that Rebekah found her presence comforting.

"Now turn," Hannah instructed.

Rebekah maneuvered the glass bottle and rag very slowly. Grace kept drinking.

"Very good," the older woman said, "and see, you

don't have to tilt it that much. She's drawing the milk out on her own."

What a difference a little guidance and a word of encouragement could make. Feeling the tension slip from her shoulders, Rebekah began to enjoy the warmth of a baby at her breast. Surely the task of mothering was more than just a challenge. It was also a delight.

Grace's eyelids closed as she surrendered to a peaceful slumber. The bottle was empty, but Rebekah didn't want to let her go.

"Best let me give her to Sadie now," Hannah said. "You'll need to change for supper. It's just about ready."

Supper...yes...

Returning upstairs, Rebekah changed into a russet-colored evening dress, then stepped in front of the looking glass to survey her appearance. A near giddiness, a feeling she rarely experienced, quickened her movements. She had never been fashionable like her friends Julia or Sally. She hadn't a beautiful smile like Emily or the vibrant green eyes with which Elizabeth and her twin sister, Trudy, had been blessed. *And yet, today, Henry said I was beautiful.*

How her heart had soared with those words. He'd said he wanted to win her. She found herself wishing to be won.

Henry was waiting for her in the foyer when she came down. He was dressed in a black frock coat and trousers. His blue silk vest matched the color of his eyes. That giddiness inside her grew. *He may not be heart-stoppingly handsome, but he is indeed a fine-looking man.*

Kathleen stood beside him, wearing her beloved yellow dress, the picture of girlish innocence. "Don't you look beautiful?" Rebekah said to her.

The girl grinned shyly. "My dress is all clean."

"Yes. We must thank Sadie for seeing to it so quickly."

Kathleen nodded.

Henry had watched the entire exchange with a look of quiet approval, a look that stirred Rebekah's emotions all the more.

"Shall we?" he said, motioning toward the dining room. The three of them sat down together.

Hannah had prepared roast chicken and vegetables. The fare was not as extravagant as what Rebekah was accustomed to in her father's home, but the meal was delicious just the same. Apparently Kathleen thought so, as well. She ate heartily.

Henry chuckled at her. "Well, pretty girl, I'd say you've worked up quite an appetite today in the garden."

She grinned again but kept on with her chicken.

He then turned to Rebekah. "I'm impressed with how well you managed both of them today."

Impressed! That was a compliment, indeed! It felt good to have someone acknowledge her successes, for she was proud of her accomplishments today, as well. Grace had been fed. Kathleen had laughed. Despite what her father had always told her, she did have something worthwhile to offer. The children were taking to her, and she was fast falling in love with them.

She wanted to tell Henry this, but for some reason, she couldn't quite formulate the words. Perhaps it was the loving glances he was giving Kathleen or the fact that he had complimented her. Perhaps it was the knowledge that this was only their second night of marriage and they still had much to learn of each other. He seemed to be struggling with words himself. The conversation between them lagged.

Rebekah ate her dinner quietly and happily, though, daring to believe she had finally come to a place where she could find what she had always longed for—peace, acceptance…affection.

After a few moments of silence, Henry said, "You spoke of interest in the balloon corp. What would you like to know?"

Everything! she thought, but Rebekah reined in her curiosity and enthusiasm, beginning with only one question. "How did you learn to pilot such a contraption?" she asked.

"I wasn't a pilot. I was only an assistant. The piloting was done by Professor Thaddeus Lowe or one of the other aeronauts. There were eight of them in the Union army."

To learn he hadn't actually *commanded* the balloon was not a disappointment to her. Whatever involvement he had she still found fascinating. "What exactly did an assistant do?"

"I drew maps, sent telegrams."

"From the balloon?"

He nodded, then gestured with his hands to explain. "On a tethered venture, a telegraph wire runs from the basket to the ground. That way the commanders in the field have immediate access to information on the enemies' movements, the location of their artillery, their strength and size…"

Given the fact they were talking about war, Rebekah glanced at Kathleen. She, however, was busy eyeing the spice cake Hannah was about to serve. "Were you ever fired upon?" Rebekah asked quietly.

"A time or two," he said.

A time or two? That was a modest answer indeed. Weren't most public officials eager to make their feats in battle known? Her brothers had been told so many times of their father's exploits in Mexico that Rebekah had learned the history of Texas independence by way of them.

"There was a particular mission during which chief aeronaut Professor Lowe and I were forced to land behind...*certain lines*."

Certain lines? She realized then what he meant. Behind *enemy* lines. He was being vague for the sake of his niece, the daughter of a rebel soldier.

"We had to remain there until we could be rescued the following morning."

"Were you frightened?" she asked.

"Yes," he admitted, a hint of a rueful smile parting his lips. "After that incident, the balloons remained tethered to the ground so they could be reeled in at a moment's notice. The army didn't want them falling into...*the other army's* hands."

Rebekah was utterly amazed, not only with the story but by her husband himself. "Why doesn't anyone talk about this?" she asked. *Why don't you?*

"There was some squabbling among the top aeronauts before the war ended," Henry said. "It eventually led to the corps's downfall. The military community never quite accepted us. Some regarded us as little more than carnival showmen."

"But you *served*. Your life was in danger just as anyone else's."

"Thank you," he said. "I appreciate you saying that. And you… I understand you served as a nurse."

The joy she felt faded. Apprehension snaked its way up her neck. Where was this conversation going now? "Yes," she replied. "I served in the Army General Hospital on Pratt Street."

"For how long?"

"A little over a year." *Then my father decided it was time for me to come home.*

"That must have been difficult work," Henry said. "Troubling, that is."

"Yes." Rebekah did not elaborate, and thankfully, Henry did not ask her to do so. The memory of those soldiers, their ghastly wounds, still haunted her. The memory of her father's words concerning them still stung. But determination outweighed her pain. *I have a new home. A new family now—and I will cultivate a place within it. I will be the mother Grace and Kathleen need. I will give them all the love that I was denied.*

She stole a glance at her husband. He was studying Kathleen as she nibbled on her spice cake, and he was smiling contentedly.

Rebekah's heart warmed. *If he truly wishes to win my affections…* The idea of being wanted, of being appreciated, nearly brought tears to her eyes. But to love him? The thought still frightened her. She'd be risking so much if she placed her heart in his keeping. The children she could let herself love, easily and fully. With her husband…she just didn't know.

Her slice of cake now finished, Kathleen pushed back her plate. "May we go into the study?" she asked Henry. "Aunt Rebekah showed me a flower book. Will you read it to me?"

Rebekah smiled at the fact that Kathleen obviously enjoyed gardening a much as she. She smiled over Henry's response, as well. "Of course," he said. "I have some reading of my own to do, and I know Aunt Rebekah would like to get a look at the newspapers."

When he turned and smiled at *her*, Rebekah's heart fluttered.

"I must get the book," Kathleen said. "It's in my room."

"Go ahead," Henry said. "Aunt Rebekah and I will meet you in the study."

The child hurried off. Henry pushed back his chair, then came to assist Rebekah with her own. Rebekah's cheeks warmed. The cuff of his coat sleeve brushed lightly against her hand as they walked toward the back of the house.

"Thank you for spending so much time with Kathleen today," he said, "and for taking such an interest in her. The past few weeks have been very hard on her."

The words weren't exactly a declaration of love or even a commendation, yet Rebekah treasured them dearly. "It is my pleasure, Henry. She is such a delightful little girl, and so is her sister."

"They are indeed."

Upon reaching the study, he went to his desk. After riffling through the day's mail, he sat down to read the various letters. Rebekah watched him quietly for a moment. His jaw was set solidly, a determined, all-business expression on his face. The look softened considerably, though, when he glanced up at her.

"You don't have to wait for me, my dear. The newspapers are on the table. Help yourself."

My dear. He had said it again. With a grin tugging

at her lips, she moved to the large, comfortable chair beside the table where the newspapers lay. She dove right in.

The *Free American*, the publication for which David and Elizabeth Wainwright worked, was lying on the top of the stack. One of Elizabeth's sketches graced the front page. Much to Rebekah's surprise, she recognized the subject. The rough-looking man had been a patient at the hospital where she had once worked. She quickly devoured the article, then those that were related. With every page her astonishment grew.

Imagine! Right here in Baltimore!

"Find anything of interest?" Henry asked.

"Yes!" she said. "This is simply amazing."

"What is?" Leaving the desk, he came toward her. Rebekah's elation grew. Here she was, reading the news of the city, of the nation, and her husband was *eager* to discuss it *with her.* She showed him the sketch from the front page of the *Free American.* Elizabeth's re-creation was most accurate. "See this man?"

A serious expression filled Henry's face. "That's Lewis Paine. He's on trial for the attempted murder of Secretary William Seward."

"Yes, but when I knew him he was Lewis *Powell.*"

His blue eyes widened. "*You* knew him?"

Rebekah wasn't in the habit of associating with assassins. She wanted to make certain her husband understood that. "He was a patient, a prisoner of war in the ward where I served. He spent only a week at the hospital, and then he escaped. No one ever figured out just how he did so, but we all suspected Maggie helped him."

"Maggie who?" Henry asked, his left eyebrow arching.

"Maggie Branson. She was another volunteer nurse."

Rebekah flipped to a second page in the newspaper. "It says here that Lewis stayed at her boardinghouse only a few weeks before President Lincoln's assassination. Maggie is being questioned about her relationship with him."

She looked again at her husband, most curious to know what he thought. "Do you think she could have conspired with these other suspects? Do you think she could have had something to do with the president's death?"

"I don't know."

Despite the gravity of the subject, Rebekah was enjoying the conversation immensely. "As incredible as it is to open the newspaper and read about someone with whom I once worked, I am not all that surprised by Maggie's story. I *never* trusted her."

"Why is that?"

"She was too friendly with the prisoners, *especially* Lewis."

"Perhaps she was only trying to be kind."

"Perhaps," Rebekah conceded, "but I think it was more than that. I think she *was* and *still is* a rebel sympathizer. Why else would she allow that man into her home?"

"There could be any number of reasons." Clasping his hands behind his back, Henry turned and walked away.

Rebekah should have taken his movement as a sign that he did not wish to continue this conversation, but she was so caught up in the tale that she continued talking. "I think they are right to hold her in custody," she said. "They should keep questioning her until they get some answers."

"If there isn't any evidence of her guilt, they should let her go."

"But she and Lewis have a history—"

Henry suddenly spun about, his face as red as war. Rebekah knew that look all too well. "If they jailed everyone in this country who had ever come in contact with that man or with Booth, there wouldn't be enough cells to hold them all!"

The newspaper fell to her lap. Quickly she lowered her eyes. *Why didn't I mind my tongue? I never should have opened my mouth! I should have kept those ridiculous newspapers to myself!*

The instinct to apologize, to beg for forgiveness, came at once, but since she didn't know which words would placate him, silence seemed best. She knew better than to trifle with a man when he was angry. Even now her cheeks burned at the memory. Her father's hand had been strong.

What punishment awaits me now?

Kathleen chose that exact moment to return. "Here is my book," she announced.

Rebekah winced. What should she do? Keep her eyes downcast and her body still to avoid drawing Henry's attention, or seek to remove the child from the room? She did not want her party to what would surely come. *But would intervention only make things worse?*

Heart pounding, Rebekah dared raise her eyes in Kathleen's direction. The girl looked thoroughly confused. No doubt she was, for the atmosphere of the room was nothing like it had been at the dining table.

"Uncle Henry?"

"Not now, Kathleen," he snapped. Brushing past his niece, he quickly left the room.

* * *

Henry jerked the door shut behind him and marched out onto the porch. The sun had dipped below his neighbors' slate rooftops. Rain was on its way, for a clammy dampness was drifting in. The weather captured his state of mind perfectly. The bright, promising evening with his wife had clouded. The warmth building between them had been snuffed out.

Her personality was blossoming before my eyes, and with one sharp comment, I withered her. Then I did the same to Kathleen.

He hated himself for wounding them, hated himself all the more for not being honest enough to mend the damage immediately. For here he stood alone, watching the last vestiges of daylight fade from the sky, when he knew what he really should be doing was apologizing to his wife and his sister's child.

He couldn't blame Rebekah for her interest in that dreadful article. *It must have been a shock to open the newspaper and read that a girl and a patient you once worked with are both implicated in the president's assassination.*

Henry wondered if, upon reading such news, Rebekah had immediately begun recalling anything and everything she'd ever said to Maggie Branson and Lewis Paine.

Or Powell...or whatever his real name is...

Certainly he had been reliving that day at the Branson Boarding House and the encounter with John Wilkes Booth in his mind time and again.

Is she afraid that she'll be questioned by the authorities?

He didn't think so. Rebekah seemed, if anything,

zealous for the truth, as if she'd gladly tell all she knew about her former fellow nurse if it would bring the president's murderers to justice.

If I confided in her, what would she tell them about me?

A sick feeling washed over Henry. Would his wife believe him if he told her that his meeting with Booth was simply innocent happenstance, that the visit with Maggie Branson was motivated purely by his responsibilities as a city councilman?

Or would she tell them that she suspected I, also, was a rebel at heart?

A great chasm in their relationship was now revealed, one Henry knew not how to bridge. His reasons for marrying Rebekah in the first place made the task of forging a successful marriage and raising his sister's children together difficult, but he had been determined to beat those odds.

He had been confident he could overcome unfamiliarity, but how could he combat suspicion? If Rebekah was studying him half as much as he was attempting to study her, she would soon notice a pattern. He had to figure out a way not to react when news of the alleged conspirators or their trial was mentioned. If he didn't, Rebekah would soon grow suspicious.

And if she were to tell her father... Henry drew in a breath, knowing he wouldn't stand a chance of proving his innocence if Van der Geld turned against him.

He raked his fingers through his hair. Caution commanded him to ride out the storm. *Rebekah will be all right come morning. She isn't expecting an explanation, let alone an apology. I'm certain her father never gave her one.*

Immediately he burned with shame. *Since when do I make Theodore Van der Geld my standard for right and wrong? I never should have started down this path! I wanted to live honorably and serve my country well, but every day that passes, I become more of the man I don't wish to be!*

I have allowed my fears to control my actions. I have courted Rebekah selfishly, and in my continual effort to hide my deceit, I have hurt her. As much as he wanted to be a good husband to her, he knew he could not, nor could he be the kind of father his sister's children needed, until he owned up to what he had done. *God forgive me*, he thought. *Forgive me for it all.*

It was obvious to him what he needed to do, and although the fear of what the truth would bring constricted his throat, Henry was determined to apologize to his wife and tell her *exactly* why he'd gotten so angry. If she rejected him, called him a traitor, then so be it.

But perhaps, just perhaps, she'll show understanding. She does care for the children. That's obvious. Surely she would not wish to see them placed in a precarious position.

He knew he'd have to come clean with Detective Smith, as well. Prudence told him to secure the services of a good lawyer first, especially given the fact that he had waited so long to come forward. *That, however, can wait until morning. Now I must make things right here at home.*

Drawing in a deep breath, he started for the study. But Rebekah was no longer there. He found her in the parlor, and the scene he discovered there was enough to melt the coldest of hearts. Rebekah was on the settee. Instead of newspapers on her lap, there sat Grace and Kathleen. *The Florist's Manual* was in Kathleen's hands. Rebekah had taken it upon herself to keep the promise Henry had not.

His guilt grew.

Snuggled against her, his nieces looked completely content. Rebekah herself was the picture of serenity and devotion until, again, she noticed him. Fear immediately flooded her face. She pulled the children closer. Did she think he had come to rail at them, that he would harm them? The thought cut him to the core.

But no doubt I made her think such. And how frightened will she be when I confess my encounters with Booth and Branson?

Closing the book, she quickly urged Kathleen from her lap. "I was just going to put them to bed," Rebekah said.

Henry couldn't help but wonder if she had actually intended to do so at that precise moment or if she was claiming that excuse to flee his presence.

"Please wait. I...need to speak with you."

She nodded compliantly, but her look of fear remained.

How could he erase it? Henry looked down at Kathleen, then bent to her level. "My dear, I am very sorry for speaking so sharply to you earlier, and for not reading to you myself. Will you please forgive me?"

Kathleen's wariness vanished at once. As a testament to her forgiveness, she threw her arms around Henry's neck. His heart lifted until he again glanced at his wife. She was holding the baby close. Her expression was now one of pain. *Why?*

Releasing Kathleen, he kissed her forehead, then

said to Rebekah, "Perhaps Sadie could settle the children tonight."

Again his wife nodded. Silently she moved to ring the bell. The maid came straightaway.

"Go with Sadie," Henry told Kathleen. "We'll be along after a while to say good-night."

Now childless, Rebekah remained before him, looking fearful of what further instructions would be given. Deeply affected by her expression, Henry reached out to touch her hand. The moment he did, the front door flew open. Rebekah jumped.

Henry turned to find his father standing in the foyer. The tension within him rose tenfold, but he tried not to let it show. "Father...what brings you home?"

"The legislature is in an uproar again," the man announced, his tone as sour as his expression.

"I see," Henry said. He glanced at his wife. Rebekah now wore a polite, albeit forced, expression.

"Welcome home, sir," she said.

His father acknowledged her with a curt nod, then looked back at Henry. "I have much to discuss with you."

Henry inwardly sighed. This had not been his plan, but he couldn't very well speak to his wife with his father breathing down their necks. *I'm sorry. I want to make things right with you. Truly I do.* He looked at her, hoping he could convey his thoughts with his eyes. Whether she understood or not, he wasn't certain. She immediately stepped into the role of the gracious hostess.

"May I fetch you some refreshment?" she asked his father.

Harold nodded again. "Coffee."

Henry watched her float from the room, her silk skirts barely making a sound. As soon as she had gone, the man started in. "Detective Smith is making his rounds. He paid me a call. Paid calls on quite a few delegates, actually."

Henry's heart quickened. Fearing Rebekah would overhear before he had a chance to explain, he steered his father toward the study. "What did he wish to see you about?"

"Lincoln, of course! Although he was very vague about it."

"How so?"

"He was asking if I knew anyone of late who had come into money or made a hefty profit in business."

Henry blinked. "Smith thinks Booth paid his fellow conspirators? He thinks the Maryland legislature was somehow involved?"

"I don't know what he thinks, and that is the problem!" His father abruptly changed course. "How's your relationship with Van der Geld?"

Henry's mouth soured as he thought of what Rebekah had shared with him concerning the man, and what Henry had seen firsthand. "There isn't a relationship, nor am I likely to cultivate one."

"What? Are you a fool?"

Henry drew in a breath. "I have been, but by God's help, I won't be in the future."

"What exactly are you talking about?"

"Father, I thought I could make this work. I thought I could keep this from her…but I can't."

The man stepped closer. "Are you suggesting what I think you are? Are you going to tell her?"

"I believe I must."

Harold Nash threw up his hands. "I can't believe I'm hearing this! You mean to tell the daughter of the most powerful man in the state, *my political adversary*, that you gave John Wilkes Booth a lift in your carriage? That you put him on the train that took him to Washington, where he subsequently murdered the sixteenth president of the United States?"

Henry could feel the anger building inside him. "Father—"

"What are you planning to do when she tells her father about that? Or do you think she won't?"

"I hope she will be able to find it in her heart to forgive me. If not for my sake, then for the sake of Grace and Kathleen."

"For the sake of— Do you honestly think *those children* will secure your future? I can tell you right now, they won't! Only power will. That's what you need— power. That's why you united yourself with her family in the first place. It certainly wasn't because you loved her. I know for a fact you didn't."

Furious, Henry slammed his fist upon the desk. He was just about to put his father in his place when he realized they were not the only two in the room. Rebekah was standing in the doorway, a cup of coffee in her hands, a devastated look on her face. A knife pierced Henry's soul, for he knew she had heard every word.

Chapter Eight

"It certainly wasn't because you loved her. I know for a fact you didn't."

Rebekah could not move. She could not breathe. The words shredded her heart. As she stood in the doorway, holding the requested cup of coffee, the dark liquid sloshed all over the saucer. Somehow she had the presence of mind to set the cup on the nearby table before it spilled onto the floor.

Henry drained pale the moment he saw her. *"Rebekah?* Oh, my dear…"

My dear? She was not dear to him. She never had been. He'd married her to feed his ambition. He was just like her father.

"Power." She'd heard the ugly word drop from her father-in-law's lips the moment she stepped into the room. *"Power. That's why you united yourself with her family in the first place…"*

As Henry started toward her, a great strength, one she hadn't realized she possessed, surged within her. Turning on her heel, she strode from the study.

"Rebekah, wait."

She heard him call but did not obey. *Let him get angry. Let him come after me with his fists raised. I am through with crying, cowering, through with trying to please!* With every step, her defiance grew. It burst forth as Henry caught her arm.

"Don't touch me!" she shouted.

Her husband's eyes widened in shock, but for the first time in her existence, a man obeyed *her* command. He immediately let go of her.

"Rebekah, please—what you heard just now…let me explain—"

Her words fired off, full of force, full of disgust. "There is nothing to explain! I understand perfectly. You weren't courting me with any sincerity. You never had any desire to court me! You were courting my father's favor! Exactly what kind of power did you hope to gain by marrying me? Do you wish to be governor after my father?"

"No!' he said emphatically.

"Then you seek his fortune? My paltry dowry is all you'll ever see. My brothers will inherit it all."

"I don't want your family's money or your father's friendship," Henry insisted.

It occurred to her then that in addition to Harold, who had remained in Henry's study, James, Hannah and Sadie were probably hearing every word of this conversation, not because they were eavesdropping behind the bannister but because Rebekah's voice was surely carrying throughout the house.

Let them hear, she thought. *Let them learn the truth of the precious Mr. Henry!* But then she thought of Kathleen and Grace. The poor children had suffered so much already. Rebekah couldn't bear the thought of them learning the true character of their uncle. She lowered her voice, but her anger did not diminish. "Your father said you married me to gain power."

"He's the one who wanted power, Rebekah, not me."

"And *he* convinced you to marry me?"

"Yes—"

Pain, like a steel bayonet, pierced her heart.

"—No!" Henry then said. "It's not like that... I admit I wasn't thinking marriage—I was trying to tell you earlier that—"

I wasn't thinking marriage? So he had never had any desire to win her heart. He had lied! "If you didn't want money and you didn't want power, than just what did you want? Why did you wed me?"

Shame flooded his features. "Protection," he said.

"Protection?" Her father was a powerful man, in good standing with both the government and the army. But why did Henry need his protection?

"This wasn't how I intended to tell you..."

Her heart squeezed. So he'd *intended* to tell her this? How cruel could he be?

"Rebekah, I give you my word—"

Your word? What good was his word now?

"—I was acting only in the role of a concerned city councilman when I visited Maggie Branson's house the day before President Lincoln was assassinated..."

Maggie? The day before the assassination? That caught her attention. Though she was sickened by the sight of him, she wanted to hear the rest of what he had to say. He told her then of a brief encounter with John Wilkes Booth. Rebekah thought her knees would buckle.

"I had no idea of Miss Branson's relationship with

Lewis Paine," Henry insisted, "and my encounter with
the assassin was pure happenstance."

"*Happenstance?*" she exclaimed. "You drove Booth
to *the train station*!"

"He told me he was going to Washington, but I had
no idea what he was planning."

His hands were again upon her arms. There was an
imploring look in his eyes, one that reached deep inside
her, tugged at her very soul. She did not wish to think
the man before her, the man who so lovingly cared for
his sister's children, capable of conspiring to murder the
president, *but if he lied so convincingly concerning his
hopes to win my affection, what else is he lying about?*

"Rebekah, please believe me."

His request served only to harden her. She'd never
believe another word he said to her, ever again. "You
are just like my father. You say and do whatever is necessary to get what you want!" Twisting free, she ran up
the staircase, then locked the bedroom door behind her.

She knew. She knew everything and she believed him
guilty of every imaginable wrong. Deception, cruelty—
even treason. He could see it in her eyes when she fled
from him.

Henry wanted to prove his innocence to her, at least
where the matter of Lincoln was concerned, but had no
idea how even to begin. Pursuing her at this point would
only further harden her heart. He had been shocked by
the spine she'd shown him, the tenacity. After years of
being told to keep silent, told what to think and when
to speak, she had stood up for herself. He was proud of
her for that, but he grieved over the fact that she'd done
so because of her sense of betrayal by *him*.

Footsteps sounded behind him. Henry turned to see his father standing calmly in the hall. He would have called the man to account for what he had said concerning Rebekah were he not so angry with himself.

"Give it time, son," Harold counseled. "She'll resign herself to the situation soon enough. Then the house will quiet."

Resign herself to the situation? So she can walk through life, sober-faced and silent like her mother? Like mine? "That is the last thing I want!"

His father blinked. "You can't be considering divorce? If Van der Geld suffers such a disgrace—"

"If Van der Geld suffers? Father, listen to yourself! She's my wife! She gave me her heart unreservedly, and I've wounded it deeply! And all you care about is how her father will react? He's the least of my concerns. But no, I'm not contemplating divorce. I want to mend the marriage."

"And just how do you intend to do that?"

Henry didn't know. He didn't even know if it was possible, but of one thing he was now absolutely certain. If he had any hope of regaining the trust and respect of his wife, his father could no longer be part of the equation. *This is my home now. This is my life. I alone am responsible for the outcome.*

"What I intend to do concerning my wife is my business," he said firmly.

"I see," the older man said patronizingly. "If Detective Smith—"

Henry stopped him with an upturned hand. Yes, the detective was part of this, as well. Henry knew he must settle that matter as soon as possible, but that was not the issue of the moment. "Father, with all due respect, I do not seek your counsel."

"You'll seek it soon enough if your angry wife starts talking," the man scoffed, "if she tells of your encounter with John Wilkes Booth."

With that, Henry realized exactly where he must start. Rebekah thought him a conspirator. If he went directly to Smith now, it would prove to her that he wasn't. *But I can't have my father undermining everything I do.* "Father, I'm afraid I must ask you to return to Annapolis."

Harold's eyes narrowed. "You are asking me to leave?"

"I am," Henry said, regretting it had come to this.

The man became indignant. Color rose to his face. "Have you no respect for your family?"

"I *am* thinking of my family," Henry replied, "and it is precisely because of them that I am asking you to go."

There was a weighty silence. Henry stared at his father. Harold stared at him. When Henry refused to back down, Harold turned on his heel. "I'll be on the six o'clock train," he called back over his shoulder. "Don't come crying to me when you have ruined your life."

Henry had no intention of doing so. Anyway, if his life was indeed about to be ruined, then it was God's judgment, his punishment for what he'd done to Rebekah.

Rebekah told herself she shouldn't be crying. She had married a liar, a traitor, an accomplice to murder. She should be planning a way to escape this terrible household, yet tears streamed down her cheeks. Great sobs shook her entire frame. She had ignored her own counsel to guard her heart. She had *wanted* to fall in love with Henry, and had naively thought he wanted to love her in return.

Reason told her it was better to know the truth now than later. What if a child had been conceived? She had at least mercifully been spared that.

Abandoning the bedpost to which she had been clinging, Rebekah paced the floor. *What am I going to do now? Where can I go?* She knew full well she couldn't return to her father's house. The disgrace of a failed marriage would be nothing compared to the consequences of disgracing *him*.

But if I told my father of the role Henry played in President Lincoln's death, if I brought another traitor to justice, then wouldn't he think differently of me? Surely he would not only welcome me back into his household but also praise me for being a patriot.

Yet as much as she longed for her father's approval and acceptance, she couldn't help but think of the two innocent children sleeping across the hall. If Henry was arrested, would Grace and Kathleen not fall into *his* father's hands?

Rebekah shuddered at the thought. Harold Nash must not be permitted to oversee the children's welfare. The man obviously cared for nothing but his own selfish ambition. *Those two little girls would be miserable, lonely...and if either of them dared to voice their complaints—*

Dreadful memories swarmed over her. An iron hand, a riding crop, a razor strap—it made no difference. Each wounded deeply in its own way. Fierce determination rose within Rebekah. There had been no champion for her, no one in her father's house to protect her from his rage. *I will not leave Grace and Kathleen to suffer the same. So help me, I will not.*

But she could not take them away from here. The children were not *her* flesh and blood. She had no legal claim to them. Rebekah crossed the floor several more times, plotting, pondering. Then she froze. She knew what she must do, and she knew how hard it would be.

Protecting them means staying...staying with a man who does not love me, one whose temper may flair at any subject, and who could be sent to prison at any moment. But if that did happen and she was here, perhaps Harold Nash would consign the children to her. *Surely he would not wish to be troubled with them.*

Rebekah drew in a ragged breath, knowing there was another reason she could not run. No matter what Henry's motives, she had made her marriage vow from the heart. *God would surely be displeased with me if I went back on it.* She had known her own father's displeasure enough. She certainly did not wish to experience the wrath of the Almighty.

So it is settled, she thought, though her heart and mind were far from experiencing any peace. *I must make the best of it. For my sake and for the children. I can manage a loveless marriage, even if I had wished for more. Mother has lasted all these years. So will I.*

Resolve dried her tears. Going to the bedroom door, she peeked into the hall. Seeing the space was empty, she crossed over to Grace and Kathleen's room.

The two little girls were sound asleep. One was in the bed, the other in the cradle. Rebekah stared at their sweet little faces, so innocent, so in need of security and love. She regretted not coming to them earlier, not kissing them good-night. She did so now, then stepped back and sighed. Yes, she would follow her mother's example of steadfast duty, but there was one thing Rebekah was determined to do differently. She would bury her pain and disappointment deep inside. She would do her best always to have a cheery countenance in front of the children.

Grace and Kathleen will never lack love from me.

Henry passed the night alone in his study. Once his father had left the house, he'd retired to the room and walked the floor for hours. His past actions tormented him, but the uncertainty of the future was even worse.

Upstairs were a wife and two little girls for whom he was responsible. Henry was determined to come clean with Detective Smith, but even so, the original dilemma remained. Once he had confessed, how could he protect his sister's children? How could he provide for Rebekah? Regardless of the reasons for their marriage, the state of it now, he was bound to her. His honor—what was left of it—demanded it. His heart wished for it, as well.

He knew he wasn't in love with her as a bridegroom *should be*, but he *did* care for her. She was a lovely woman. He thought her highly intelligent, caring. He enjoyed her company, and *before tonight, she seemed to enjoy mine*.

Henry couldn't help but wonder—if circumstances had been different, if politics and war had not been part of the equation, would they have fallen in love? He sighed heavily.

It does no good to speculate now. This is my reality, and somehow I must manage it as best as I can for all involved.

But his management thus far had been severely lacking. He was in over his head. He had been from the very first day he'd taken charge of Grace and Kathleen. No matter how much he wanted to make things right for them or for Rebekah, he was only making things worse.

From somewhere in the back of his mind, familiar words emerged: *"For the good that I would I do not: but the evil which I would not, that I do."*

Henry recognized the words of the Apostle Paul from his mother's bedtime Scripture readings. When he was a child, she had reminded him often,

"You cannot be good on your own, Henry. As much as you may wish to, you cannot keep the law well enough to please God."

"Then how does one please Him?" he had asked.

"By confessing your faults to Him, by accepting His grace... Remember, 'there is therefore now no condemnation to them which are in Christ Jesus...'"

No condemnation? Could that really be the case? If anyone deserved condemnation, it was he. Rebekah's words sliced through his memory.

"You are just like my father!"

Shame turned his stomach, for Henry realized she was exactly right. He had done and said things to manipulate her for his own benefit. *I am a liar. I have been arrogant, thinking my past mistakes could be hidden. I am self-righteous, seeing the flaws in others' characters but not recognizing them in myself.*

The revelation pierced him to the core. What was he to do now? He couldn't right the damage he had done to Rebekah, and in his present state, he was likely to cause more unintentionally.

Again the Scripture verse whispered through his

mind. *"There is therefore now no condemnation to them which are in Christ Jesus..."*

He contemplated the meaning of those words. Their weight was suddenly staggering. Unable to stand on his own power, Henry bent his knees. *Oh, God, how can you show such mercy to a man like me?*

He recalled another verse. *"For the law of the Spirit of Life hath made me free from the law of sin and death..."*

The Sprit of Life, he thought, *the spirit found through accepting Jesus Christ as Savior.*

Going to the shelf, Henry found his Bible. He turned to the book of Romans, chapter eight. Hungrily he read the words his mother had taught him. No, he could not be good enough on his own, but God knew that and loved him, anyway. The secret to life wasn't living by his own wits or in his own strength. It was living in the grace that Christ would provide.

Who shall separate us from the love of Christ? Shall tribulation, or distress, persecution or famine, or nakedness, or peril, or sword? Nay, in all these things we are more than conquerors through Him that loved us.

Henry sighed once more. If only he had remembered such promises. If only he had read them before he'd let his fears of prison and ruined reputation consume him. *I could have saved my wife much heartache. God loves Grace and Kathleen even more than I. Would He not have provided for them without my interference in the course of justice?*

*For I am persuaded that neither death nor life…
nor things present, nor things to come…shall be
able to separate us from the love of God…*

The Scripture testified boldly that nothing could
make God stop loving Henry—not his fears, not his
failures, not even his most deliberate sins—but inside,
his soul was still churning. *God may grant mercy, but
Detective Smith may not.* Once more he bowed his head.
*Help me God…help me to trust You. Help me believe
that Kathleen, Grace and Rebekah will be looked after.*

He spent the rest of the night reading, praying, thinking, planning. Shortly before sunrise, Henry climbed
the staircase. He went to his room, shaved and changed
his wrinkled clothing. James, Hannah and Sadie were
beginning to stir, but the rest of the house remained
quiet. Grace and Kathleen had thankfully managed a
restful night. Henry wondered how Rebekah had fared.
For a moment he thought of knocking on her door, attempting to speak with her, but he decided not to.

It would benefit neither of them to repeat last night's
argument, nor would it help the girls. Forgoing his
wife's room, he looked in on the nursery. Much to his
surprise, he found Rebekah there. She was curled up in
the bed beside Kathleen. Grace was bundled between
them.

So that is why the little ones passed a silent night.
Henry found himself smiling, though his expression
was a sad one. Rebekah truly cared for the children.
Again, he couldn't help but think what this household
might have been like if their marriage had begun on
different grounds.

God, help me. I know I must move forward. Give

me courage and the faith to believe You will take care of them. Shutting the door quietly, he left the house. Deciding to seek legal representation before visiting Detective Smith, he went first to see attorney William Davis.

The streets of Baltimore were still relatively quiet at this hour. Early sunlight pushed its way through gaps between buildings, bathing the streets in a rosy-gold glow. Henry would have thought the morning beautiful were it not for the heaviness of his heart and mind. Reaching the home of Mr. Davis, he rang the bell. The attorney himself answered the door.

"Why, Councilman Nash, what brings you here?"

Henry removed his hat. "Business, I'm afraid. I apologize for the earliness of the hour, but it is important. Have you a few moments to spare?"

"I do. Please, come in."

He followed the attorney to his library. The man offered him a seat across from his desk.

"I hear congratulations are in order," Davis said as he claimed his own chair.

Henry didn't know how to respond to that, so he simply stated a fact. "My wife and I were married several days ago."

The older gentleman nodded pleasantly. "Mr. and Mrs. Wainwright stopped by yesterday. They told me the news. I daresay once my daughter, Emily, returns from Washington, she'll be showering your Rebekah with gifts." He paused to chuckle. "In fact, all the girls will. You'll soon have a parlor full of tea cakes and chattering females."

Probably not now, Henry couldn't help but think.

Davis then turned serious. "Well, you said you were here on business. What may I do for you?"

"I may be in trouble with the provost marshal," he said.

Davis offered a somewhat sarcastic smile. "You wouldn't be the first Maryland man. Does it concern some political opinion you have expressed?"

"Well, you know my father wasn't particularly fond of Lincoln, and he made no secret of his disdain for his policies. I also had a brother-in-law who served in the rebel army."

Davis nodded. "And you believe you are now suspected of disloyalty because of this?"

"Yes. Because of those issues and an unfortunate series of encounters." Confiding in the attorney, he told of his visit to the Branson Boarding House and the carriage ride with John Wilkes Booth.

Davis leaned back in his chair, listening wide-eyed. "Well," he said after taking it all in, "you've certainly done nothing *criminal*, but given the current climate, the frenzy over the assassination, I can understand why you're worried."

"Detective Smith has been turning up quite a bit here lately."

"Has he already questioned you?"

"No, but I know he suspects something. I can just tell. Do you think I should go to him and explain what happened?"

Davis thought for a moment. "Concerning Booth and Miss Branson—and through her, Lewis Paine—you have no information to give that Detective Smith doesn't already know, but I do believe it would be best to be forthright. Unfortunately, it may lead to a bit of hounding on his part, but if he's been turning up already, as you say, he was bound to question you at some point."

"That's what I was afraid of."

"Don't worry. I've dealt with many cases just like yours. We'll see that this matter is ended soon enough."

"How soon?" Henry asked, remembering the councilman Smith had investigated previously. His life had been turned upside down for nearly a year.

"Probably not as soon as you'd like. Even though you would be offering a sworn statement, the detective may not be satisfied entirely with that. He may seek to hold you in custody until your story is corroborated."

That was exactly what Henry had feared. The Baltimore authorities were notorious for letting lengthy amounts of time pass before a story was corroborated. "I am now responsible for my late sister's children. Two young nieces. The youngest is not yet three months old."

David nodded again thoughtfully. "I will stress that fact to the detective. I should think that Smith will take into account your reputation as a city councilman and your good standing in the community."

Davis glanced at a small appointment book on his desk. "I was to meet with another client at nine, but I could reschedule. Detective Smith was in Annapolis yesterday, but it is my understanding that he returned to Baltimore this morning. We could do our best to resolve your issue today, if you like."

Fear prickled Henry's skin. He wanted resolution, yes—but would today bring relief or the beginning of something far worse? Of one thing he was certain, however. Doing nothing would solve nothing. *Lord, give me courage. I believe this is the path You wish for me to take.* "I'd appreciate if you would reschedule your other client, sir."

The attorney nodded. "I'll have my assistant deliver the message."

"Thank you," Henry said, "and, if you don't mind, there is another matter…"

"Yes?"

"I'd like to make a few changes to my will."

Rebekah woke to the sound of Grace crying. It was feeding time again, and the baby wanted to be certain Rebekah understood that. Hearing her sister's demands, Kathleen soon stirred, as well. She rubbed the sleep from her eyes, then blinked at Rebekah. "Did you stay with us?" she asked.

"Yes," she answered, though she did not tell her exactly why. "You had fallen asleep before I could kiss you last night."

"Sadie said you and Uncle Henry would come when you could, that Grandfather had come and you had to visit him."

"Yes," was all Rebekah could think to say.

Kathleen slid from beneath her blankets, then made her way to the wardrobe. Opening it, she stared at her dresses.

"Let me see to your sister first. Then I'll help you."

"Yes'm." The little girl plopped down on the floor to wait.

Sunlight was filtering through the shutter slats, proclaiming a beautiful spring morning. Despite her smiles to the children, Rebekah felt no joy, only trepidation. What awaited her downstairs? Would she be able to face Henry and his father, make suitable conversation with them for the sake of the girls? Dare she ask God for His assistance? *Since my request is really on behalf of the children, will He answer it?*

Sadie's soft rapping was heard upon the door. "Breakfast is about ready, miss," she announced. "Mama set two places. One for you and one for Miss Kathleen."

"Just two?"

"Yes, miss. Delegate Nash left the house last night. James says he returned to Annapolis. And Mr. Henry's done left for the mornin'."

So they were both gone? Rebekah felt relieved to know her father-in-law was no longer under the roof. She wasn't quite sure what she thought about her husband, however. *Where has he gone? What is he doing, and how will it affect the children?*

"You want me to take Miss Grace and get her fed?" Sadie asked.

Given her state of mind at the moment and the tremble in her hands, perhaps that was best. Besides, Kathleen needed dressing. Rebekah did, too, and she did not wish to keep Hannah and breakfast waiting.

"Thank you, Sadie. I'd appreciate that. I'll see to the next feeding."

"Yes'm."

Fifteen minutes later, with laces drawn and hooks and eyes all fastened, Rebekah and Kathleen entered the dining room. Kathleen seemed not the least bit bothered by Henry's empty chair, yet Rebekah found herself staring at it repeatedly. Was it really only yesterday that he had sat there and told her of his service in the balloon corps? How intrigued Rebekah had been. How her heart had pounded as she'd hung on his every word.

Now it squeezed with pain. *Then we stepped into the*

study. Then he grew so angry when I spoke of Maggie Branson. Then his father said those horrible words...

She never wanted to step foot in the study again, but she did still wish to know what was happening with the trial, especially now that it could involve her own husband. When James came into the dining room a moment later to see if she had need of his services, she asked him if he would bring her the newspapers.

"Yes, miss. Straightaway."

He returned shortly with the stack of publications. Rebekah thanked him and then began scouring the headlines.

Notable Baltimore attorney Reverdy Johnson had resigned as Mary Surratt's defense council, and a new man had taken his place. One publication speculated that Johnson had decided he could not in good conscience defend such a woman. Another ventured he was withdrawing because he had taken a case he realized he could not win. Still another suggested he was doing it for Surratt's benefit—that as a Maryland man, his loyalty was under suspicion by the military tribunal, as well. The new attorney, a war hero named Frederick Aiken, would ensure a more fair trial for the woman.

Rebekah did not know what to think of Reverdy Johnson or Mary Surratt or anyone else. *This world is full of liars, cheats, crafty people willing to do or say anything to save their own skin*, she thought. *This household is proof.*

A chill spread through her as she laid the paper aside. She realized Henry's troubles with Detective Smith were not only his own. *I very well could be implicated in some way or, at the least, questioned rigorously be-*

cause I am his wife. Also, I worked in that hospital. I knew Maggie Branson and Lewis Paine.

She looked across the table at Kathleen. Unaware of the grave circumstances, the child was innocently sipping her milk. As she watched her, Rebekah's anxiety grew. The newspapers were also full of stories of those *connected* with the trial. Anna Surratt, Mary Surratt's daughter, was practically a prisoner in her own home while she waited to learn her mother's fate. Even the daughter of a respected New Hampshire senator was not exempt. Lucy Hale, who had reportedly been John Wilkes Booth's sweetheart, was now being ostracized by Washington society.

Will Kathleen and Grace suffer the same fate?

The little girl set down her now empty glass. "Can we go into the garden?" she asked hopefully. "You said yesterday there are still weeds to be pulled."

Rebekah had no desire now to improve upon Henry's landscape, but Kathleen had so enjoyed digging in the dirt, and she did not wish to disappoint her. Perhaps the feel of the earth between her own fingers would give Rebekah a measure of peace.

She did her best to smile. "I did say that, didn't I? Yes. We can go out into the garden, but first, let's go back upstairs and change into an older dress."

"Will you take Grace outside, too?"

"Yes, of course." She shepherded Kathleen to the foyer. They were halfway up the staircase when a knock sounded on the front door. Rebekah froze. It was still rather early. Just who was paying them a call at this hour?

"You go on upstairs," she told Kathleen, hoping the

nervousness in her voice was not apparent. "I'll be there directly."

The little girl climbed the rest of the steps. When she reached the upper landing, Rebekah turned. James had already opened the door. He shut it again before Rebekah reached the foyer floor.

"Letter for you, miss," he said as he held out an envelope.

Rebekah breathed a shallow sigh. "Thank you, James. Who was that?"

"It was Mr. Davis's man."

Mr. Davis? William Davis, the attorney? Why would he be sending her a letter? A sick feeling washed over her.

Knowing she would wish to read her news in private, James moved on. Rebekah stared for a moment at the envelope in her hand, then slowly opened it. She hadn't recognized the handwriting—she hadn't seen it before—but she soon spotted the signature. She was tempted to crumple the letter and throw it in the wastebasket when she realized it was from her husband.

What more could you possibly have to say to me? she thought, but she forced herself to read. Amid Henry's profound apologies was a promise to do right by her and the children.

I have gone to seek out Detective Smith. I will not return until I have told him everything that occurred the day John Wilkes Booth was in Baltimore. In the event that I am implicated in the conspiracy, please return the enclosed document to William Davis. He will assist you.

Rebekah looked then at the document he had included with the letter. Shock ripped the air from her lungs. Henry Nash had just signed over his home, all his worldly processions and the guardianship of his two nieces to *her*.

Chapter Nine

With gut-wrenching anxiety, Henry told the young corporal at the front desk that he wished to see Detective Smith.

"To what regard?" the soldier asked.

Henry swallowed hard. "John Wilkes Booth."

The infamous name garnered an immediate response. Henry and Davis were quickly ushered into the presence of the detective. Pleasantries were short, perfunctory.

William Davis came straight to the point. "Sir, my client has some information that may be of interest to you."

"Regarding Booth?"

"Yes."

Henry's ears were thudding. His collar felt tight. Detective Smith's eyes narrowed as he looked him up and down. "Are you ill, Councilman Nash? You look out of sorts."

Just how should he look, considering why he was here and what had happened between him and his wife?

Whispering a prayer and drawing in a deep breath,

he told Smith of his chance encounter with Booth. He described the carriage ride to the train station and his visit to the Branson Boarding House.

Smith listened silently. His steel-gray eyes seemed to penetrate Henry's very soul.

"I assure you, Detective," Mr. Davis said, "this man had no knowledge of Booth's plan when he met him, nor had he any knowledge of the connection with Miss Branson and Lewis Paine."

Smith again focused his attention on Henry. "Did you know Paine was a patient at the Army General Hospital on Pratt Street?" he asked.

"Not at the time, sir. I only learned of that after the fact."

"How?" Smith asked.

Henry's first thought was Rebekah. She had told him that detail, but he did not wish to bring her name into the conversation. "The newspapers," he said. It was true, after all. She had been reading them. That was how she had recognized Paine as being Powell, the escaped prisoner from her ward. Henry had read the article for himself early this morning.

"I see," Smith said. "And why tell me all of this now?"

"I had thought to come to you earlier," he said.

"But you didn't."

"No, sir."

"So you mean that as the trial of the conspirators progressed, you thought you, yourself, might soon be under suspicion."

Henry swallowed again. "That did cross my mind, Detective."

Davis then handed the man Henry's statement. "May

We'd like to send you two free books from the series you are enjoying now. Your two books have a combined cover price of over $10 retail, but are yours to keep absolutely FREE! We'll even send you two wonderful surprise gifts. You can't lose!

Each of your FREE books is filled with joy, faith and traditional values and women open their hearts to each other and join together on a spir journey.

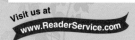

GET 2 FREE BOOKS!

CLAIM NOW!
Return this card today to get 2 FREE Books and 2 FREE Bonus Gifts!

YES! Please send me the **2 FREE books** and **2 FREE gifts** for which I qualify. I understand that I am under no obligation to purchase anything further, as explained on the back of this card.

2 FREE BOOKS

102/302 IDL GKCJ

FIRST NAME

LAST NAME

ADDRESS

APT.#

CITY

STATE/PROV.

ZIP/POSTAL CODE

READER SERVICE—Here's how it works:

I point out, Detective, that Councilman Nash did come to you of his own free will, and he has graciously provided you with documentation of these events."

Smith eyed the paper shrewdly before laying it aside and once again leveling his penetrating gaze at Henry, who held his breath for what seemed like an eternity.

"Councilman Nash," Smith said finally, "I know all about your ride to the train station and your ill-timed visit to the Branson Boarding House. I have known from the beginning."

Henry's jaw dropped. "You've known from the beginning? How?"

"Witnesses, of course. You'll be pleased to know that they each insisted your only crime could be kindness or, at the most, a bit of *campaigning.*"

Henry could feel himself reddening. *All of this for nothing...? Why didn't I just tell the truth to begin with? Oh, God, forgive me for my weakness. If only I had...if only I had reached out to You in the first place...*

"So you see, Councilman, you've wasted the attorney's valuable time, not to mention mine, and you have vexed yourself for no good reason. I advise you to return home, look after your new bride and leave me to my business. I have bigger fish to catch." He called for the corporal. "Show these men out."

Dazed and bewildered, Henry exited the provost marshal's compound.

"Well, that certainly went easier than I expected," Davis said.

"Indeed," Henry replied. "Do you think this will be the end of the matter?"

"It would seem so...but should the detective approach you again, do not hesitate to call upon me." He handed Henry his card, then added, "And might I suggest, if there is indeed a next time, do not wait so long to do so."

Henry took the card and then shook the man's outstretched hand. "Yes, sir. Thank you."

They went their separate ways. Walking home, Henry told himself he should be relieved, but he wasn't. His life was far from settled, let alone happy. He wondered exactly what he should say to Rebekah when he saw her. "I'm sorry... I'd like to make this work... The children need a mother and you are so good with them"?

Nothing sounded right. Nothing seemed sincere. He had hurt her deeply. He did not wish to do so again. *God help me. I want to start over completely with her...but I don't even know where to begin.*

Sunlight was filtering through the large oak tree. Grace lay on Rebekah's lap, staring up at its gently swaying branches. Kathleen was seated beside them. She had found an inchworm crawling on a nearby rock. Mesmerized, she studied the creature intently.

The garden provided the serenity and solace that each of them seemed to need. Kathleen was enthralled with the world around her. Grace was content, and as long as Rebekah focused on her present surroundings, on the colors, scents and sweet faces before her, she felt peace. The moment she dared think of the past or the future, however, the knot in her stomach tightened.

And it shows on my face. She knew that for a fact, because when Rebekah had gone to fetch Kathleen after receiving Henry's unexpected letter, the little girl observed, "Your face has lines."

Rebekah smiled, hoping to wipe away any such

traces. Whatever Kathleen had spied clearly troubled her. "I was deep in thought," she said.

Kathleen scooted from her bed. The wary expression remained. "'Bout what?"

Rebekah drew her close to her heart, wanting to reassure her. "Nothing you need concern yourself with, love. All is well."

She had said the words but knew how hollow they actually were. Life was far from well. Kathleen had lost her mother and her father. Was she about to lose her uncle, as well? How Rebekah wanted to shelter her and her little sister.

"I love you," she said as she brushed a wisp of hair from Kathleen's cheek.

The child turned to her, her eyes blue as a clear September sky. She smiled. "I like havin' a' Aunt Rebekah."

Rebekah kissed the top of her head. Kathleen then returned her attention to her inchworm. Grace now stared at Rebekah, her dark blueberry eyes intense and alert.

What is going through her mind? Rebekah wondered. *Does she think I am her mother? Her real mother?* Rebekah would have felt privileged to claim the honor but knew herself to be insufficient for the task. She was mastering feedings, diapering and rocking, *but can I actually be the mother she and Kathleen need? Can I do it alone if it comes to that?* Would she even be allowed to do so? If Henry could no longer care for them, would Delegate Nash contest his son's decision to give her custody?

Rebekah shut her eyes tight, wanting to pray but hesitant. God would not wish to be bothered with her fears. What was she, after all, to the likes of Him? A failure, a weak-willed woman, a sinner.

Rebekah's head snapped up as the door to the house opened. Henry had returned. She didn't know whether to feel relief or resentment, thankfulness or fear.

Kathleen waved to him happily. "Come and see what I found!"

He came at once, a smile on his face, although Rebekah noted it seemed a bit forced. There were lines on his face, as well, particularly his forehead. Kathleen failed to notice them.

"See my worm?"

As he bent down to appreciate Kathleen's discovery, Rebekah stood. Taking Grace, she moved to the opposite side of the garden. The daylilies there would soon be in bloom. Rebekah studied their long green pods intently, searching for the first hints of orange. After a moment, she heard Henry approaching. The gravel was shifting beneath his feet.

"Rebekah? May I speak with you, please? It concerns Detective Smith..."

The fear she'd felt previously had given way to a different emotion: anger. She did not wish to speak to Henry about this subject—or any other, for that matter—but knowing Kathleen was watching, Rebekah obliged. Biting back all she wanted to unleash, she turned to face him.

"I spoke with the detective just now," he said, his voice low. "He did not believe my actions to be criminal. Therefore, we will have no further trouble from him."

Rebekah forced herself to take a breath. She told herself she should be grateful. Grace and Kathleen would not face a future of ostracism from society, but her agitation only grew.

"We will have no further trouble..."

We. He'd said the word as if they were actually a couple. *We may be bound by law but not love.* Grace, dissatisfied with the way she was being held, wiggled. Rebekah shifted her from one arm to the other, then returned her attention to the unopened lilies. The petals trapped inside the pods were struggling to burst free.

"Did you receive my letter?" he asked.

"Yes," Rebekah replied, refusing to meet his gaze. She wouldn't chance doing so. If she did, she was certain her temper would make itself known.

The letter was still in her skirt pocket. She felt like tossing it in his face. She wasn't fooled by his false apologies and promises of wealth. She knew why he had written it. She knew what it *really* was. She could recognize a bribe when she saw one.

Her father had been a master. The rings, the dresses he gave his wife, were payment for her acting the part of a supportive, contented woman in public. Nights at the theater or other outings were designed to make the voters think him attentive and in love with the woman he had married.

And now you seek to do the same...

Henry stepped closer. The smell of soap powder from his freshly laundered shirt overpowered the scent of the garden. It nauseated her.

"Rebekah, please understand... I know I have done wrong and I am truly sorry. I know I haven't sought the Lord's counsel much in these past few weeks, but I make you this promise—I will from here on out. I want to make this marriage work. I want to be a good husband to you and a loving father to Grace and Kathleen."

"A loving father..." The words shouldn't have cut

her so, but they did. He loved Grace and Kathleen. He just didn't love her.

The baby began to cry. Rebekah's eyes blurred, also. All her life she had wished to be dear to someone—her father, her husband, God... What was so wrong with her that she was unable to secure affection?

Henry touched her on the sleeve. "Rebekah, please look at me."

She couldn't, *wouldn't*. Hoisting Grace onto her shoulder, Rebekah forced herself to speak. "I understand, Henry. I, too, want what is best for Grace and Kathleen."

She kept her attention on the flowers until at last the gravel shifted again. Henry returned to Kathleen. Rebekah swallowed back her pain.

Separate spaces, she thought. *Separate rooms. We'll come together only for the good of the children, or when his work deems necessary. I'm destined to relive the life I saw my parents live.* But she told herself there was no point in being angry or disappointed. *My marriage is what it is. I have a roof over my head, plenty to eat. I have more than most. The sooner I resign myself to this arrangement, the better off the girls and I will be.*

She tried her best. That night, she dined with Henry and answered his questions politely concerning what she and the children had done before his arrival. Later she helped Kathleen dress her dolls and comb their hair. She fed Grace and rocked her to sleep, then put both her and her sister to bed. Afterward she went to her own room. Finding her knitting needles, she started a swaddling blanket for the baby.

She did the exact same things the following day.

On Sunday they went to church. It seemed odd to be

claiming Henry's pew, when *her* family was seated six rows ahead on the opposite side of the aisle. Rebekah studied them. With her father absent, her brother, Teddy, was seated in his place, just as he always was whenever the head of the house was in Annapolis.

Rebekah returned her focus to the family with her. Wrapped in her newly finished blanket, Grace slept soundly in one of Rebekah's arms. Kathleen leaned upon the other while quietly thumbing through the hymn book. A few moments later, she switched to leaning on Henry.

Rebekah sang the customary hymns and did her best to concentrate on the sermon Reverend Perry delivered rather than think of the man sitting just inches from her.

Anger bubbled inside her. Disappointment burned her soul. She loved the children and they cared for her, but she wanted more. She had always wanted more.

She looked again at Reverend Perry, finding herself irritated with him now, as well. Where was this all-encompassing peace, this soul-satisfying love of which he spoke? *God must be selective in whom He grants it*, she thought.

Just as the preacher was concluding his message, smack in the middle of the congregation's most reflective moments of silence, Grace woke with a jolt. Whether she was wet or hungry, Rebekah wasn't certain, but she was most definitely cross. Her face twisted in protest. Rebekah knew what was about to follow. She bounced the baby lightly, hoping to keep her quiet.

"Nothing," her father had always insisted, was *"more disruptive in a service than a crying infant!"*

And cry Grace soon did.

"Shh," Rebekah pleaded. "Shh." She put the baby on her shoulder, patted her back.

Kathleen eyed her with a look of distress. Rebekah could feel Henry's gaze upon her, as well, his and everyone else's behind them. Grace's head bobbed side to side. She arched her back. Rebekah stroked her rigid spine, but to no avail. The baby began to wail.

Cheeks burning, Rebekah quickly scooted from the pew and hurried for the front door. Once outside, she took up post beneath the maple tree and continued to bounce the child.

Sunlight now upon her face, Grace was soon perfectly happy, as if she had wanted only to leave the confines of the sanctuary and experience the fresh air. Rebekah ceased her bouncing, but the anxiety inside her did not fade. Was she the cause of Grace's distress? Had the baby sensed the tension inside her?

Can everyone else sense it? Is my inadequacy obvious to everyone in the church? What should she do? Perhaps her mother could offer her some advice. While Rebekah wouldn't call her a shining example, she had raised five children and had always excelled at keeping up appearances.

A few minutes later, the church doors opened, and the congregants began descending the steps. Rebekah spied her mother and siblings. Moving toward them, she offered a greeting. Her mother nodded to her as though she was little more than a stranger and then continued toward the carriage. Her brothers did the same, with the exception of Joseph, who waved at her enthusiastically.

Rebekah watched them go, the great emptiness inside her deepening. Henry's shadow soon fell over her. He slid his hand around her waist. For a second she dared to think he had perceived her hurt and was trying to comfort her. Her heart desperately longed to believe it, but that couldn't be the case. He was a politician, just like Rebekah's father. The congregation, the voting citizens of Baltimore, were watching their every move. Henry Nash wanted to look like a caring husband. That didn't mean he actually wanted to be one.

How can they be so cold? Henry wondered.

He'd seen the look of disappointment, of pain on his wife's face when her family had passed her. Even though they were in public, his first thought had been to draw her close, offer her the comfort and support he could see she craved.

Babies cried in church. It was a fact. It didn't mean Rebekah was a poor mother.

His wife, however, did not wish for his encouragement, and she'd made it known. The moment Henry slid his arm around her waist, he'd felt her stiffen. He had no doubt she would have pulled away from him completely were it not for her friends' arrival.

The ladies swarmed around them, offering hugs to Rebekah and congratulations to him. Poor Kathleen was nearly consumed by the bell-shaped skirts. Backing into Henry's legs, she tugged on his frock coat. He scooped her up into his arms.

"The girls and I were so surprised to hear of your wedding," Mrs. Julia Ward said, her own child in her arms, "but we were oh so pleased."

Henry swallowed hard, wondering how his wife would respond to such a comment. He wondered, too, what his own face revealed.

"Y-yes," Rebekah stammered. "Thank you." She moved Grace from one arm to the other.

"What a beautiful family," Miss Sally Hastings said. "Rebekah, you must come to the sewing circle once you have gotten settled in your new home. And bring the children. We have missed you so."

"Yes," Mrs. Elizabeth Wainwright added. "It has been so long since you've joined us."

Rebekah nodded—rather sullenly, Henry thought. She had not mentioned attending any circle before, but he didn't want her forgoing it simply because she had married him.

"We are looking for a new project," Miss Trudy Martin—Mrs. Wainwright's twin sister—announced. She then said to Henry, "In the past, we have knitted socks for soldiers, sent clothing to prisoners."

"It sounds like a noble effort," he replied. He could see the interest, the longing on his wife's face.

"When are you planning to meet again?" she asked.

"As soon as we can agree upon whose turn it is to host," Julia replied.

Rebekah repositioned Grace upon her shoulder. Henry was trying his best to read his wife. Did she wish to attend the meeting? Was she worried about managing the children in a friend's home, especially given what had just happened in church?

"Perhaps the ladies would care to join you in our home," he said to her. "Dare I say it would be easier with the children, rather than bringing them somewhere else?"

The look she gave him was one of surprise, then something else he couldn't quite read. Appreciation? Suspicion?

"I believe it would be easier," she said.

"Then it's all settled," Mrs. Ward said, clearly delighted. From there they determined a date.

"Oh, this will be wonderful!" Miss Martin said. "Rebekah has never hosted before."

Oh no, Henry thought. Had he just volunteered his wife for something she didn't wish to do? She was smiling at her friends, but was it genuine or for appearances' sake only?

He asked her straight out as they walked home. "Did I inconvenience you by inviting your friends into our home?"

"No," she said.

He'd hoped for more than a one-word answer. He tried to encourage further conversation. "You seemed interested in attending, but then when Miss Martin said you had never hosted—"

"I never hosted because my father wouldn't—"

She stopped, her jaw tightening, as if she'd said something she wished she hadn't.

Kathleen looked up at them both. For her sake, Henry didn't push any further, but Rebekah's dangling sentence tormented his thoughts.

Your father wouldn't, what? he wondered. *Welcome a group of young women into his home?* He remembered how Miss Martin had mentioned making and gathering clothing for prisoners. Did she mean rebel prisoners of war? Had Van der Geld forbidden his daughter to assist?

How will it look to Detective Smith if—? He clipped the thought short. *No. This is a matter of Christian charity. I will not discourage her from helping someone in need, no matter what the provost marshal's office may or may not think.*

Rebekah's attention was now fully on Kathleen. She asked about the child's Sunday school lesson and discussed the flowers they'd passed in their neighbors' front gardens. She was putting on a cheery display, but Henry could see a different set of emotions in her eyes.

When they reached the house, his niece went off with Sadie so she might change out of her Sunday dress. He and Rebekah were alone in the foyer for the space of a minute. Henry wanted to broach the subject of her family again, but before he could open his mouth, Grace began to fuss.

"She's hungry," Rebekah said. "If you'll excuse me…"

"Of course."

He could hardly detain a hungry child. *And if Rebekah does not wish to discuss her family with me, that is her prerogative*, he told himself. He had wanted this arrangement to work for the sake of his sister's children, and it was clear that Kathleen and Grace were doing splendidly in Rebekah's care. But now he realized he wanted this union to succeed for his sake and Rebekah's, as well. He wanted to be her place of comfort, security. He wanted to be the place where she built her home.

But knowing he could no more manufacture feelings of affection than he could his own righteousness, he let her go.

Chapter Ten

The latter days of May passed slowly. Rebekah cared for the children. Henry cared for the citizens of Baltimore. Each morning he rose with the sun and left early for City Hall. One day, however, she came down the stairs, girls in hand, and found him waiting in the foyer. He was dressed in his silk vest, tie and black frock coat. Rebekah tried to ignore how handsome he looked.

"I thought you would be at City Hall by now," she said.

"The council isn't meeting today, and the Wainwrights are coming later to conduct their scheduled interview."

Scheduled interview? Rebekah didn't remember him ever mentioning anything of the sort. She knew from that day at the Merchant's Exchange that there was *to be* an interview, but Henry had never told her a specific day or time.

For one quick moment, she was tempted to blame herself for not being prepared for the arrival of guests, but she quickly shoved that thought aside. *It isn't my fault.* "I was not aware that this was scheduled for today," she said.

Kathleen crossed the space between them. Henry lifted her into his arms. When he nuzzled her neck, she giggled.

"I know," he said to Rebekah. "I apologize. I forgot to tell you. In fact, I didn't remember myself until just this morning."

Oh, gracious. That means extra work for Hannah. She told herself she was angry, but it was hard to remain that way toward a man who apologized, especially one who showed such affection to children. "Have you anything to serve your guests?" she asked, her sense of duty taking over.

"Hannah has tonight's dessert already prepared. We could serve that, if it is not an inconvenience to you."

"It is of no inconvenience to me," she said.

He nodded. "Sadie has offered to take the girls for a stroll when the Wainwrights visit. I would appreciate it if you would stay here to greet our guests."

And there it is, she thought, her emotions swinging back to their previous state. *Another political request.* He wanted her there so the refreshments would be served and they could present the appearance of a happy, well-functioning home. *Just like he wanted me to host the sewing circle.* She was tempted to tell him to serve his own cake at both events, but *Elizabeth is a friend of mine. It would be rude not to greet her today... and I have so missed visiting with our other friends.*

Rebekah sighed. "Very well. I will do so, but I need to change my dress."

"Of course."

Sliding from his arms, Kathleen scampered toward the dining room. Henry held out his hands. "I'll take Grace to Sadie," he said.

Resisting the urge to keep the child to herself, Rebekah handed her to him. Grace's little legs wiggled with excitement, especially when Henry held her at eye level and smiled. "Good morning, pretty girl. How are you today?"

Swallowing back the lump in her throat, Rebekah returned to her room. There she exchanged her simple cotton day dress for the blue taffeta tea bodice and skirt she'd worn on the rare occasions when she'd received a social call in her father's house. Removing the pins from her bun, she brushed out her long, dark hair, then rolled and braided it into a more fashionable style. Henry had never said a word about her hair. Had he even noticed it the night it lay loose about her shoulders?

What does that matter now? she asked herself as she steeled her resolve for the duty that lay before her.

When David and Elizabeth arrived, Rebekah greeted them warmly, served the lemonade without spilling a single drop, then sliced Hannah's spice cake and distributed the pieces.

"Thank you, my dear," Henry said when she gave him his.

The words that had once made her heart swell now grated on her. *My dear.* She knew he did not mean that. She was not dear to him. He was speaking that way only because David and Elizabeth were listening. Her task now finished, she turned to go.

"Please stay."

Stay? Rebekah froze. She told herself once again that Henry was asking only to make a good impression on his guests, but her curiosity got the better of her. She had never been included in such a gathering before. She *would* like to stay, if only to learn more of the world outside her new home. Cautiously she claimed the seat beside her husband.

Across from her, Elizabeth was already sketching away. David was balancing a reporter's journal on one knee and his dessert on the other. Henry asked him how his newspaper was faring.

"Very well," he said. "We've yet to match the *Baltimore Sun*, but our circulation is improving." He glanced at his wife and grinned. "I think Elizabeth's artwork has a great deal to do with that."

A pang of jealousy struck Rebekah, and she immediately scolded herself. It wasn't right for her to begrudge Elizabeth's happiness. *Forgive me, Lord. I'm sorry.*

The conversation shifted from pleasantries to more pressing matters. David asked about the business of the council in regard to the president's death.

"Well, as you are aware, there have been no riots, no public disturbances, so the police force is no longer on high alert," Henry said.

David nodded. "For that we can be grateful. With the war ended and those suspected of conspiring against Lincoln now on trial, do you think the city will see a return to peace and prosperity?"

"I do hope so," Henry said. "Economically, things are looking up. Several banking and trading institutions are already reestablishing business connections with the South. That will be helpful not only locally but also to the other cities."

David scribbled down the quote. Elizabeth continued to capture Henry's likeness. Rebekah watched the proceedings with a measure of intrigue and cynicism.

"I'm told by a reliable source that the federal government plans to maintain a military presence in Baltimore throughout the remainder of the year," David said. "Do you think the soldiers' presence will be a help or a hindrance?"

Only then did Rebekah see her husband hesitate. When his jaw shifted slightly, she couldn't help but wonder if he was thinking of the prison he had so desperately hoped to escape or the one he now found himself trapped in with her.

"I hope the soldiers will be a help," Henry said. "Transitioning from war to peace has not been easy, especially now, with the assassination. There is a lot of uncertainty about which way the country should go."

David nodded. "Indeed. Some citizens want tighter federal control. Others want the power returned to the states. What would you like to see?"

"As a councilman or a private citizen?"

"Both."

Again, Henry paused. "I hope we never again witness what we've seen the past four years. Hundreds of thousands dead, including the president..." He shook his head sadly. "I hope the local, state and national leadership will never forget the suffering this nation has endured. I hope we will seek divine wisdom in the days ahead, for surely history shows we aren't wise enough on our own."

As angry as she was with him, Rebekah had to admit, it was one of the most humble answers she had ever heard.

"There is also the matter of funding the Freedmen's Bureau," David said next. "Now that Lincoln is dead, many fear the money to assist the former slaves will be cut off completely."

Henry nodded. "The council is looking into measures, ways to assist locally, should that happen."

"I'm glad you brought that up," Elizabeth said. Laying aside her drawing pencil, she turned to Rebekah. "I was thinking, given the current circumstances, that perhaps the sewing circle could do something to help."

Rebekah was surprised that David and Henry had allowed the interview to change focus, but she was highly intrigued by Elizabeth's suggestion. "*Help?* In what way?"

"We could make clothing, knit socks, other items. We've done it before for others."

Yes, they had, only she had not been allowed to participate. A sense of pride, of purpose, surged within her. *I will participate this time, regardless of the circumstances, regardless of Henry's reasons for arranging them. This is how I will manage. I'll care for the children. I'll help those less fortunate. I'll stay so busy that I have no time to mourn the life I had hoped for.* "That sounds like a wonderful idea," Rebekah said.

"Then you'd like to join us?"

"Oh yes."

"Splendid!" Elizabeth said. "We can discuss it further with the girls next week."

"Very good," Rebekah replied. "I shall look forward to your arrival."

Henry had thought the interview with David and Elizabeth Wainwright had gone well. He had enjoyed the couple's visit, but more so, he had enjoyed having Rebekah beside him. At first he'd taken Rebekah's interest in matters at the Freedmen's Bureau as a positive sign. She was intrigued. She was smiling. She was engaging her guests in conversation; perhaps eventually she would do the same with him.

However, the moment Mr. and Mrs. Wainwright departed, so did her lively manner. When Henry tried to tell her he thought her desire to assist the freedmen was charitable indeed, she immediately withdrew from him.

"I've fabric to purchase," she said. "I'd best do so before the shops close."

"Have you enough money?" he asked, although he was fairly certain she did. Rebekah was downright frugal with her personal allowance, never spending a dime, at least as far as he could tell.

"I do," she said. She thanked him for the inquiry, but her tone lacked warmth. He did not wonder why.

He started to tell her how pretty she looked in that ruffled dress, with her pagoda sleeves trimmed in white lace and ribbon. She'd dressed her hair, as well, rolling and plaiting it as she had that night he'd come to dinner in her father's home. He didn't say anything, however, for Sadie had returned. Rebekah was now delivering instructions concerning the children.

"I won't be gone long," she promised.

He watched as she kissed each child. An odd feeling resonated inside him. Was he jealous of her affection for the girls? How could he be? Didn't he want her to love them?

When Rebekah left the house, Kathleen turned to him.

"Can we read the books?" she asked.

Henry smiled genuinely despite the conflict within him. "Of course, pretty girl."

Sadie took Grace upstairs for a nap. He led Kathleen

to the study. She chose her customary atlas. Nestled on his lap, she turned the big, dusty pages.

"Look at this one," she said. "It's a funny shape."

"That's Michigan," he said. "Soon you'll be big enough to read the names of the states for yourself." Not that he was in a hurry to forgo moments like these. He kissed the top of her head, only to discover Kathleen's hair smelled of lavender water. *Just like Rebekah's.*

"I'm learning my letters," Kathleen announced. "Aunt Rebekah is teaching me." She found a capital *K*. "See, that's in my name."

"Yes, it is," Henry said. "Very good."

The conflict inside him intensified. His wife's bond with Grace and Kathleen was strengthening. The ties that bound her to him, however, were weak and thin. He knew he couldn't force a relationship with her, even if he did truly wish there was more to what they presently had. Henry supposed he'd been naive in thinking a prayer of confession and an apology would be enough to start over. Was complimenting her dress and hair what was needed? Or if he did so, would she think him even more insincere than she already did?

Tired of the atlas, Kathleen asked for another book. "What about a Bible story?" Henry asked. "I'll read you the one about Esther."

"Who's that?"

"Esther was a beautiful young lady whom God used to save her people from a very bad man."

"She was a 'portant lady?"

"Yes. She was very important. She was a queen." He squeezed her gently. "Just like you."

The little girl giggled, then hurried to fetch the Bible. Following the story, Rebekah returned. She called for Kathleen from the hall. Sliding from Henry's lap, the little girl hurried for the door. He trailed after her.

Rebekah greeted the child with a warm embrace and a smile. Her enthusiasm faded when she noticed him. Henry forced himself to ignore the chill her frostiness invoked.

"Was your shopping successful?" he asked.

"Yes," she replied with all the cordiality one would give a complete stranger. "I've all the fabric I need."

Rebekah led Kathleen toward the staircase. Not knowing what else to say or do, Henry returned to his study. Frustrated, he blew out his breath.

How do I mend the damage, Lord? His Bible was still lying on the table. He picked it up. He'd spent much time in the Scriptures lately. It was here he had once learned the principles of honest business and public service. It was here he was certain he'd find the secret to a happy marriage. He knew God wished for children to be reared in a loving, Christ-centered home. He'd heard Reverend Perry say such words before. Henry wished now he had paid more attention.

He wasn't certain exactly where to look, but he thought he remembered seeing instructions among Paul's writings concerning husbands and wives. Finding what he was looking for, he settled himself into a chair and began to read.

"Husbands love your wives, even as Christ also loved the church and gave himself for it..."

He heaved another sigh. *Christ is perfect. I am far from it.* He realized that as much as he wanted to, he could not love his wife as he should. He could not undo the damage he had done. *But God can...*

And so he continued to read.

* * *

The city council was to convene at noon. Henry was just leaving the house the day Rebekah's friends arrived for the sewing circle. He spoke with them momentarily in the foyer.

"I understand good news is in order," he said.

Rebekah knew exactly what he meant. She'd seen the one encouraging newspaper story among the rest of the disheartening articles. The prison camps were closing, and the former rebel soldiers were returning to their families. Julia's brother, Edward, and Trudy and Elizabeth's brother, George, had been held at Point Lookout as prisoners of war.

"Oh yes!" Julia exclaimed. "Our brothers will soon be returning home! At long last, the war is finally coming to an end!"

"Indeed," Henry replied with a smile, "we are so pleased for you." When he looked to Rebekah, his smile faltered.

Her heart squeezed. *He will never look at me the way Sam does Julia, nor the way David looks at Elizabeth. Never.* "Yes," Rebekah forced herself to say cheerfully, looking to her friends. "We are very pleased."

With that, Henry bid the ladies good day and went on his way. Rebekah was grateful he did not linger any longer. The tension between them would soon be obvious to anyone in the room. How was she to explain their circumstances to her friends? They were newly married. They were expected to be happy.

As the front door closed behind him, Rebekah determined to put all thoughts of Henry aside. *I will waste no more time thinking about him today. I have other matters to attend.* The ladies commandeered the parlor. Rebekah settled Kathleen and Julia's two-year-old daughter, Rachael, on the settee in the corner of the room. She handed them each a cloth doll that she had fashioned from fabric scraps last evening. When the little ones were content, Rebekah showed her friends the fabric she had purchased for the freedmen.

"This will make good, suitable clothing," Elizabeth said.

"Indeed," Julia replied, "but before we begin, there is another matter."

"Oh," Rebekah said. "What's that?"

A round of giggles ensued as brown paper packages emerged from sewing baskets. They were soon thrust in Rebekah's direction.

"What's the meaning of this?" she asked, although she had a fairly good idea.

"You didn't think we would let you get married without a proper start," Julia said with a laugh.

A proper start... Rebekah swallowed back the lump forming in her throat and tried to smile. "You are too kind."

"Go on!" Trudy said impatiently. "Open them!"

"Yes," Sally added. "Don't keep us waiting!"

Rebekah felt awkward, but what else could she do, given the circumstances? Her friends were insistent. Reluctantly she untied the string on the first package. Beneath the paper was a delicate lace pillow.

"That's mine," Sally said.

"How lovely! Did you make this?" Rebekah asked.

Her friend blushed. "I did. I thought it would look nice in your parlor."

Rebekah was truly touched. *All the work that went into this...* "It's beautiful."

"And now for the next one," Trudy insisted, handing her another package. She had given Rebekah a copy of *The American Frugal Housewife*, a book full of cleaning remedies, housekeeping strategies and anything else a woman would need to know about managing her home.

Elizabeth presented her with a large box of candles. Julia gave her a painted silk fan and a flowerpot full of seedlings.

"What's this?" Rebekah asked, not recognizing the plant.

"Chinese balloon flower," Julia said proudly. "I thought you would like it. I'm told Martha Washington once grew it in her garden at Mount Vernon."

Rebekah's throat tightened even further.

"Do the blooms really look like little hot air balloons?" Trudy asked.

"Indeed they do," said Julia. "They are *floating* all over my garden right now."

Rebekah did her best to keep back her emotions, but all she could think of was the night Henry had told her about his service in the aeronaut corps. How much she had wanted to float through the clouds with him! "You are too kind," she repeated. "Too kind indeed..."

"There's one more," Sally said, handing her a rather large package. "This is from all of us. We finished it only yesterday."

Rebekah unwrapped the paper to find a beautiful nightdress, its neckline embroidered with, of all things, tiny pink roses. Unable to contain her emotions any longer, she burst into tears.

"Oh," Trudy gasped, looking almost equally distressed, "don't you like it?"

"It's lovely," Rebekah tried to say through her choking sobs. "It's just… I don't *deserve* it."

"Oh, of course you do," said Sally.

"No…really… I don't…"

Julia and Elizabeth exchanged knowing glances.

"It's happened, hasn't it?" Elizabeth said.

Rebekah's cheeks burned with shame. *So it is obvious. Everyone knows my marriage is a lie!* She stared down at the gift in her lap, a gift she knew she'd never wear.

"You and Henry have had your first quarrel, haven't you?"

First quarrel? Her head came up. Is that what they all thought? It went way beyond a simple quarrel, but Rebekah couldn't bring herself to admit this. All she could do was cry.

From the corner of the room, Kathleen was eyeing her with a look of concern. Rebekah tried for her sake to rein in her emotions, but was unable to stop the tears. Thankfully, Sally took it upon herself to distract the children. She scooted in between Kathleen and Rachael, marveling over how well they had, or at least, had *tried*, to dress their dolls.

"I suspected there had been a quarrel when we met Henry at the door," Julia said. "He just didn't seem himself."

"Indeed." Elizabeth smiled sympathetically. "And neither did you. But rest assured, Rebekah. All will be well soon enough. If it makes you feel any better, David and I weren't married twenty-four hours before we had our first disagreement."

Julia gave a little laugh. "Samuel and I weren't *even married* before we had ours…"

"Yes," Elizabeth said, "we all remember that. Here we were making lace for your gown, and we worried there wasn't even going to be a wedding."

"At least Henry doesn't have to worry about losing Rebekah," Trudy remarked. "They are already married."

Yes, Rebekah thought. *We are.* She knew her friends were trying to console her, and she appreciated that. *But if they only knew...*

Elizabeth looked again to her. "Would it help to talk of it?" she asked.

Absolutely not, Rebekah thought. She could feel herself reddening further. "I don't think so..."

The women respected her privacy and after a few moments decided that, given the circumstances, they should go. As they prepared to depart, Rebekah felt a mixture of relief and guilt. Here it was, her first opportunity to host the circle, and her guests were leaving early because she couldn't conceal her emotions.

If I am going to remain in this arrangement, I must learn better self-control—if not for my sake, then for the sake of Grace and Kathleen. It will not benefit either of them to be surrounded by rumors of their aunt and uncle's unhappiness. "Perhaps you could return here next week," Rebekah said, "and we'll work then on the clothing for the freedmen."

"That is a lovely idea," Elizabeth said.

The women each hugged Rebekah before leaving. "Don't be discouraged," Julia whispered. "I'm sure whatever has happed between you and Henry will work itself out. Disagreements come to all relationships. It is how they are navigated that determines the future. You love Henry and he loves you...just keep that in mind."

"I will," Rebekah said, but only she knew how empty that promise really was.

She walked them to the door. After they had gone, Rebekah stood in the foyer until she felt Kathleen tugging on her skirt. "Why did the ladies bring you presents?" she asked. "Is it your birthday?"

Her eyes were wide with interest, as blue and captivating as those of her uncle. Rebekah did her best to smile. "No. It isn't my birthday. They brought presents because I have married your uncle Henry."

"Oh. When I get married, will I get presents?"

"I imagine so." The thought of Kathleen one day finding herself in a loveless union sent a shiver down Rebekah's spine. *But surely Henry would not allow such a thing, not when he adores this child so... Surely he would want her to be loved as much as I do.*

Rebekah lifted her into her arms and planted a kiss on her forehead. "Thank you for playing so nicely with Rachael while the ladies visited."

"She's little," Kathleen said, as if the maturity difference between two and four was incalculable.

"Yes, she is, and I appreciate you being so kind to her. You are a good girl."

Kathleen smiled broadly.

"Would you like to help me put the presents in their proper places?" Rebekah asked. "Then, when your sister wakes from her nap, we can go outside."

Kathleen nodded and slid from Rebekah's arms. They placed Sally's pillow on the parlor settee and Elizabeth's candles in the cabinet where Hannah kept the others. Kathleen carried the potted balloon flower to the back door, while Rebekah took the remaining gifts to her room.

Rebekah mentioned none of presents to Henry when he returned home that evening. As much as she appreciated her friends' kindness, it didn't seem right to take joy in wedding gifts when their marriage was anything but joyous.

Henry had hoped the time spent with her friends would be good for Rebekah, that he'd return home to find her in a more cheerful mood. However, she was as formal and guarded toward him as ever and seemed even sadder than usual. At dinner it was Kathleen who told him about the wedding gifts.

"There was a pillow, a book, candles, flowers for the garden…"

"Is that so?" Henry glanced at his wife. She was staring at her plate, a flush on her cheeks. Evidently she was embarrassed by her friends' generosity or perhaps thought he would be. He wasn't. "That was very kind of your friends to think of us," he said.

"Yes, it was," she replied without looking at him. Her attention was on Kathleen. "Finish your supper and we'll go to the parlor."

Kathleen nodded eagerly, then looked to Henry. "Aunt Rebekah promised she was gonna to teach me how to sew."

It warmed his heart to see the way Rebekah was mothering the child and how Kathleen was responding. "Is that a fact?" Henry asked as cheerfully as he could. "I'd like to see that. Would you mind if I joined you?"

Rebekah turned her attention to him with a look of surprise. Kathleen offered the same.

"You're gonna learn to sew?" his niece asked.

"No," he said. "I think teaching me would be too much to ask of your Aunt Rebekah."

Kathleen giggled. "You'd pro'lly stick your fingers."

"Probably," Henry agreed.

Rebekah gave no indication whether she wished for his presence or opposed it, but Henry knew there was no hope of building a relationship if they did not spend time together.

The meal now concluded, Sadie brought in Grace.

"She's all fed and diapered, miss," the maid said.

"Thank you, Sadie," Rebekah replied. "I'll manage her for the rest of the evening."

"Yes, miss."

As Rebekah took the girls to the parlor, Henry went to the study to gather his letters and various proposals the city council was considering. Returning then to the front of the house, he claimed the chair next to his wife. Again, she said nothing.

It was a chilly night, especially for early June. A steady rain had settled in over the city, and James had lit a small blaze in the parlor fireplace. As the flames danced and flickered, Henry found himself distracted from council business. It wasn't the now cozy temperature of the room, nor the soft glow of the hearth. It was the look on Rebekah's face as she tended to his nieces.

Grace lay in the basket beside her chair, cooing and playing with her toes. Rebekah would reach over every now and again to speak to her or pat her on the belly. Henry couldn't help but think of how, just a short time ago, the baby had cried incessantly unless held. Grace was becoming secure in her surroundings. Kathleen was, as well. She was seated on Rebekah's lap, concentrating hard on the fabric and threaded needle in her hands.

"Like this?" she asked.

Rebekah's voice was full of tender affection and encouragement, rich like coffee, smooth as silk. "Yes, good. Try to keep your stitches in a nice straight line, and make them as small as possible."

"It's hard."

"It is, but it will get easier with practice."

Henry was captivated. It was more than just appreciation of Rebekah's patient way with Kathleen, more than the fact that she was willing to help raise the girls despite her and Henry's flawed marriage. It was as if he was seeing her for the very first time.

Her long, delicate fingers gracefully guided the child's stitches. Lamplight mingled with firelight, softly caressing her beautiful chocolate-brown hair. Henry suddenly felt the urge to take the pins from it, run his fingers through the thick tresses. "Rebekah, you are very lovely."

The blurted compliment made Kathleen look up from her stitching and grin, but *stunned* wasn't word enough to describe the look on his wife's face now.

Henry held her gaze. *Yes, I mean it. I truly do...*

It seemed she didn't believe him. Distrust darkened her features as she returned her attention to Kathleen. "Yes, love, that's it. Very good."

Henry was disheartened by her lack of response, but he supposed he could not blame her for turning away from him. She had obviously taken his words for empty flattery. He tried to recall what he'd read from the Scriptures. How did God win hearts? *By being a servant.*

While Rebekah continued teaching Kathleen, Henry

silently contemplated the meaning of the word. *A servant doesn't demand his way, claim his rights. He does his job, thanklessly, consistently, quietly...*

If his father or his fellow council members knew what he was thinking, surely they would laugh in his face. Undoubtedly they'd say he couldn't manage his own household and therefore was not capable of managing anything else.

But I'm not accountable to them in this case. I'm accountable to God.

So when Grace cried out for want of a dry diaper, Henry laid aside his work. "I'll see to her," he promised. He did not pause to gauge Rebekah's reaction then. He simply claimed the baby and saw to her need.

Rebekah didn't know what had surprised her more—Henry's compliment or his willingness to tend Grace. She had rarely seen a man claim a fussy child before. She'd certainly never seen her father do so. Nor in all her years at home could she remember him sitting quietly in the parlor with her mother. The only room they ever shared was the dining room.

But Henry had passed the evening in her presence as if he *wanted* to be with her. He had told her she was lovely. Had he actually meant it, or was he simply saying what he wanted Kathleen to hear?

Surely he is trying to give Kathleen what she once had—loving guardians. She would not begrudge a child her uncle's love, no matter how oddly he might show it. She kissed the top of the little girl's head. Kathleen looked up at her and smiled.

"I think you are pretty, too," she said.

Rebekah's heart swelled. "Thank you, but no one is as pretty as you, love."

The mantle clock struck the appointed hour. Rebekah laid aside the fabric, much to the child's dismay. "It is time for you to go to bed now."

"Do I have to?"

Do I have to? Rebekah knew she must remain firm, but she couldn't help but take pleasure in Kathleen's protest. She would never have dared to question her parents' command. Kathleen, however, felt she could—and truly wanted to spend more time with Rebekah.

"Do as your Aunt Rebekah says," Henry said from the doorway. His tone, however, was far from forceful. He looked then to Rebekah. "Grace was yawning, so I laid her down."

He saw to her needs and put her to sleep? "Thank you," was all she could think to say.

Kathleen reluctantly moved from Rebekah's lap and went to say good-night to her uncle. Henry surprised her not with a hug but by scooping her into his arms. He tossed her in the air. "The balloon goes up," he said dramatically, "and…it comes down."

Kathleen giggled. "Again!"

"Only if you promise me you'll go straight to bed," he said.

"I will."

Henry honored her request. Kathleen again laughed. Rebekah watched the entire episode with a lump in her throat. All her life she had longed for her father's embrace. Did Henry realize what he was bestowing on these children?

"I'll see to her, as well," he said.

Her heart was so full, all she could do was nod. As

Henry carried away a still-giggling Kathleen, Rebekah wiped away a tear. She was grateful for Henry's devotion to the girls, but oh, how she longed for such affection from him, as well.

No! I mustn't think of such things. I mustn't pine. Nothing good will come of it.

Determined to bury her emotions, she picked up her own sewing. *I'll use the time I would have spent settling the children to finish another shirt for the freedmen.*

Rebekah was fully aware of the hardships the former slaves faced. While her father might not have given her opportunity for reading newspapers or abolitionist pamphlets, Rebekah still had eyes. She had seen many a slave on the streets of Baltimore. She had ears, as well. She'd heard the discussions of abolitionist visitors at the hospital. It was there Julia had loaned her a copy of Frederick Douglass's book, the narrative of his life as a slave. Rebekah had read it during her meal breaks.

Even now she shuddered as she remembered reading the tales of backbreaking labor, the beatings, the humiliation of being owned by another. She'd blushed at the horrible stories of white masters fathering slave children. Many of those same women then suffered the despair of seeing those children sold away.

Now, as Rebekah sat in her husband's comfortable parlor, she couldn't help but feel condemned for indulging in self-pity over her own circumstances. *I have nothing of which to complain. I never have. I should be grateful. I have much more than most.*

Once more resolved to discount her own pain, she returned to her sewing. A few moments later, Hannah came into the room. In her hands was a cup of tea. "I thought you might be in need of this," she said, "with the night bein' so chilly and all."

"Thank you, Hannah. That is very kind."

"No, Miss Rebekah, thank you."

She lowered her needle, blinked. "For what?"

"For the work you are doing to help the freedmen. For the way you love Miss Grace and Miss Kathleen. Mr. Henry was tryin' his best, but it's hard to raise children on one's own. I know."

Rebekah's curiosity got the better of her. Perhaps she shouldn't have asked, but she couldn't help herself. "Hannah, did you love Sadie's father?"

The older woman smiled. The answer was clear. "I did. I loved my Robert with all my heart, and he did me."

"What happened to him?"

Her smile faded. "He was a slave like me. He was sold away before my belly grew round."

Rebekah winced. "So he never saw his little girl?"

"No. A few years later, the master sold me and Sadie, as well. That's how we came to be with Mr. Henry."

Rebekah blinked, her thoughts suddenly shifting. "Henry told me he never owned any slaves."

"He didn't, least I reckon, not for more than five minutes. He freed me and Sadie the moment he claimed our papers. James, too."

Oh...so he told the truth about that.

"When Mr. Henry learned about my Robert he tried his best to find him. Then came the war and—well, he says now that the fightin' has ended, Robert might turn up yet. He's been askin' of him at the Freedmen's Bureau, askin' of him by way of his friends in the government, as well."

Rebekah swallowed hard, that conflicted feeling rising inside her once more. *How many men would spend the time, the money to track down a former slave? No wonder Hannah thinks so highly of Henry.*

The woman then turned the conversation in a way Rebekah had not expected. It told her Hannah knew more about her and Henry's relationship than Rebekah realized.

"You and Mr. Henry will settle in time," she said. "The good Lord will help you."

Rebekah didn't know how to respond to that. From what she had experienced, the Almighty did not concern himself with her. Jesus had died for her sins, yes, and Rebekah had bowed the knee, promised to serve so that she could escape eternal punishment. But even though the Scriptures testified to the existence of a supreme *loving* Father, Rebekah could not conceive any guardian who did not forcefully subdue and rule those weaker than He.

And yet, something deep down told her otherwise— that the example her father had given her was not the true reality. There was something more. There *had* to be. Something that made Hannah believe in the return of the man she had once and still loved. Something that made Henry do what he had done tonight.

Was there more to God the Father than punishment and perfection? Rebekah would have liked to believe so. She would have liked to believe that her husband was more than just a vote seeker, a man hungry for power.

But believing something, no matter how sincerely, doesn't necessarily make it true.

Chapter Eleven

Summer sunshine baked the streets of Baltimore. In the Nash home, however, a chill remained. Rebekah never displayed any hint of coldness before Grace and Kathleen. When they were present, she engaged Henry in polite everyday conversation. She smiled. She even laughed once or twice when he made silly faces at Kathleen. The moment the children were out of sight, though, so was she.

As Henry's father had so ruefully predicted, Rebekah appeared to be resigning herself to the present situation. She dutifully and efficiently managed his household, cared for his children and attended public worship at his side, but was never alone with him. Henry did his best to encourage interaction, to engage her in meaningful conversation. He complimented her often on her skill with the children, sometimes asked if she would care to take a stroll about the garden with him.

She always declined, insisting she had charity work that must be completed. Rebekah had already managed to sew more shirts for the Freedmen's Bureau than he could count. It wasn't that she was behind in her charitable responsibilities. She just didn't want to be with him.

Henry was surprised at how badly her rejection stung. If she was content with the way things were, shouldn't he allow her peace? The problem was, he wanted more from his wife than distant courtesy, and he was at a loss for how to go about achieving it. How did you court a woman you had already wed? Especially one who did not wish him to do so?

One oppressively warm morning at City Hall, Henry was trying his best to concentrate on his civil responsibilities, yet his wife remained prevalent in his thoughts. Apparently most of his fellow council members were having a hard time focusing on the business of Baltimore, as well. All they seemed to want to discuss was the ongoing aftermath of Lincoln's assassination.

While Michael O'Laughlen's and Lewis Paine's cases had proceeded to trial, Maggie Branson's had not. She and the rest of the members of the Eutaw Street boarding house had been set free.

"The trials won't last much longer," one councilman predicted, "and that Surratt woman will be executed with the rest of them."

Henry sighed. He didn't know if Mary Surratt was guilty or if she had simply been drawn into events beyond her control by her son and his associates. But whatever the truth indeed was, Henry certainly couldn't imagine the United States government executing a woman, especially a widowed mother, no matter what role she might have played in the president's death.

His shoulders rose, then fell with a labored sigh. He would be grateful when the entire matter was put to rest once and for all. As long as the Lincoln assassination was still a topic of conversation, he would be reminded of his foolish fears. *And as long as Rebekah is reading the newspapers, she will be reminded of them, as well.*

"I don't like this," George Meriwether whispered.

Henry pulled himself out of his reverie and looked at the man seated beside him. "You don't like what?" he asked.

George gestured toward Mayor Chapman and their fellow councilmen. "All this discussion of the trials… all it does is generate anger and suspicion. It keeps us from our local issues. We have veterans in need of work, former slaves who are struggling to assimilate into society. They need our attention far more than Mrs. Surratt or Mr. Paine."

Henry nodded in agreement. He couldn't help but think again of his wife, this time with a smile. She was already seeing to the needs of former slaves, and with such dedication. Beneath her defensive exterior was a kind heart, one he admired and respected. One he deeply wished to know better.

When the council adjourned that afternoon, Henry started down the front steps of City Hall, eager to be on his way home. Having remembered that Rebekah had once expressed an interest in the education of freedmen, Henry wanted to tell her how he and George had persuaded the council to set aside funds for books and slates today. He had just stepped onto North Holliday Street when Detective Smith came up alongside him.

"Well, if it isn't the honorable Councilman Nash," the man said. "I see you have been hard at work, as usual."

Henry stopped. He wasn't certain if the comment was a compliment or a cut. The detective had a knack, it seemed, for injecting suspicion and fear into every situation.

"Your name came up in a conversation I had recently," Smith said.

"Is that so?" Henry replied, wondering where Smith was going with this.

"Evidently Miss Branson knew your wife."

Henry immediately felt the hair on the back of his neck stand on end. His pulse quickened.

"Why didn't you tell me they were employed together at the hospital?" Smith asked.

"I didn't think it important. There were many people employed there."

"Indeed. Countless numbers...countless wounded and convalescing men. It must have been a dreadful place for a lady. No wonder your wife chose not to continue."

Henry's fists clenched in indignation. Was Smith implying Rebekah hadn't the stomach or stamina to serve her country? *Or is he implying something in reference to Lewis Paine's escape from the hospital?* He called him to account immediately. "Detective, are you implying that my wife might have aided in your suspect's escape from the hospital? If you are—"

"Of course not, Councilman. Your wife had an impeccable record of service. I understand she served for well over a year and received several commendations. When she left, it was at her father's request."

Henry wasn't surprised to learn she had left "at her father's request," but he was taken aback by the mention of commendations she had received, not because he didn't think her *capable* of earning such but because she had never told him. The thought that Smith knew more about his wife's service than he gnawed at him.

"What exactly is this about, Detective?" Henry asked.

"I assure you, Councilman, I mean no disrespect to your lovely wife. It was simply a matter of conversation."

Conversation? Since when did this man ever engage in simple conversation?

The detective tipped his blue kepi. "Well, no doubt you are anxious to return home... A good evening, sir."

Henry watched Smith walk away, thoroughly confused by the entire exchange. He didn't know what direction the man's investigation was now taking, but he couldn't shake the feeling that somehow, despite Henry's innocence, Smith was working his way back to his family.

Sweat soaked his collar, yet a chill shimmied down his back, strong enough to make him shiver. Henry hurried up Holliday Street. Rebekah wasn't in the house or the garden when he arrived, and neither were the children. The shiver remained. *It isn't like her to be gone.*

He asked Hannah what she knew.

"Miss Rebekah left after the midday meal," the cook said.

"Did she say where she was going?"

"No, but she asked for a bottle for the baby."

"And she didn't say when she would return?"

"No, sir."

Henry tried not to worry. Rebekah could be in any number of perfectly safe places. Still, he could not get Detective Smith's conversation out of his mind. The dinner hour came and went, yet Rebekah had not returned. She might not have been in the habit of spending time with him personally, but she had never once neglected a meal or strayed from the children's routine.

Something is wrong.

Heart pounding, Henry donned his sack coat and hat, determined to search for her. Just as he laid his hand on the front door, it opened. In walked his wife, the baby asleep in her arms, her skirt hem stained with mud, and an equally dirt-dusted four-year-old at her side.

Henry didn't know what he felt more, relief or resentment. Didn't she realize how she had worried him? "Where have you been?" he immediately asked. "I have been waiting for you all afternoon!"

Rebekah blinked, clearly taken aback by the question. "I took Kathleen and Grace to the public gardens."

Having heard voices, Sadie came to claim the children. All was well, but even so, Henry's nerves were on edge. After the maid had gone, he said to Rebekah, "It would have been good of you to let me know. I had no idea where you were. Neither had Hannah. I was just about to come looking for you."

"Why?" Rebekah asked.

"Why? Why do you think?" *Because I was worried!* He didn't want to say exactly *why* he was so worried. He didn't want to tell her about the encounter with Smith, the fact that her name had come up in a conversation about Maggie Branson. Henry didn't want Rebekah to think he suspected *her* of some wrongdoing.

But for her protection... "I think it best for you to remain at home until—"

She visibly stiffened, lifted her chin. "Until what?" she snapped. "Until I prove my worthiness? Until you are assured I will do nothing to embarrass you?"

Embarrass me? "Rebekah, I—"

"You are just like my father! You'd keep me captive to your plans!"

There it was again, that charge. Henry's frustration was building. Yes, he'd given into fear of imprisonment. Yes, he'd made a political pact he had no business entering into. Yes, he had used her—and deserved her ire and distrust for doing so. But he was trying to make amends. He wanted their life to be different. Couldn't she see that? "I am nothing like your father! I am trying to protect this family!"

"Protect it from scandal, no doubt! You insist I play the role of charitable hostess, and you think by buying me off—"

"Buying you off?"

Stained skirt swishing, Rebekah strode to the parlor fireplace. On the mantle behind the matchbox was a piece of paper. Henry didn't know what it was until she tossed it at him. It was the document he had instructed her to give to William Davis in the event of his arrest. His heart was crushed. So was his pride. "You think I signed my property over to you as a bribe?"

"Didn't you?"

"Rebekah, I signed my property over to you *because you are my wife*, because I wanted to be certain you'd be *cared for* in the event of my imprisonment or death! And as for playing hostess... I asked you to stay with me during the Wainwrights' interview because I thought you would find it *interesting*. And the sewing circle? I thought you would enjoy spending time with your friends. I am not trying to make you a prisoner! I'm trying to be good to you. You, however, won't let me!"

She said nothing to that. The look on her face was stone-cold. Clearly she did not believe him.

Henry was exasperated. *Why can't you see? What more can I do to make you understand?* Suddenly, from out of nowhere, he had the strong desire to pull her into his arms and kiss her. He bit back the foolhardy desire, however, and just in time. Kathleen came bouncing into the room. Rebekah's hardness quickly turned to a look of fright. Obviously she hoped the child had not heard any of the previous exchange.

"I changed my dress," Kathleen announced. "All by myself." She twirled to show off her accomplishment.

Henry wasn't going to let his niece see how conflicted he was. Offering the best smile he could muster, he patted her shoulder, then turned on his heel. Going to his study, he shut the door behind him. He ripped off his coat and tie, tossed them to the desk. Then he paced about the room. *I am so sick of all of this! Sick of politics, sick of Detective Smith and this colossal trial!*

But what affected him most of all was the tension between him and Rebekah. Never in his life had he felt so inadequate, so incompetent. *How is it I can get opposing council members to find common ground for the people of Baltimore, yet I cannot communicate, let alone make any progress, in my relationship with my own wife?*

And how on earth could he be so angry with himself and with her, yet long to take her in his arms at the same time? The desire to march back into the parlor and kiss her was as strong as ever.

What would she do if I suddenly did so? Slap my face, most likely, he thought, for he'd seen the scathing look, the mistrust in her eyes. He remembered her biting words.

"You are just like my father!"

Henry sighed. His anger spent, discouragement alone remained. *God forgives, but a woman wronged does not forget*, he thought. *Help me, Lord, please...if not for our sake, then for the sake of the children.*

Going to the shelf, he once more picked up his Bible, sank into the nearby chair and tried to read. He could barely concentrate on the words, much less retain them. Even so, he continued, for he had nowhere else to turn.

Sometime later, Henry noticed Rebekah had come into the garden. Grace was once again tied to her bosom. Little Kathleen was at her side. Laying his Bible on the table, Henry moved to the window. He watched as Rebekah ran her hand over the orange daylilies, now in the peak of bloom. His heart was stirred by the sight. He'd observed some time ago that she seemed most at peace when surrounded by God's creation.

For a moment, he wondered how much happier she would have been to marry a simple farmer or even a wandering aeronaut. He remembered how her eyes had danced when he'd told her of drifting over green fields and groves with nothing but the whisper of the wind in his ear and the warmth of the sun on his face.

Henry couldn't help but think of a letter he had received a few days ago. One of his old comrades from the balloon corps, Allen Tilney, had written to tell him of a new venture in which he was now involved.

"Two hundred acres of farmland," Tilney had written. "The richest soil in Ohio. Come and see it, or better still, come and give me a hand."

Henry had not yet replied to the letter, but he had passed off the offer with a laugh at the time. Farming wasn't his forte, yet now he seriously wondered if a drastic change of lifestyle wasn't exactly what his family needed. Rebekah had been born into a society in which every word and deed was carefully calculated, observed by those in powerful positions and weighed for worth. She in turn now did the same.

What would happen if I took her away from this life? Would she be happy if we left behind politics for good? Would he?

The question plagued him for the rest of the evening.

Rebekah could not sleep that night. Those moments in the parlor with Henry troubled her deeply. *Of course Henry would have been concerned over the children,* she thought. She knew she shouldn't have let her temper get the better of her. She knew it even while she was letting it happen, but the rage inside her demanded to be unleashed.

One of these days I will go too far.

She feared she had done so today. She'd seen that look of intensity in Henry's eyes. She was certain she would feel his hand, bear the mark of her disobedience upon her cheek. *Then Kathleen came into the room, and he left. Was I rescued by a child? Or did he actually mean the things he said? Does he truly wish to be good to me? Am I the one keeping him from doing so?*

Questions hounded her. Answers evaded her. Rebekah didn't see her husband for the rest of the evening. He didn't come to supper, and he didn't join them in the parlor afterward.

Kathleen had asked where he was. Rebekah had told her he was doing important work and could not be disturbed. She tried to teach her a new stitch, but the girl was not interested. She wanted her uncle.

For the past few nights, Henry had taken it upon himself to read aloud to her. They were navigating the Old Testament, reading all the familiar stories—creation, Noah's ark, David and Goliath. Kathleen loved it. Rebekah found it torturous.

The sound of Henry's voice as he read to the child, the way he sheltered her on his lap, made Rebekah long for things she knew would never be. Henry would never speak to her that softly, nor hold her so gently. To him she was little more than a governess, an employee, *and an unruly one at that*. How long would it be before his patience wore thin?

A child's sudden cry forced Rebekah to her feet. Snatching her dressing grown, she hurried across the hall. Grace was still asleep in the cradle, but Kathleen was tossing fitfully, trapped in a nightmare.

"Mama! Mama!" she cried.

Rebekah gently brushed the matted hair from the little girl's forehead and spoke tenderly. "Wake up, love. You are dreaming."

Kathleen only cried louder. "No! No! Mama!"

Rebekah's heart broke for her. The child had done so well these past few weeks. Rebekah couldn't help but wonder if the tension exhibited today between her and Henry had caused this insecurity. Guilt raked her heart. *This is my fault. I know it is. God, please forgive me...*

Rebekah took Kathleen in her in her arms. Rocking, she held her close and whispered in soft, soothing tones, "Shh...it's all right, love, it's all right. I'm here..." *I'll always be here for you. No matter what.*

The poor girl never fully awakened, but as Rebekah continued to speak comforting promises, Kathleen eventually began to settle. Rebekah had hoped to quiet her before Grace was awakened, or worse, Henry. The former still slept. The latter, however, was now standing in the doorway.

How long he had been there, she did not know, but his presence made her heart pound.

She inadvertently drew Kathleen closer. "I'm sorry she woke you," she said.

He crossed the room and ran his hand lightly over the sleeping child's head. "I couldn't sleep, either," he said.

Rebekah tensed even further when he claimed the chair beside Kathleen's bed. Clearly he intended to stay. Why? Was he waiting for her to apologize for her earlier behavior? She didn't want to find out what would happen if she missed the opportunity.

"I'm sorry I lost my temper before," she said, "and I'm sorry I didn't let you or Hannah know where I was taking the children. I didn't think I'd be gone so long."

"I know you didn't." He heaved a sigh. "I'm sorry, as well."

He was staring at her with the same intensity as earlier, but the harsh tone was no longer there.

"I didn't mean to get angry with you," he said. "Despite how it sounded, I was truly worried about your well-being."

"*My* well-being?"

Rebekah laid Kathleen back upon her pillows as Henry told her of an encounter with Detective Smith. "It was foolish of me to think the conversation today would be cause for alarm. The detective does not suspect you of any wrongdoing. He said so."

Rebekah breathed a sigh of relief, for she had wondered this herself.

"I let my past fears commandeer my reasoning," Henry said, "and for that I am sorry."

He had said nothing about *her* accusations. Rebekah's heart was pounding, not with fear but with a feeling she'd never experienced before and could not name. Rapturous as it was, the moment was all too fleeting.

"I understand you were quite the nurse," Henry then said. "The detective told me you received several commendations for your service at the hospital."

Rebekah's cheeks warmed, not with pride but with shame. Quickly she returned her attention to Kathleen.

Henry saw the look of apprehension come across her face. Obviously she did not wish to discuss her time at the hospital. But why? Had the repeated deaths she'd surely witnessed there wounded her, or was there a particular soldier she'd been fond of? Had her father put an end to the relationship because he'd thought the soldier unsuitable? Was that why she had been forced to leave?

Is that why she has no interest in me?

He wanted to know, not because he felt he had a right as her husband, but because he yearned to understand. There was so much he didn't know about her, so much he wanted to learn.

She was tucking Kathleen's blankets around her, carefully avoiding his eyes.

"You are so good with her," he said. "One would think you had been mothering all of your life."

Her jaw twitched. "My brother Joseph had frequent nightmares," she said. "I was the one to comfort him."

"*You* were? What about your mother?"

Again, the twitch. It was followed by a shrug. "She never seemed to know what to do for him."

Henry felt his indignation rise, not toward her but

again toward her family. *What kind of a mother doesn't comfort her children's nightmares?* In what kind of a household exactly had Rebekah been raised?

How thankful he was to have had a mother who offered affection. Both he and his sister had known their parents' marriage was not a happy one, but neither had ever doubted they were loved by their mother or, for that matter, God. Henry and Marianne had been nursed through illnesses, given numerous second chances when they failed and taught that mistakes could be forgiven. His Heavenly Father knew he was far from perfect, and He did not expect Henry to be. What He did expect was Henry's willingness to let God change his character.

Sadly, I haven't always done that, but not a day went by now that Henry didn't pray for God to take control in his life.

"Your brother was fortunate to have you," he said, "fortunate to know your love."

Rebekah didn't say anything to that, but his compliment seemed to have struck a chord. He could tell by the way her mouth shifted and by the expression in her eyes as she turned to him. She looked so vulnerable. Everything within him wanted to reach for her. Caution, however, kept him where he was.

"Your family wasn't all you hoped they would be, were they?" he asked. "*I'm* not all you hoped I would be."

Even in the moonlight, he could see the blood rushing to her cheeks.

"Talk to me, Rebekah. Tell me what you are thinking."

She fiddled with the blankets once more. "I'm not thinking anything."

Allen Tilney's invitation to Ohio again crossed his mind. "Have you ever considered leaving Baltimore?" he asked. "Have you ever thought of going somewhere entirely new?"

"What?"

He quickly told her about his friend's letter. The look of alarm on her face slowly gave way to one of quiet reflection. Rebekah was listening intently but offered no indication of what she actually thought.

Taking a chance, Henry left the chair in which he had been sitting. He moved to the edge of Kathleen's bed, claiming the space beside his wife. Rebekah looked as though she'd suddenly forgotten how to breathe. Was it because of his proximity or because of what he had suggested?

"It wouldn't have to be Ohio," Henry assured her. "We could go anywhere you wanted to go."

"What about your position on the city council?" she asked, her voice quivering slightly. "Your political future?"

"I'd give it up for you."

She looked at him as if he had lost his mind. Perhaps he had. All Henry knew was, he wanted to make her happy. He took her hand in his. It was trembling.

"Rebekah, I…" Dare he say it? Was he actually in love with her or did he simply wish to be? He didn't know. He had never been in love before. He had told her less than the truth when they had wed. He never wanted to be dishonest with her again. "…I care for you," he said instead.

Her dark blue eyes were searching his, as if she was desperately trying to decide whether or not he was sincere. Henry stroked her hand lightly with his thumb. For a moment *he* forgot how to breathe.

From across the room, Grace began to whimper. Rebekah immediately ripped back her hand and rushed to the cradle.

Henry watched her closely. Her long brown hair was bound in a braid that fell down her slender back. Her dressing gown swished slightly as she settled the baby. Rebekah must have felt his eyes upon her, for she then said, "The council convenes early tomorrow, doesn't it?"

It was a veiled request, but he recognized it for what it was. It was a request for him to leave. "It does," Henry said. Swallowing back his disappointment, he rose. "Thank you for looking after the children," he said, and he quietly stepped from the room.

Chapter Twelve

The cobblestone streets were silent. Silver stars twinkled over the slate rooftops of the city. Grace was now content, and Kathleen had long since returned to sleep. Rebekah, though, was as restless as ever. Returning to her bedroom, she walked the floor for hours, chewing on Henry's words.

He said he was sorry. He said he cared for me. Does he really mean the things he said, or is he only speaking the words he thinks I want to hear?

She tried not to be drawn in by the memory of those moments, but she couldn't help herself. Moonlight had revealed a trace of stubble on his jaw, a firm yet gentle set of his mouth. He had spoken to her tenderly. He had taken her by the hand. Did Henry know how his touch affected her? Did he realize how badly she wished for him to take her in his arms, yet how much she feared it at the same time?

Charm was indeed a politician's skill, but the way he had treated her tonight was causing her to question seriously the defenses she had erected against him. Henry wasn't a forceful man, at least she didn't believe so—

not anymore. Not after he'd responded to her temper with gentleness and apologies. Was the selfless, humble nature with which he engaged the children and that he had demonstrated to her tonight the real man?

He had talked of giving up politics, of leaving Baltimore behind. *He'd said he would do so for me. Father has never given up anything, for anyone.*

Though running away had been a desire of Rebekah's for years, running away *with Henry* was another matter. If she were to go to Ohio, or anywhere else, would she find the life, the love she had always dreamed of, or would she discover further heartbreak?

At least here in Baltimore, I have my friends. I have my work for the Freedmen's Bureau. I have my own family. The last might not be all she wished them to be…*but better the trouble you know than the trouble you don't*, she thought.

Sighing in exasperation, she sank to the bed. Hannah had said that in time things would settle, that Rebekah would ease into the task of being a wife and mother, that Henry would learn to be a good husband and father. She wanted to believe that was true. *He has admitted his faults and apologized for them. He tells me he seeks the Lord's counsel, that he wants to start again.*

Could they? Who exactly was Henry Nash? *Can I risk giving him my heart once again?*

By the time Rebekah dressed the following morning, her husband had long since left the house. Kathleen showed no memory of her nightmare, but the effects of a disturbed rest were evident. She was quiet, if not cross, while Rebekah brushed her hair and braided it into place. At the morning meal she showed little interest in her eggs or even the possibility of playing in the garden. By early afternoon, Rebekah had Sadie put her down for a nap.

Truth be told, Rebekah wished for one, as well, but her friends were soon to arrive. Though her unresolved feelings toward Henry still weighed heavily upon her mind, she made certain she was all smiles when the others entered the parlor. Rebekah served the tea and cake and talked of the sewing projects for the Freedmen's Bureau. Her friends were impressed with the clothing she had crafted thus far and were eager to begin their own sets of shirts and trousers. Needles threaded, thimbles in place, they soon set to task.

"I received a letter from Emily yesterday," Julia announced as she finished off a seam, then snipped her leftover thread.

"Did she say what she and Evan will be doing now that the war is over?" Trudy asked.

"They are to remain in Washington until the bulk of the military hospitals are closed," Julia told them, "but Emily says Evan is eager to return to Baltimore. He would like to set up house here in the city."

"I imagine they would wish to be near her parents," Elizabeth said, "especially now that they have little Andrew."

"Did she say anything in particular about the baby?" Sally asked.

Julia grinned. "Only that her stern-faced military husband melts whenever his son smiles at him."

Rebekah shifted in her seat. She was glad Evan Mackay took pride in his family, but she still didn't know what exactly her husband thought of his. She couldn't shake the feeling that this offer to leave politics was simply a play for some grander scheme. *But what?* she wondered. *And in what role would I be cast?*

"Are you all right, Rebekah?" Sally asked. "You look rather pale."

Her thoughts must have again shown on her face. Rebekah inwardly scolded herself. "Kathleen didn't sleep well last night," she explained. She didn't tell who else couldn't sleep, either. The memory of her husband's nearness, the tenderness of his voice, made her skin tingle.

"Is Henry home today?" Trudy asked.

"No," Rebekah replied. "He's at City Hall."

"Are things better this week?" Elizabeth asked.

Rebekah felt the heat creep up her neck. It must have shown on her face, as well, for her friends giggled. Her embarrassment grew. She knew what they were assuming. *We share a home, the child-rearing responsibilities, but nothing more...* Rising quickly, she moved to fetch the teapot. For one quick second, her vision blurred.

I must be more tired than I thought. Thankfully, no one seemed to notice. They were once again busy with their work.

Rebekah refilled the teacups, then moved to shut the parlor window closest to her. A steady breeze was blowing the draperies, one much too strong for her today. She felt a little chilled. Upon returning to her seat, Sally mentioned the trial of Mary Surratt. Apparently she had been following the newspapers, as well.

"Do you think she really is guilty of conspiring to assassinate the president?" Rebekah asked.

"I don't know whether she is or not," Elizabeth said, "but David tells me they are holding her in the most deplorable conditions, that the cell is barely habitable."

"Has he seen her?" Julia asked.

"No, but a source where she is being held says conditions are filthy. David thinks they are treating her that way on purpose, to make an example of her."

Rebekah did not comment on any of the discussion. The topic hit all too close to home. To think that Henry married her in the first place to escape the possibility of similar prison conditions was positively nauseating.

And yet, she couldn't help but think, *if he hadn't, I would still be in my father's home. I wouldn't be hosting the sewing circle, and I would never have known Grace and Kathleen.*

"Did they ever release the actors from the theater?" Sally asked. "I heard they were holding them, as well."

"All but one," said Elizabeth. "Although I believe he is a stagehand."

Rebekah tried to steer the conversation in another direction. "I'm surprised you were able to join us today," she said to Elizabeth. "I thought you'd be busy at the paper."

"Actually, I must head back there soon."

"Another interview?" Rebekah asked.

"No. The editor has called a staff meeting."

"And how is your Mr. Carpenter?" Sally asked.

"Oh, he's not my Mr. Carpenter," Elizabeth said with a grin. "He's Trudy's."

All eyes immediately turned to Elizabeth's now red-faced twin sister. Even Rebekah was curious.

"Are you courting?" she asked.

"No," Trudy said quickly.

"But she hopes to be soon," Elizabeth teased.

She, Julia and Sally giggled. Rebekah did not. The last thing she found humor in now was potential romance. *Be careful*, she wanted to tell Trudy. *He may*

*not be all he appears to be. Be certain you find out who
he really is before you agree to anything.*

"I never said I wished for Peter Carpenter to come
calling," Trudy insisted.

"You didn't have to," Elizabeth said. "It's been written all over your face since the moment you started
working at the paper."

"Are you an artist now, as well?" Rebekah asked,
again hoping to nudge the conversation in a more comfortable direction.

"Oh no, nothing like that," Trudy said. "I have no tal-
ent for such things. I'm a proofreader. I've been working one day a week, just to help them."

"Them or *him*?" Julia teased.

Blushing once more, Trudy owned up to what was now
obvious to everyone in the room. "Well… I suppose…
both."

A round of laughter ensued. Rebekah's throat, however, felt tight. In fact, it had been that way all afternoon.

"Rebekah, are you certain you are all right?" Sally
asked. "You don't look well at all."

"I know what's wrong with her," Julia quickly answered. "I can tell by the look on her face." She turned
to Rebekah. "Have you called yet upon my father?"

Rebekah blinked. *Your father is a physician. Why
should I call upon him?* Had Dr. Stanton some concoc-
tion for wiping away the pain of the past? Had he a pre-
scription that enabled one to discern truth? She glanced
about the room. Knowing looks and smiles passed over
the faces of her other friends. She realized what they
were thinking.

"No…" Rebekah said, quickly shaking her head,
"No. It's not that—it isn't possible."

"You've been married now for more than a month," Julia observed. "It *is* possible."

"No," Rebekah insisted. "It is not."

At that, Julia only laughed. "What do you think, Elizabeth? Will there be a future city councilman or a gracious hostess of society?"

Blood was coursing through Rebekah's ears, thudding so loudly it surely must be heard by everyone in attendance. She didn't think her throat could get any tighter, but it had.

"Hush, Julia," Elizabeth chided. "Can't you see you're embarrassing her?"

"Am I?" Julia asked as if the thought had never occurred to her. "I'm sorry, Rebekah. I'm just happy for you."

You shouldn't be. "Julia, I am *not* with child."

Her eyes narrowed. "Are you certain?"

A forceful knock sounded upon the front door. Anxious to put this particular conversation to rest, Rebekah hurried to answer it before James could reach the foyer. She should have let the man attend to the matter, however, for Rebekah was not at all prepared to receive the guest who stood before her.

Cold dread washed over her. "F-father," she stammered, "what a surprise."

Chest out, jaw sharp, he glared at her. "I am here to see your husband," he said.

Rebekah swallowed hard. *Why?* "I-I'm afraid he isn't here."

Theodore Van der Geld's frown deepened. That all too familiar chill seized her again.

Noticing James, her father pushed past her and commanded him, "Fetch me a sheet of paper and an envelope. I wish to leave the councilman a note."

James did as he was told. Rebekah watched in horror as her father then strode toward the parlor, only to stop at the threshold when he beheld her friends.

"Well, I see you are frittering away your time as usual," he said to her.

We aren't frittering, she wanted to say. *We are helping the freedman. We are doing important work! Work you would surely be proud of if only you would take the time to notice!*

"Ladies, that is all for today," he said, as if *he* owned the house.

Not one of her friends moved. They simply looked to her.

Stay! Rebekah wanted to say. *This is my house. Not his!* But the expression of absolute authority on her father's face kept her silent. She knew what would happen if she crossed him. She dared not have her friends witness it.

James returned then with paper and ink.

"Never mind," her father said to him. "I will wait for the councilman's return."

Her father waved James away, but the man hesitated. She saw the concern on his face. *Do you wish to dismiss me?* he seemed to be asking. She wanted to tell him to throw the man out, but what authority could a freed slave assert over a state legislator? She could not put James in such a position.

Rebekah nodded, tried to smile. "Thank you, James. We won't be needing a letter after all."

He nodded to her and turned to go. Her father was now glaring at her friends. Not one of them had ventured to close her sewing basket, so he stepped into the parlor to *encourage* them to do so.

"I'll wait here for your husband's return," he told Rebekah as he commandeered the chair in which she had been sitting.

The women looked at her the same way James had, all except Julia. Rebekah spied the scowl on her face.

No, Julia. Don't say anything. It will only make things worse.

At that moment, the front door opened. Rebekah turned to see Henry stepping into the foyer. The tension within her mounted.

"I d-did not except you home s-so soon," she stammered.

He laid his hat and gloves on the table. "We adjourned early."

She wondered if her friends could hear the unsteadiness in her voice. It was bad enough to have her father interrupt their gathering and reveal his disdain for her. Now her friends would once again witness the strained relations between her and her husband.

She moved toward the front door so she would at least be out of their view. Henry thought she was coming to greet him personally. He smiled at her. "How goes the sewing circle?"

He brushed her arms lightly with his hands, as if he was seeing if she would welcome an embrace. Rebekah shivered at his touch, embarrassed once more by Julia's speculation of pregnancy, further disconcerted by her own conflicted heart. She wanted to trust her husband. She wanted to be sheltered, especially right now.

She could hear her father's heavy footsteps approaching.

"Councilman. I wish to speak with you."

Rebekah did not turn to face him. She was too busy

watching her husband's reaction. Henry's look hardened. "Delegate Van der Geld." He then looked back at her. "Are your friends still here?"

"Y-yes."

"Councilman—"

Henry held up his hand. "One moment, Delegate."

Fear chilled Rebekah's spine. Snatching her hand, Henry led her to the parlor.

"Ladies," he said, "forgive me for not greeting you sooner. How good to see you again. I trust all is well."

Rebekah's heart was beating rapidly. What would her friends do now? What would her father do?

"Yes," Elizabeth said. "We are well, and we were just leaving."

"Oh?" Henry looked back at Rebekah, then again to her friends. "You don't have to go on my account. Stay. Finish your work."

She felt him squeeze her hand. She knew what he was expecting. He was expecting her to follow his lead. But at this point Rebekah didn't wish for anyone to stay. She tried her best to keep her composure, to formulate some sort of response to her friends, but her mortification at her father's rudeness toward them and now Henry's handling of the situation was so great, she couldn't find the words.

"Thank you," Sally said sweetly, "but you've obviously much to which you must attend. We should go."

Rebekah nodded her approval, tried to smile. The moment she did so, Henry let go of her hand. He bid the ladies a good day. His tone toward them was pleasant, but she knew he was angry with her. She hadn't followed his instructions. She chanced a glance behind her. Her father looked just as angry, even though she *had* followed his.

The women gathered their sewing supplies and headed toward the door. Julia hugged her before leaving.

"I'm sorry for teasing you so," she whispered.

"It's all right," Rebekah managed, for Julia's gentle needling had disturbed her far less than what had followed.

"We'll meet again next week," Julia insisted. Rebekah did her best to offer Julia a smile. Then she shut the door behind her.

James had already seen to Henry's gloves and hat, so Rebekah quietly moved toward the staircase, intent on looking in on Grace and Kathleen. Her stomach was churning. Her head was pounding. All she wanted to do was escape the presence of her father and her husband before whatever battle they were intent on having commenced.

Henry called for her. "Rebekah, come here, please."

She froze, sucked in a breath. She didn't want to go anywhere near that parlor.

"Rebekah?" Henry was now standing in the entryway.

She reluctantly returned. "Y-yes?"

Her husband drew her up beside him. Rebekah instinctively resisted at first, but gave in. Across the room, her father had reclaimed her chair. He looked like a king on his throne.

"Now, Delegate," Henry said. "What is so urgent that you thought it necessary to disrupt my wife's charitable activities?"

The tone with which he spoke made Rebekah cringe. *What is he doing?* She'd never heard anyone speak to her father in such a way before. No man dared think himself entitled to speak to him—much less scold him—as an equal.

Her father certainly seemed to take offense at Henry's tone. Standing, he puffed out his chest. His eyes narrowed. "I have come, *Councilman*, to solicit your presence for an upcoming campaign rally."

"Yours?" Henry asked.

"Yes."

Rebekah held her breath as they stared at one another. She wanted to flee from this showdown of authority. Henry, however, kept hold of her. *Why are you so intent on keeping me here? What is it you want from me?*

"I will not be attending your rally, Delegate Van der Geld."

Rebekah gasped.

Her father was equally surprised. "You won't?"

"No," Henry said firmly. "I do not appreciate you coming here and—"

"Councilman, if I were you—"

"You are *not* me, sir, and—"

Henry did not have the opportunity to finish the sentence, for Sadie then stormed into the room. Her cry spilt the charged air like lightning. "Mr. Henry! Miss Rebekah! Come quick!"

Rebekah's heart dropped from her throat to the pit of her stomach. A mother's instinct told her something was the matter with one of the children. Henry knew, as well. The look on his face instantly changed.

"What's wrong?" he asked.

"It's Miss Kathleen. She's burnin' up with fever!"

Rebekah raced toward the staircase. Sadie followed

close behind. All determination to do battle with her father apparently evaporated, for the last thing she heard Henry say was, "Sir, I am confident you can see your way out of my house."

Then he came charging up the stairs, as well.

Chapter Thirteen

All thoughts of her father and the way Henry had responded to him vanished. Rebekah's mind was filled now with only one person—little Kathleen. Reaching the nursery, she confirmed Sadie's description of fever.

"I'll have James fetch Dr. Stanton," Henry said.

Rebekah saw the fear in his eyes, felt the same emotion in her own heart. The poor child was lying on the bed, pale except for her flushed cheeks. Her skin blazed like fire.

"I thought she was a little warm when I put her down to rest," Sadie explained, "but then so was the room. That's why I opened the window. I didn't think she had fever. I'm so sorry…"

"It's not your fault, Sadie," Rebekah insisted. *It's mine. I should have known… I should have seen it… I'm supposed to be the one caring for her.*

Rebekah reached for the nearby water pitcher. The liquid was only tepid at best, but she soaked a cloth in it, then laid it to the child's forehead. *I never should have taken her yesterday to the public gardens. She must have come in contact with the fever there.*

"You did well to call us when you did," Henry said to Sadie. "But if you would, take Grace down to your mother."

Rebekah watched the maid claim the baby from the cradle. Her guilt grew, as did her fear. *I am such a fool. I should have removed Grace immediately. Are not most fevers spread by inhalation? The baby is in danger now, as well.*

Sadie immediately took the child from the room. When they had gone, Henry stuck his finger in the water pitcher. "This will do no good," he said. "I'll fetch cooler water, and I'll see if Hannah has any ice."

"Ice. Yes. Thank you." *I should have thought of that, as well...*

Kathleen was whimpering, tugging at her sheets, but it was no nightmare plaguing her now. Rebekah's heart ached for her. "It's all right, love. I'm here. I'm here..." She continued to blot her forehead. *How many times did I do this at the hospital? And how many times did those soldiers—?* She shoved the thought aside.

Henry returned with the pitcher of water. He'd secured a large amount of ice from Hannah. The water was so cold, Rebekah could barely touch it.

He sensed her hesitancy. "It's what she needs," he insisted.

Without word, Rebekah plunged the cloth into the swirling water. In this matter she trusted his judgment far more than she trusted her own.

Dr. Stanton arrived, and Rebekah relinquished her place beside Kathleen. From one end of the room, she watched him examine the child. Henry watched from the other. When their eyes met, Rebekah felt as though every thought of hers, every action and every failure lay bare before him. Unable to stand such scrutiny, she looked back to Dr. Stanton. He had finished his task, and was now covering Kathleen with her bedding.

"You were wise to remove the baby," he said to Rebekah, as if she had been the one to think of it.

"Do you know what it is?" Henry asked.

"I can't be certain as of yet, but my best guess at this point would be scarlet fever."

Scarlet fever! The breath lurched in Rebekah's lungs. As children, she and her brothers had been spared this particular killer. The house next door, however, had not. Six siblings had once resided in that home. Now there were only two.

A horror unlike anything she had ever experienced before gripped her. For a moment, she thought her knees would buckle. *No!* she told herself. *Now is not the time for weakness. Now is the time for action!*

"Keep her head cool and her body warm," Dr. Stanton said to her. "We'll know for certain in a few hours. The rash follows the onset of the fever."

Rebekah nodded firmly.

The gray-headed physician then looked to her husband. All this time, Henry had been standing against the wall, a grave expression on his face. "I'll return to look in on her first thing in the morning," Dr. Stanton said. "But send for me straightaway should the situation worsen, or should the baby—"

He didn't finish the sentence, but Rebekah had no trouble finishing it in her head, or recognizing its gravity. *Should the baby contract the fever...* She shuddered at the thought. Grace was too little to survive such an illness. Rebekah could not bear the idea of something happening to her. What would it do to Henry? What would it do to *her*?

As Henry escorted Dr. Stanton out, Rebekah returned her attention to Kathleen. She sponged. She prayed. *Please, God...please, have mercy on them. Don't punish Kathleen or Grace because of my sinfulness. Please... I'll do anything you ask. Anything...*

Henry returned to the room to find Rebekah had donned a pinner apron and a pair of white oversleeves, looking every bit the army nurse as she hovered over Kathleen. Soaking the cloth in the ice water, she laid it to the child's forehead, then repeated the procedure.

He came alongside her, touched Kathleen's head. She was so hot and yet she shivered. How was that possible? It was as though a war was waging inside her little body. He looked then at Rebekah. There was a war going on inside her, as well. He could see the tears in her eyes, yet her jaw was set with fierce determination. Henry had no doubt she would spend every ounce of energy she possessed, offer every prayer she had, to bring about his niece's recovery. He'd do whatever it took, as well.

"Dr. Stanton suggested we send Grace away," he said.

"Away?" Rebekah's blue eyes were wide with alarm. "Too whom? For how long?"

"For as long as necessary. He suggested we send her to his daughter, Julia. Her child has already had the fever. So if Grace—"

He couldn't bring himself to finish the rest of the sentence. He didn't want to think about what would happen if a baby not yet four months old contracted scarlet fever. He had buried his mother. His sister and his brother-in-law were in their graves, as well. *God, not a child...please...not Grace or Kathleen.* "I told Dr. Stanton to take her. Hannah and Sadie are gathering up the bottles and diapers now."

The tears in his wife's eyes spilled over. Henry instinctively reached for her. Her reaction was the same as it had been downstairs when he had tried to comfort her. Her spine stiffened. She immediately pulled away.

Why did she insist on keeping her distance from him? *What am I doing wrong?*

Henry realized he probably hadn't handled her father's visit in the way he should have. When the arrogant man had stepped out of the parlor, announcing that he had business to discuss, Henry had thought his blood would boil. It wasn't the demand for an audience that caused his reaction. It was the look in Rebekah's eyes. She had been obviously frightened.

No doubt her father had burst through the door and taken it upon himself to clear the parlor of Rebekah's friends. They had been embarrassed and in a hurry to leave even though Henry had encouraged them to stay.

Did I come across as too forceful? Possessive? He'd wanted to show acceptance, of his wife and of her friends. He'd wanted Rebekah to feel valued, protected. She had come to him for help, or so it had seemed at the time. *And instead of easing her mind, I frightened her. She fears her father, and she still distrusts me.*

Rebekah once more laid the cloth to Kathleen's forehead.

Lord, help me. I want to understand. I want her to feel secure...

"I think we need more ice," she said.

"I'll fetch it."

Going downstairs, he thought more of the emotions she had displayed before coming to him today in the foyer. He remembered a similar expression the night he had first raised his voice to her. *She looked as though she thought I was going to strike her.* He recalled what she'd said when she'd learned why he had married her.

"You are just like my father!"

Henry suddenly realized just what those words meant. The man in charge of her protecting her, the man who was supposed to love her, had done just the opposite. Henry literally felt sick to his stomach, sickened by what had happened to her, sickened further that he had unknowingly perpetuated her fear.

Oh God, forgive me... I should have realized... I should have put the pieces together long before this. She fears me because of him. And every time I've acted in a way that resembles her father, in stance, in word or in deed, I have reinforced that fear.

Returning to the nursery, he set the water pitcher on the table, then took up post in the chair opposite Kathleen's bed. Rebekah's face was flushed, her jaw still tight with emotion.

Oh God, help me... What do I say? What do I do? He knew what he wanted to do. He wanted to take his wife in his arms, promise her no one would ever hurt her again. *But my rush to action caused much damage before.*

He'd never known being a husband, a father, would be so hard. It was a maddening feeling, seeing someone you loved so ill, and another so hurt, knowing no matter how much you wanted to, *you* could not heal either one of them.

Kathleen was growing worse. Now she was thrashing about, calling for Marianne and John.

"Mama! Papa! Don't leave me! Don't leave me!"

Her cries tore at his heart. Henry watched Rebekah cradle the girl in her arms, much as she had the night before. He reclaimed the space beside his wife, gently laid his hand upon her shoulder. She flinched, but he held his place. "It's all right," he whispered. "It's going to be all right." How he prayed his words would prove true, for all of them.

Rebekah rocked Kathleen, hummed a soft tune. The music and the ice water did little to help. The fever continued to rage. Sadie came to report that she and James had delivered the necessary items for Grace to Julia Ward. Hannah brought fresh cloths and food, but neither he nor his wife could eat a bite. Rebekah kept her vigil. He silently kept his.

By nightfall, what they had fearfully suspected was confirmed. The area around little Kathleen's mouth was as pale as cream, but her cheeks blazed red as if she'd been burned by the sun. Her back and her chest bore the telltale rash, as well.

"Dr. Stanton was right," Henry said. "My sister looked just like that when she had scarlet fever."

"D-did the fever weaken her heart?" Rebekah asked in a thready voice. "I-is that why she d-died?"

"Don't," Henry immediately said. "Don't think that way. Kathleen is not Marianne. She'll come through this."

Rising, Rebekah quickly walked to the opposite side of the room, but not before Henry saw the conflict on her face, saw the fear, the pain, the longing. His heart ached for her.

"I don't know what to do for her," she said.

"Yes, you do. You are doing it. You have treated fevers before. You are an accomplished nurse."

"No, I'm not!" Tears sprang from her eyes, ran down her cheeks. Her words tumbled out like a confession. "My commendations at the hospital were for following orders, Henry, for keeping the ward tidy! My soldiers *died*."

He approached her slowly. "Wounded men often die, Rebekah. It's a sad fact of war. You can't change it."

"My father thought I should be able to."

"What do you mean?"

"He said if I were a more successful nurse, I'd be transferred to a ward with US officers rather than rebel prisoners…that I'd be assigned to more *respectable* men."

How could Van der Geld say such things? How could he place such unspeakable blame on his own daughter? Henry forced himself to swallow back his disgust. He could not allow what he felt toward her father to invade this moment with *her*.

"The army kept you where you were needed," he said, "among the prisoners of war. They outnumbered wounded US officers greatly." He paused, taking her hands in his. They were so delicate, so warm, and again, they were trembling. "Is that why your father made you give up nursing?"

Rebekah drew in a ragged breath. She had never looked more vulnerable. "He said I was becoming too attached. He said he wouldn't abide tears for traitors. He never stood for tears…" She pulled her hands from his, quickly wiping her eyes, as if *he* were the one who couldn't abide her crying. "I'm sorry," she said.

"You needn't be."

He slid his hands up her arms. Her cotton dress was soft to the touch, but the limbs beneath were taut with fright. "Rebekah," he whispered. "You don't have to be afraid of me. I will not hurt you."

She stared at the floor. "But this is all my fault."

Henry gently lifted her chin, looked into her eyes. They were vacant and glassy. "What is your fault?" he asked.

"Kathleen..."

"*Kathleen?* You think *you* are responsible for her illness?"

She nodded, sucked in a breath. She was trembling all over now. "I should have realized. I should have known last night something was wrong. And now if Grace—"

She started to pull away. He refused to let her go. "Rebekah, I was here, as well. I didn't know anything was wrong, either."

"But today...if I had not been busy with the sewing circle... I was the one that invited them this time. If I had only—" She hung her head. "Surely God is *punishing* me."

She had never really spoken to him about her faith, and to Henry's shame, he had never asked. He'd seen her reading the Scriptures, overheard her more than once speak of God's role as creator and sustainer of the universe to Kathleen in the garden. She bowed her head at mealtime and when putting his nieces to bed. *But for all of that, her faith is apparently more out of fear and duty than joy.* His heart squeezed.

"Rebekah, please look at me..."

She slowly raised her eyes. They were full of shame.

"Why do you think God is punishing you?"

"I-I am n-not as I should be."

"Neither am I. You are fully aware of my sins."

"But... I am your wife. I am to please you. I am to obey, not challenge your authority, nor flinch when you touch me."

"Rebekah, that is not a wife. That is a slave, and you know how I feel about slavery." Wrapping his arms around her, he drew her close. Despite the circumstances, it felt so good to hold her. She was so fragile, so in need of protection. Henry vowed he'd spend the rest of his life proving she had nothing to fear from him.

"I know what your father did to you," he whispered. "I know he struck you...repeatedly."

"Only when I deserved it."

At those words, Henry didn't know what he felt more—anger toward his father in law, or pain for his wife. "My dear, you *never* deserved it. And it's over now—you are safe here. You are safe *with me*. I will never let anyone hurt you again, and I will make it known to your father that he is never to step foot in this house again."

He could feel the tension draining from her body. She sagged against him, overwhelmed by emotion and exhaustion. Henry tightened his arms about her. "And Kathleen's illness is *not* your fault. God is *not* punishing you. He loves you. I—"

He stopped, realizing Rebekah's stance had moved well past surrender to his embrace. She was limp in his arms. "Rebekah?"

Her eyes were closed, and the flush on her face was due to more than tears. She was hot with fever, as well.

Sweeping her into his arms, Henry raced for the hall. "Hannah! Hannah!"

The cook came running, meeting him at the door to Rebekah's bedroom. A cry escaped her throat the moment she saw them, instantly recognizing what was wrong.

"Help me," Henry pleaded.

He placed his wife upon the bed, then reached for the water pitcher. "I'll fetch the ice."

An apron, a dress and a collection of ladies' underpinnings littered the floor by the time he returned to the room. Hannah had somehow managed to get Rebekah into a nightdress and pulled the pins from her hair. A long chocolate braid now tumbled down her shoulder. Embroidered pink roses encircled her neck.

Henry set the pitcher of water on the table beside the bed and helped Hannah cover her with blankets. Rebekah was now shivering uncontrollably, yet like Kathleen, she burned with fever.

"I'll fetch you another blanket," Hannah said. "Then I'll look after Miss Kathleen. Sadie can mind the kitchen."

"Thank you, Hannah."

The woman hurried off. Henry laid the cold cloth upon Rebekah's forehead. She opened her eyes. "Grace... Kathleen..."

"Grace is safe," he told her, "and Hannah will see to Kathleen."

She uttered something unintelligible, then suddenly twisted as if she were about to be violently ill. Henry immediately reached for the washbasin. He was just in time.

Rebekah collapsed back upon her pillows, eyes

glazed and vacant. Evidently she was now oblivious
to his presence.

"God…please…forgive me!"

Her cry broke his heart. Henry grasped her hand.
"He does forgive you. Rest easy, my dear."

"I'm sorry… I'm so sorry…please…"

She gripped his hand tightly but drew the blankets
close to her body with the other, as if she was trying to
hide from someone. Her words soon revealed whom.
"Father, please… I'm sorry. I'll try harder…"

Once more Henry felt his emotions swirl. "Rebekah,
you're safe. *I'm* here. *I* will protect you. *I will never* let
your father hurt you again."

The hours wore on. She continued to toss and turn.
The rash that marked Kathleen now covered Rebekah,
as well. She was in full delirium, calling out, writhing
in fright and pain. Down the hall, despite Hannah's
care, Henry could hear as Kathleen cried again and
again for her mother.

His heart rent in two. Was he to lose them both? *God
please, please spare my family. My wife…my children…*

As far as Henry was concerned, Grace and Kathleen
were now *his daughters*. And as for Rebekah, he could
no longer imagine his life without her, any more than
he could live without his own breath.

Once he had pledged to her his fortune, his freedom
and his life. Now he did so not out of a sense of obligation but because she was the woman he had come to
love. *Love*…he was certain of it now. He loved her for
the affection and care she bestowed upon Grace and
Kathleen. He loved her for staying with him, despite
his failures. He loved the strong spirit she tried so desperately to keep chained inside her delicate carriage.

He loved the honest, sometimes overly frank, vivacious creature struggling so to find her place in this world.

Henry carefully drew her feverish body close to his. He didn't know if she could hear him or not, but he prayed she could. "Rebekah, my dear, *darling*...please... do your best to get well. *I love you*."

Chapter Fourteen

Rebekah rubbed her eyes and blinked but could not clear her hindered vision. A mist seemed to shroud the room, and though it was early morning, the hospital ward seemed uncommonly dark. She could barely see the beds before her, but she could hear the moans of pain from the ill and wounded soldiers in her care.

"Maggie, before you go, you must light the lamps," Rebekah ordered.

But the young nurse paid her no mind. She was tugging at Rebekah's apron and her oversleeves, as if she would take them from her.

"Maggie, stop this foolishness! Unhand me! The soldiers...can't you hear them? We must help them!"

But Maggie didn't listen, and she wasn't any help with the wounded. She flittered off, giggling, as if the disfigured men around them were something to laugh about. Rebekah tried to reach the suffering soldiers, but now the attending physician blocked her path. He took hold of her arms. He called her by her Christian name. "Rebekah... Rebekah...you must rest..."

But she couldn't rest. She had to help those men.

She had to do her duty. Billy, the Kentucky private, was gasping for breath. Corporal Clark was shuddering with fever. A Virginia sergeant whose name she did not know was writhing in anguish because of infected wounds. Tommy, the young drummer boy missing the left side of his face, swore he would take his own life.

She pushed against the physician but could not break free of him. "Please! Help me! God, please! Help me!" But neither the Almighty nor anyone else came to her aid. Rebekah watched in horror as one by one the soldiers met their ends and were covered with their sheets, their emaciated faces hidden from view.

Silence blanketed the ward. Her father then desecrated the stillness. His booming voice was like a cannonade.

"No tears! I forbid you to return to this hospital! You are useless! You will stay at home. You will learn to manage a proper household!"

Proper. Yes, proper... Rebekah tried her best to do so, but tea was spilt and statesmen's frock coats were stained. Her manners were never refined enough, and her apologies did not suffice. She felt his fist against her jaw. Her ears began to ring.

But somehow, someway, she at last found her courage. "I will not stay here any longer!" she shouted. "I will run! I will escape! I will go where you cannot find me!"

Rebekah took off through the darkness. The city was a maze of twisting streets, and soon she lost her way. Buildings were draped in black. Little children were crying. Paralyzed by the heartbreaking sound, she wanted to comfort the children but didn't know how.

Shame pressed heavily upon her. "I'm sorry! I want to help you..."

She heard a voice. *"Rebekah... Rebekah...this is not your fault."* The voice was firm but kind. It spoke of promise. *"I will never let him hurt you again."*

She turned toward the direction from which the soothing voice had come, but suddenly her feet and hands were bound. She could not move, could not even breathe. Rebekah tried to cry out, but her tongue was parched. Her throat was so sore.

Then she heard other voices, other whispers, soft and kind. Who were they? Did they know she was in trouble? *Please...please help me... Don't leave me in this darkness...*

Soon a pair of hands, ones that commanded strength and authority, took hold of her. Rebekah was frightened but far too overcome, too exhausted to resist. She felt herself being lifted. She was again being called by name.

"Rebekah... Rebekah... I love you."

Darkness still surrounded her, but a warmth now flooded through her. Rebekah was powerless to move, yet she no longer feared, no longer questioned. Wherever she was, she was safe. She was valued. She was loved.

Rebekah's fever had continued to climb, but at long last, she appeared to be resting a little easier. Her breathing was less labored. Her body was not as tense. Whether it was holding her close that gave her a measure of security or simply God's mercy, Henry did not know, but he prayed the effect would continue.

James and Sadie moved in and out of the room,

bringing fresh water and clean cloths. Henry sponged Rebekah's forehead, held her and prayed. Dawn brought Dr. Stanton's return, but he had little encouragement to give. Kathleen continued to burn in one room, his wife in the other. The physician felt Rebekah's wrist while looking at his watch.

"She's been seeing things," Henry told him. "She's calling out for people at the hospital, nurses, doctors, dying soldiers."

The man nodded gravely as he placed Rebekah's arm beneath the blanket. "That's to be expected with a fever this high."

"I pack her head with ice. All it does is melt. Is there nothing else I can do?"

"I suggest you cut her hair."

"Cut her hair?"

"To cool her head."

Henry would do what the doctor ordered, of course. He knew the command had been issued in Rebekah's best interest, but the thought of robbing her of her crowning glory seemed tantamount to sacrilege. Would she forgive him? Could he forgive himself? Henry grieved the fact that he'd never run his fingers through those long, dark tresses, never fully appreciated her physical beauty until now that sickness sought to destroy it.

Sadie brought in a tray of tea and toast for him and a bowl of broth for Rebekah. Henry knew neither he nor his wife could swallow an ounce, but he thanked the young maid just the same.

"Fetch you anything else?" she asked.

Henry hesitated, but he knew it had to be done. He

would seize on any remedy that might lessen even a degree of Rebekah's fever. "Please bring me the scissors."

The look on Sadie's face was one of immediate pity. She must have known *why* he wanted them, what he intended to do. Silently she left the room. When she came back a few moments later, she handed him the scissors.

"Poor Miss Rebekah," she breathed, and with that, she quickly fled.

Rebekah's long dark braid lay upon her left shoulder, the one nearest to him. However, Henry couldn't bring himself to touch it. He instead handed the scissors to Dr. Stanton. In an instant, the physician had snipped the bound locks, laid them on the bedside table. "It will grow again," he said, sensing Henry's lament.

If she survives, he thought. *God, please...please...*

"Keep watch over her," Dr. Stanton said. "Sometimes patients become so delirious, they wander from their beds. She could unintentionally harm herself."

She had already tried twice to do so. Thinking she was still on duty in the wards, Rebekah had thrown back the covers, insisting she must tend to the wounded prisoners. Henry had caught her both times and restrained her before her feet had hit the floor.

"Be assured," he said, "I will not leave her."

The examination finished, he rang for James. The man quietly escorted Dr. Stanton out. Henry returned his full attention to his wife. She was once again shivering. What remained of her hair now curled about her ears.

Sighing, Henry wrapped a chocolate-colored ringlet about his finger. He couldn't help but remember the feel of her hair as it had brushed his chin, how their breath had harmonized when he had held her. For those few brief seconds, Rebekah had seemed at peace. Henry wanted desperately to offer her that forever, but he wondered if he could truly give her what she needed. He knew all too well what emotions bubbled inside him.

He despised her father. For that matter, he despised his own. *And the Scriptures testify repeatedly that love and hate cannot coincide.* But how did one go about forgiving someone who had intentionally inflicted pain upon another? *Her father should have protected her, loved her. My father should have done as much for my mother. I've done so for Grace and Kathleen...*

But he knew full well that ability hadn't come from within. Henry's attempts at procuring a loving, stable home for the girls had been disastrous. He'd made decisions based on fear, not love, and he had reaped the terrible consequences. *And God has forgiven me. I need to extend the same grace to Theodore Van der Geld.* He sighed heavily, knowing it would take even more of the Almighty's grace for him to do so. *Lord, help me... Help me to forgive her father... Help me to forgive my own...*

When James returned to the room to see if he had need of anything else, Henry asked him to bring paper and a pen. He felt he should notify Rebekah's parents of her illness, regardless of their lack of a relationship. It was only right. *And the presence of sickness will surely keep Van der Geld from reentering this house anytime soon.* He also needed to send a message to the city council, letting them know he would not be joining them today.

James brought him the necessary implements. Henry scratched out the two missives, then gave them to the man.

"I'll get these off straightaway," James promised.

"Thank you. I'd appreciate that."

Henry straightened Rebekah's coverings once more. He felt her cheeks and forehead and in doing so tried to keep faith. Rebekah wasn't any cooler, despite losing her hair.

The following morning, Hannah came into the room. "I've good news," she said. "Miss Kathleen's fever broke just after sunrise."

Henry laid his head in his hands. He heaved a sigh. *Thank You, Lord. Thank You.* "I'm pleased to hear that," he said to Hannah.

The woman came forward. "She's resting peacefully now. Sadie's sittin' with her." Hannah looked at Rebekah. "How is she?"

"No change," Henry said. He could hear the fatigue in his own voice, the discouragement. Hannah could, as well.

"You should rest, Mr. Henry. I'll look after her for a while."

"No, Hannah, but thank you. I want to stay. I want to be here when she wakes."

She nodded slowly, then peered into the nearby pitcher. "Have you been able to get her to drink anything?"

"Not much."

"I'll bring you some fresh water and somethin' for you to eat."

He appreciated that but didn't want her to go to the trouble. She needed rest, as well. "Don't bother about me," he said.

To that, the older woman only smiled. "But that's my job, least till Miss Rebekah gets back on her feet."

Hannah wasn't the only one who felt the need to look after him. By that afternoon, word had gotten about of the sickness plaguing the Nash family, and there was a steady stream of souls wishing to help.

George Meriwether was the first to arrive. He came bearing notes from the council meeting, promising to keep Henry abreast of any developments, especially in regard to civil unrest. The trial of the Lincoln conspirators had come to conclusion, a guilty verdict having been rendered. The man whom Rebekah had nursed in the hospital—Lewis Powell, now Paine—had been sentenced to hang for his crime. So had several others, including the widowed mother, Mary Surratt.

Henry wasn't surprised by the first verdict, but he was by the second. Although he and apparently the rest of the council doubted she'd actually be executed, Mayor Chapman suggested that the city police force again be put on high alert in case any Southern sympathizers sought to stir up trouble. Henry laid the council minutes aside. He certainly hoped there would be no trouble, but he would leave the business of Baltimore to his fellow councilmen. Right now, his family was more important.

Sam Ward came next. He delivered to James a pot of soup that his wife insisted on sending and the good news that Grace was still unaffected by fever.

"Thank You, God," Henry breathed when James told him the news.

"He said Miss Hastings and Mrs. Wainwright plan to send food tomorrow and the next day," James then reported.

Henry took comfort in their friends' concern. Still, it grieved him that there had been not one word from

Rebekah's family, not even a token gesture. *Do they not care at all that she is so ill?* He supposed it unreasonable to think her father would be concerned with her suffering, but Henry had thought that at the very least, her mother would show some sort of attention.

How hard-hearted can they be? Feeling the anger burning inside him, once more he prayed for the grace to forgive.

He still didn't know if leaving Maryland politics was best, for Rebekah had shown little interest when he'd mentioned the opportunity in Ohio. If they did remain in Baltimore, Henry certainly wasn't going to campaign for a man who treated his daughter with such little respect.

But I must do my best to live in peace with him, for her sake. And so he continued to pray for the ability to do so.

Rebekah's eyelids fluttered open. The veil of murky darkness had finally lifted. She beheld Hannah's familiar face smiling at her.

"The Lord be praised," the woman said. "Welcome back, Miss Rebekah."

Back? Where exactly had she been? A host of mottled memories drifted through her mind, hospital wards…dark streets…but Rebekah wasn't certain any of them had been real.

"You've had the scarlet fever."

Rebekah blinked. So her memories of wandering had been fever dreams? Vaguely she remembered Hannah helping her into a nightdress and before that, sitting with Kathleen. Then she remembered why. Her pulse quickened. "The girls—"

"They are just fine," Hannah reassured her. "Miss Grace is with the Ward family, fit as a fiddle, gettin' fat and sassy, and Miss Kathleen is on the mend. Her fever broke early this mornin', and that rash of hers is completely gone." Hannah sponged Rebekah's forehead lightly, studied her for a moment. "I'd say yours is fading nicely, too." She put the cloth into the washbasin. "Miss Kathleen has managed a few helpings of beef tea today and now even a little toast. Are you feelin' up to tryin' some?"

Just the mention of food made Rebekah's stomach rumble. She felt as though she hadn't eaten in weeks. "Yes, please. Thank you…and thank you for taking such good care of us."

Hannah smiled as if she possessed a wonderful secret. "I was happy to tend to Miss Kathleen. But when it came to lookin' after you, miss…that wasn't me," she said.

She glanced toward her right. Rebekah's eyes followed. There, just a few feet from her bedside, sat Henry. Chin pressed to his chest, he was sound asleep.

"This is the first he's slept in three days," Hannah whispered. "I s'pect he'll be put out with me for not wakin' him, but the poor man is spent. He just wouldn't leave your side. Nursed you the entire time."

The entire time? So it was *his* hands that had cooled her forehead? It was his comforting voice she had heard? Rebekah searched her memory. What exactly had he said to her?

"They had to cut your hair," Hannah said.

My hair? Rebekah's heart sank. Her one and only beauty was gone?

"Sadie said it 'bout broke Mr. Henry's heart to ask

for the scissors. Couldn't bring hisself to do it, in the end. Dr. Stanton had to take command."

It broke his heart?

"You lay still now. I'll fetch you that tea. Then, when you're up to it, I'll help you into a fresh gown."

Hannah wisely knew Rebekah was too weak to even raise her head, though she wished she could change gowns now. The sweat-drenched cotton was as uncomfortable as it was embarrassing. Glancing down, she realized what nightdress she was wearing—the one her friends had so painstakingly embroidered. Henry had seen the gift for himself now, but not at all in the way it had been intended.

Heat crept up her neck as Rebekah stole another glance at him. How unkempt and indiscreet she must have appeared during those hours of fever. *And yet he stayed with me? Never once relegating the task of my care to someone else?*

As Hannah tiptoed from the room, Rebekah continued to study her husband. On his lap was not the daily newspaper, or matters of business, but an open Bible. His shirt was soiled. His hair was mussed, and his customarily clean-shaven face now bore the beginnings of a beard. It was far from the polished look of a city councilman, and yet there was something so endearing, so very handsome about him.

Rebekah then remembered those last moments in Kathleen's room, before her knees had weakened and the darkness rushed in. Henry had been speaking of her time at the hospital and of her father. He knew everything, and he had promised no one would ever hurt her again.

She remembered being lifted in his arms, remembered exactly what words she had heard.

"Rebekah, I love you..."

Her heart came undone. Great tears filled her eyes, and a sob she could not contain choked her throat.

Startled by the sound, Henry's neck snapped up. He immediately came to her side. The expression on his face was one of fear. "God, please...please help her..." Evidently he did not think her lucid.

"Henry..." she whispered.

Relief melted his taut features. "Oh, thank You, God. Thank You." Brushing his lips lightly against her forehead, he said, "I thought I was going to lose you."

Rebekah's heart was so full, she could not speak. She stared up into his blue eyes. Fatigue lined them, but even so, they were as sincere and inviting as the summer sky. What could she say to this man? She'd thought she had known him, understood him, but clearly she had not. How could she even begin to express her gratitude for his faithfulness, his tender affection?

"It's all right," he said. "It's all right. You are safe. Kathleen is well. Grace is, too." He brushed away her tears with his fingers. For the first time she truly welcomed his nearness, his touch.

Hannah returned with the promised tray of food.

"Do you want to try a bit of tea?" Henry asked.

Rebekah nodded.

"Can you sit upright?"

"Y-yes..." Or at least she would try, since he so seemed to wish for it.

Bending low, her husband encircled her with his arms. The muscles Rebekah had once seen as means for control, for domination, she now saw as something else entirely. Henry's strength was a means of help, of protection. As Elizabeth had once said, he was a man with a true servant's heart. Rebekah leaned against his chest until she came to rest upon a pile of pillows. Henry then stepped back.

"There now," Hannah said. "This will fix you." As she brought forward the tray, he backed quietly to the door and slipped into the hall.

Watching, Rebekah silently wished he had remained.

Chapter Fifteen

Henry stepped from the room and sank against the hallway wall. He was physically drained but emotionally overjoyed. God had answered his prayers, in more ways than one. The fever had finally abated, and in the process, something else had changed. His wife now looked at him with different eyes. He saw it when she spoke his name, saw it again when he leaned her against her pillows. A smile tugged at his tired mouth, for he sensed this was the beginning of a real courtship, a true union, one with commitment and affection on both of their parts.

Thank You, God. Thank You...

Across the hall, he heard the sound of Kathleen's voice. She was chattering away to Sadie. His smile broadened. *Another prayer answered.* His strength renewing, he made his way to the little girl's room. Kathleen was lounging upon her own pile of pillows, showing Sadie the cloth doll Rebekah had created for her.

The young maid smiled and stepped back when she

saw him in the doorway. Kathleen grinned, as well. "I'm better," she announced.

"I can see that," Henry said as he came to her.

Kathleen's pert little mouth then turned down with a frown. "But Sadie and Hannah say I can't go outside."

"No, not yet," Henry said, "but soon."

Her expression brightened. "How soon? When Aunt Rebekah gets better?"

He nodded and hugged her tightly. Kathleen giggled but pulled her face away from his.

"You're scratchy," she said.

Letting go of her, Henry ran his hand over his chin. She was right. He shouldn't have been surprised. It had been days since his face had seen a razor. "What say I remedy that? Then I'll take you to see your Aunt Rebekah."

Kathleen nodded eagerly—a little *too* eagerly, perhaps. Suspecting she would toss back her blankets and hit the floor, Henry told her, "Wait here with Sadie and play with your doll until I return."

She nodded again, this time with a little less enthusiasm. Satisfied she'd stay put, Henry went to his room. After making the necessary changes, he returned to fetch her.

"You were gone a long time," Kathleen said.

Henry heard the statement with a smile. Her impatience was a sign of recovery. "Forgive me," he said. "I wanted to make myself handsome for you and Aunt Rebekah."

She reached up, her chubby little hand feeling his chin for herself. "You did good. It's soft now."

Kathleen put her arms around his neck as Henry carried her across the hall. "Now we mustn't visit long," he said. "Aunt Rebekah is still very tired. She needs her rest."

"When she isn't tired anymore, will Grace come home?"

"Yes," Henry said. "Then we can all be together again." He could hardly wait for that day. For now, though, he knew he must also heed his own command to show patience. Rebekah was out of danger but still far from health. She needed time to heal, not only from the effects of scarlet fever but also from many other scars.

Lord, help me to remember that. Help me to be patient. I don't want to overwhelm her.

When he reached his wife's doorway, Henry found Hannah had left and taken the food tray with her. Before going, she had managed to get Rebekah into a new nightdress. His wife looked fatigued but content.

"Someone wants to see you," Henry said. "Is that all right?"

Rebekah immediately smiled. Despite the ravages of fever, the frail eyes and cropped curly hair, Henry thought her beautiful. He carried Kathleen forward and set her on the edge of the bed, then claimed the chair beside them.

"How are you, love?" Rebekah asked. Her voice was weak, but Henry could plainly hear the motherly concern, the affection.

"I'm all better," Kathleen told her. She again lamented the fact that she wasn't yet allowed to play outside.

"Soon," Rebekah promised.

"That's what Uncle Henry said."

His wife offered another fragile smile. "You must listen to what he says. He loves you, and he knows what is best for you."

Henry felt his confidence swell. He didn't always *know* what was best for any of them, but he wanted to *do* what was best, and if God would grant him the wisdom and the grace, he'd spend the rest of his days proving how much he loved them.

Kathleen noticed her aunt's hair. "It's short," she said.

"Yes," Rebekah replied, embarrassment darkening her cheeks.

"I think it is beautiful," Henry said. "Don't you, Kathleen?"

The little girl nodded. "It's twisty now." She reached out and felt one of her aunt's curls. As she did, Rebekah's eyes moved to his. They seemed to speak volumes. For a moment, Henry could barely breathe.

Hannah then came back into the room. "Well, Miss Kathleen, your bed is all fresh and ready for you."

The little girl frowned. She knew what was implied by such a statement.

As much as Henry was enjoying this moment, he knew it was time to go. He could see that Rebekah was growing more tired by the second. "Remember what I told you," she whispered weakly to Kathleen. "You must listen to Hannah, as well."

Kathleen nodded once again, but her frown remained.

"That's a good girl," Rebekah said. "May I have a kiss?"

The child readily bestowed one. Rebekah embraced her as long as her drained muscles would allow. When her arms slipped back to her sides, Henry claimed Kathleen.

"All right, pretty girl. Aunt Rebekah needs her sleep."

He was gazing at his blue-eyed child, the one who looked so much like his sister, and remarkably so much like himself, but Henry could feel his *wife's* eyes upon *him*. Did Rebekah know how badly he wished to remain with her? Did she wish for him to do so? If he did stay by her side, would she find his company enjoyable or taxing? Choosing to err on the side of caution, he and Kathleen turned for the door.

Hannah met him. "I'll take her, Mr. Henry," she said, holding out her arms and smiling. Then in a voice barely audible, she whispered, "I think Miss Rebekah wants you to stay."

Rebekah's heart leapt as she watched Henry pass Kathleen to Hannah. Was he going to stay with her for a little while longer? It might be selfish, childish for certain, but she had wished for him to do so, at least until she was again sleeping.

Fever had marred much of her memory of the past few days, but of one thing she was certain. He had told her he loved her. He had held her in his arms, and she had felt safe in his embrace. She had wanted to hear those words again, feel the beating of his heart.

Henry turned back to her. "Shall I fetch you anything?" he asked.

"N-no," Rebekah whispered.

He stood there for a moment as though unsure of what to do or say next. Rebekah didn't know, either. There was so much she *wanted* to say to him, so much she wanted to ask. She tried to thank him, but her tongue was tied, her thoughts jumbled, especially when Henry settled carefully beside her. He had shaved and changed his clothing. His pressed white shirt was crisp and smelled of that familiar soap powder. He was dressed as though he had very important matters to attend, *but he is sitting here with me.* "You took care of me," she said.

"I did."

"W-why?"

He smiled gently. Rebekah felt a flutter in her chest. "You are my wife," he said. "It is my privilege to care for you."

His privilege? No one had ever even so much as hinted it was a privilege to care for her. In her father's house, she had been an imposition.

My father. She immediately shut her eyes tight. Those moments in the downstairs parlor ripped through her mind. Henry had stood toe to toe with him while holding her in his guard. She had taken her husband's actions for possessiveness and arrogance. Now she realized they were something else entirely. Henry had been demonstrating to her father that she was now part of his household and that she was no longer subject to her father's control.

He was defending me, she thought, but instead of feeling joy, shame flooded though her. *I've been so wrong about him. More than once I accused him of being just like my father. Nothing could be further from the truth.* She tried to voice her thoughts. "Henry, my father—"

"Shh," he soothed her. "It's all right. You don't have to worry about anything concerning him. For now, darling, just rest. We can speak more on that subject later if you like. You'll feel stronger in a day or two."

Darling...not a contrived *my dear*. He was speaking from his heart. Tears filled her eyes. "I'm so sorry... I misjudged you so..."

"Shh," he said once more. "There is no need for that, no need..."

"You are such a good man."

"No, I'm not. I'm far from it. I'm simply a forgiven man." Leaning close, he kissed her again on the forehead. "And I love you."

Closing her eyes, Rebekah let his words, his scent wash over her. Before long she fell asleep. The nightmares that had plagued her previously did not invade her mind this time. Rebekah instead found herself dreaming of pleasant things. Kathleen was romping through a field of daylilies. Grace was rocking back and forth on her plump little legs, crawling for the first time.

When Rebekah awoke, it was evening. Twilight had colored the sky orange and purple. The curtains danced at the windowsill, a steady breeze blowing, but Rebekah no longer felt chilled. Henry was still at his post, seated in the chair beside her.

She smiled at the sight of him. He grinned in return. "Feeling better?" he asked.

Rebekah shifted beneath her blankets. Her arms and legs no longer felt so weak, but she was ravenously hungry. She told him. Henry leaned his head back and laughed. The sound was like music to her ears.

"That's a good sign," he said. "Kathleen herself is much the same. I believe you are both truly on the mend."

Thank You, God. Thank You... Rebekah noticed then

the Bible spread open across his lap. She was curious. "What were you reading?" she asked.

"Romans," he said. "It's my favorite book."

His favorite? She'd read the Scriptures as commanded, but could she really say she had a favorite book? So many of the passages reminded her of her shortcomings. And the verses of peace, joy, a gentle and quiet spirit? That was something she had never been able to obtain. *The Bible condemns me more than it comforts.*

"Chapter eight is my particular favorite," Henry said.

"Why is that?"

"The Apostle Paul has just laid out how impossible it is to keep God's law, how one can never live up to His holy standards, and then he tells us God loves us anyway, that those who've asked for His mercy are no longer condemned."

No longer condemned...?

"Christ took the punishment for the wrongs we have done."

Rebekah nodded in agreement. All this she knew. "So that we might spend eternity in Heaven."

Henry nodded in return. "Yes, but so that we might also know His love, His peace, here on earth."

Know His love? God was a father. Rebekah understood mercy, a reprieve from eternal punishment, but *love*?

Henry leaned closer. She could see the earnestness in his eyes. "God doesn't see you as a failure or an inconvenience, darling. You are *His daughter*. He thought you were worth dying for. He'd have gone to the cross just for you. That's how much He loves you."

The words gripped her heart. Jesus would have died

to rescue her alone? She could see God giving His life for Kathleen or Grace or Henry, but *for her*? It was simply incomprehensible.

"What your father displayed to you, what he did, is *not* a representation of true fatherhood."

Deep down, Rebekah knew Henry was speaking truth. She knew it because of what she'd seen *him* display toward Kathleen and Grace. But to believe that God loved her in spite of her temper, her impatience, her resistance to authority? She couldn't believe that. *He might have saved my soul from eternal darkness, but isn't He eagerly waiting for my character to improve? And isn't Henry waiting, as well?*

Heat crept up her neck. Here her husband had just told her he loved her, had just spent the last several days caring for her needs, and she couldn't even properly thank him, let alone express all she was feeling inside. Why couldn't she tell him how the sight of his smile made her practically giddy or how cherished she had felt when she opened her eyes to find him still watching over her?

Henry closed the Bible and laid it on the table beside his chair. "You said you were hungry." He rose. "I'll fetch you something."

Henry could see the wheels turning in his wife's mind. She was puzzling through what he had said, but she couldn't quite bring herself to believe it applied to her. He wondered what type of relationship he would have with God if he had grown up in a household where both parents had been cold.

Most likely I would see the Heavenly Father as indifferent and as stern as she does.

More than anything, Henry wanted Rebekah to find the peace that he had. His character was far from perfect, and his future was uncertain. He had two young children dependent on him and had probably made a powerful man very angry because he had not agreed to assist in his gubernatorial campaign. Henry's city was still as fraught with tension as it had been the day of Lincoln's assassination, and no one knew what would happen if the convicted conspirators were actually executed.

Theodore Van der Geld may very likely take it upon himself to go digging up my past associations and try to connect them to any rabble-rousers should there be trouble.

But Henry was not fearful, not this time. He knew God was with him and with his family. *I know the road ahead may not be easy, Lord, but I trust You will give me the courage and the wisdom to travel it. Give Rebekah the same.*

He brought her a bowl of soup. After she had eaten it, she asked if she might borrow his Bible. Henry took that as an encouraging sign. "Of course," he said. Removing the tray, he then handed the book to her. "I'll leave you to the quiet. I'll look in on Kathleen."

"Give her a kiss for me," she said.

"I'd be happy to."

As he moved toward the door, he could hear Rebekah turning the delicate Scripture pages. He wondered what she was looking for, exactly. He wondered if she would notice he'd written her name alongside his in the marriage record. He had listed Grace and Kathleen as their children, as well.

Henry couldn't help but wonder if the day would ever

come when he would add another name to that list. He certainly hoped so, but for now it was too early even to think about having more children together.

The night that passed was a peaceful one. Both Kathleen and Rebekah slept soundly for the first time in days. Henry looked in on them several times before taking to his own bed. Sleep claimed him almost the moment his head hit the pillow.

Morning dawned on not only a brand new day but also a new month. The strong July sun made the upstairs rooms feel like a bread oven. Kathleen jumped at Henry's invitation to join him in the shade of the garden. Rebekah was equally delighted. After Hannah had helped her into a comfortable sacque dress and pinned up her curls, Henry carried Rebekah downstairs.

"I think I could manage the walk today," she said.

It wasn't a protest, but rather a statement of hope. Henry was thankful she was feeling stronger, but he wasn't going to forgo the opportunity to hold her close, especially when she smelled of lavender water and fit so perfectly in his arms.

"Why waste your strength navigating the staircase when you could spend it picking flowers?" he asked.

She smiled softly. Henry wanted to kiss her right then and there but held back. At present she was captive in his arms, and he wasn't going to press forward with affection until he was absolutely certain she wished him to do so. She no longer flinched, but nervousness still darkened her cheeks whenever he touched her.

He settled her in a chair beneath the oak tree. When Rebekah was slow to slide her hands from his neck, Henry's heart beat a little faster.

"It's good to be outside again," she said.

"The fresh air will do you good."

It was already doing so for Kathleen. Eyes bright, smile wide, she was poking the dirt with a stick, searching for inchworms. He and Rebekah watched her for a moment in silence before Rebekah asked, "When will you bring Grace home?"

"When do you wish for her to return?"

"Now," she said. "Yesterday."

He smiled at her. "I miss her as much as you do, but *now* might be a little too soon. You need to regain your strength to be able to see to her care. What if I ask Julia to keep Grace until Monday?"

"What day is it now?"

"Saturday."

He recognized the look on her face, the regret over lost time. The week had been as much a blur for him as it was her.

"I suppose that is best," Rebekah said. "I can't believe she's been away so long…"

He sensed where her thoughts were headed. Kneeling down, he rested his arms upon his raised leg. "Don't worry. While it is true Grace may feel a little out of sorts from being passed about, I'm confident you'll soon have her smiling again."

She looked at him with eyes full of amazement. Dare he think even admiration? "You think so highly of me. Why?"

"Because I love you." Rising slowly, this time he did not kiss her forehead. He kissed her cheek. Henry heard her sigh. Lingering, he hoped she would turn her face toward him, meet his lips. She did not, however, so he backed away and stood upright.

"I'll send Sam and Julia word," he said. "I'll ask them to bring Grace on Monday."

"Thank you." Her words seemed to hold more meaning than the obvious, as if she wanted to say more but couldn't.

Give her time, he thought. He returned to the house. After scratching out a letter to the Wards, he gathered up the newspapers. He figured Rebekah would want to catch up on what had been happening in the world. Tucking them under his arm, Henry went to find James. He would ask the man to deliver the Wards' letter. Then he would return to the garden.

Henry stepped into the foyer to find James already taking charge of a missive. Immediately his muscles tensed, for the person delivering the particular letter was Rebekah's former maid, Fiona. *So communication from the Van der Geld household has finally come*, he thought.

Fiona curtseyed when she saw him. "Mornin', Councilman Nash. I brought a letter for Miss Rebekah."

James handed it to him. Henry tried to smile. "Thank you, James, and thank you, Fiona. You are looking well."

She blushed slightly and curtseyed again. "Thank you, sir. You are very kind. I'd best be off. The missus will be lookin' for me. A good day to ya."

"And to you, Fiona."

When she had gone, James shut the door and then asked about the other envelope in Henry's hand. Henry explained the details concerning Grace.

"Yes, sir. I can deliver that to Mr. Ward right now." Taking it, James quickly headed out.

Henry stared then at the remaining envelope. He had

accepted it graciously from Fiona but was not eager at all to deliver it to his wife. Despite recovering still from her illness and missing Grace, Rebekah seemed happy. He did not wish to do anything to change that.

Henry did not know if the communication from the Van der Geld household would be charitable or chastising. Given the history, he suspected it would be the latter, so he slipped the envelope into his coat pocket. Deciding to keep it there, at least for now, he returned to the garden.

Chapter Sixteen

The dappled sunlight danced over Rebekah while a warm breeze caressed her face. She told herself she should be content. Grace was well and would be coming home soon. Henry had promised such. He missed Grace as much as she did, but his delay in fetching the baby was due to his concern for *her*. Henry wanted to be certain Rebekah was well recovered before resuming the challenges of motherhood.

He shows me such kindness. And how can he think I am beautiful when I feel anything but? And his confidence in me? He was so certain she'd be able to settle Grace upon her return. *No one has ever believed in me as he does. He does not lord my mistakes over me. He never even mentions them!*

Henry came back into the garden. He was carrying a stack of newspapers. "James delivered my message to the Wards," he said, "and I thought you might be interested in these."

She was indeed. She knew before falling ill that the trial of the conspirators was to conclude any day. She was particularly interested in finding out what was to become of Mary Surratt. "Thank you," she said. "I appreciate that."

Henry gave them to her, then went to join Kathleen. She was still digging in the dirt, searching for worms. As he sat down beside her, she handed him a stick. He happily accepted it. Watching, Rebekah couldn't help but smile. What other statesman would think poking in the garden with a four-year-old child worth his time?

Especially when the newspapers are proclaiming such perilous headlines...

Three of the Lincoln conspirators had been sentenced to prison at a remote army fort in the Gulf of Mexico. The other four, including former hospital patient Lewis Powell and the widowed mother Mary Surratt, had been sentenced to hang.

Rebekah read further. David and Elizabeth's paper talked of a petition drive to commute Surratt's sentence to life in prison. Another publication predicted civil unrest if that happened. Still another projected rioting in the streets if the hanging *was* carried out. Rebekah laid the papers aside. *The war might have ended, but peace has yet to come to Baltimore, or to me.*

Henry loved her. He had proclaimed such and had demonstrated it by his continued care. She could see the longing in his eyes when he looked at her, felt the quickness of his breath when he was near. When he had kissed her face just moments ago, Rebekah had wanted nothing more than to turn to him and lose herself in his embrace.

But once again, she held her back for reasons not even known to her.

Why do I still feel so agitated? What is keeping me from him? What was keeping her from the God Henry had spoken of? Did she think His love would fail to be as liberating as her husband claimed?

Rebekah couldn't help but remember then what Henry had said: that when God looked at her, He saw not her sins and failures. He saw His son's likeness. The verse she'd read afterward came back to her, as well. *"There is therefore now no condemnation for those that are in Christ Jesus."*

No condemnation…that meant acceptance, just the way she was, flaws and all. It meant feeling secure in such a love. Rebekah wanted that, desperately.

Still…

From across the garden, Henry must have seen the look of distress on her face. He returned to her. "Are you all right?" he asked.

"I was just reading the headlines."

He frowned slightly. "Perhaps I shouldn't have brought them to you, at least not yet, given the subject matter. But I knew you had been following the trial."

The events surrounding President Lincoln's death had been a reminder of Henry's lowest moments, of his most questionable character. *Yet he no longer seeks to hide that fact. He has never once denied me the ability to follow the trial.* Again, Rebekah marveled at her husband's humble spirit.

"I was following it," she said, "and I thank you for bringing them. It's just…" How was she to voice all that was swirling inside? Did she even truly wish to do so? The last thing she wanted was for Henry to think she was still angry with him or that her doubts were directed at him. "So much is happening… So much *could* happen."

"I know," he said, kneeling down beside her. Evidently he thought she was still speaking of the trial. "The council is concerned, as well. George Meriwether has been keeping me abreast of the situation."

"I suppose you'll be going back to work now," Rebekah said, though deep down she dreaded the thought.

"The council can manage without me," he said. "I would rather be here."

"Here?" Had he really just said that?

Henry smiled. "George and the others are trusted men. They will do what is best for the city. Don't misunderstand me. I value my position on the council greatly, and I care deeply about what happens to the people of this city. But darling, I *love* you. *You* are more important to me."

You are more important... Her heart swelled. "So what you said about moving to Ohio was true? You have no interest in advancing politically?"

"I was offering to move for your sake. I don't want you living in a politician's shadow any longer." Earnestness was written all over his face. So was something else. Love. Pure, self-sacrificing, glorious love. "Rebekah, I once let my associations, my fear of public opinion, rule my actions. But what others may think of me now is of no consequence. My only concern is your happiness."

Suddenly it made sense. It all fit together. Everything she had been reading, everything he had said, everything she had seen. Henry wanted to give up his prestige, his power for her. It was the same in regard to Christ. He had left Heaven, allowed Himself to be nailed to a cross, had even died an agonizing death not because it was *His duty*, or because His own Father insisted on it, but because He *wanted* to do so. *He wanted to demonstrate His love for me!*

Her defenses crumbled. Tears sprang to her eyes, tears not of shame but of wonder. Henry didn't know that, however, and he immediately took her hand. "Darling, please don't cry. We don't have to go to Ohio if you don't want to do so. We could—"

"No, it's not that. It's what you said earlier."

He blinked, then handed her his handkerchief. "What exactly did I say?"

"When you were talking about the passage in the Bible... I have always thought of God the Father as a harsh tyrant, demanding His way or dispensing punishment. But He isn't like that at all, is He? He's like you."

Henry's jaw dropped. "*Me?* Oh, Rebekah, I don't think—"

"You were patient with me. You loved me even when I wanted nothing to do with you. You took your sister's children—the children of a Confederate soldier—into your home, knowing the difficulties that choice would bring. You are willing to sacrifice all that you have worked so hard for if I ask it of you."

"Rebekah, do not think too highly of me. I am a very flawed man. I struggle with even the simplest of matters." From his coat pocket he withdrew an envelope and held it out. "This came earlier for you. Fiona brought it."

Fiona? Rebekah's breath hitched. She knew who it was from.

"I didn't want to give it you because I wanted to keep you from being hurt. I considered reading it myself first, giving it to you only if the message was kind, but I did not wish you to think I *expected* to be privy to all your correspondence."

She could see how torn he was. She felt it herself. For a moment she wished he had simply burned the letter. She wished it had never come at all.

"Would you rather I read it?" he asked.

Yes, she wanted to say, for what if the words were indeed less than charitable? What if the letter was full of scolding reminders that she was a statesman's daughter, the child of the next governor, and she owed him her allegiance?

But I have a husband who loves me and a God who does, as well. Isn't it time to face my fears? My father need not control my life any longer.

However, she wasn't quite brave enough yet to forge through on her own. She looked at Henry. "Will you read it with me?"

Henry's chest swelled. The feeling of pride her request evoked was tempered only by the circumstances in which it had been asked. Neither of them knew what was in the letter, but they would face it together, as husband and wife. He again took Rebekah's hand.

"Come with me to the study," he said, gently pulling her to her feet.

Rebekah rose willingly but after two steps froze. "What about Kathleen?"

"She'll be all right. We'll ask Sadie to look after her."

The young maid was in the hall, feather duster in hand, when he and Rebekah stepped inside. "Sadie, would you mind keeping an eye on Kathleen in the garden for a few moments?" Henry asked.

"Yes, sir."

"We won't be long," Rebekah added.

The maid hurried off. Henry steered Rebekah to the

study. She had spoken cheerfully to Sadie, but he could feel the tremble of her hand as she leaned on his arm. Reaching the room, Rebekah stopped in front of his desk. She stared at the envelope but did not reach for it.

Henry picked up the letter opener from the desk and sliced through the paper. The tension between his shoulder blades eased somewhat as he perused the page. "It's from your mother," he said, and the first line contained an apology.

"My mother?" Rebekah claimed the page and began to read aloud. "'Dear Rebekah, First I must tell you how sorry I was to hear that you were ill. Your husband informed us readily of the case.'"

She stopped and looked up. "You did?"

"I thought they should know."

Nodding in agreement, she returned to the letter. "'I wished to come to you but could not for fear of your brothers then taking ill, as well. I hope you will understand. I was greatly relieved to receive your husband's second letter, not only to learn you were improving but also because I took the communication as a sign of Providence.'"

Rebekah's jaw dropped. Henry's did, as well. A sign of Providence?

His wife continued to read but now silently. She sank to the floor, her skirts spreading out around her like a great island. Henry's pulse quickened. Kneeling beside her, he slid his arms around her.

"What is it, darling? What's wrong?"

"Nothing."

Nothing? Tears were now trickling down her face.

"This letter reveals a side to my mother that I hadn't known existed," she said.

"How so?"

Rebekah handed it to him. Henry read quickly.

> Your husband's letters gave me courage to be-
> lieve that my lack of intrusion in your marital ar-
> rangement was indeed the right course of action.
> I hope you will forgive me for such. I assure you,
> I was not as indifferent to your future as it might
> have seemed.

Not indifferent? He read further.

> While your father's motives for arranging this
> marriage were based solely on what he intended
> to gain from it, I sincerely believed you capable
> of finding contentment with Henry Nash. Though
> I might have kept silent where your father's deci-
> sion was concerned, I had pleaded your case be-
> fore the Lord for many years. I prayed that God
> would send you a considerate husband, one to
> protect you, guide you, give you opportunity to
> grow and experience life in a way not possible in
> this household.

Henry was stunned.

> I believe God has answered my prayers. He
> has given you a man who truly cares for you. It
> is evident in the words he writes and his effort to
> ease a mother's concern. I remember how fright-
> ened you were about becoming a bride. Have no
> fear, child. If you have not already done so, give

Henry your whole heart. I am confident that you will be well cared for.

He didn't know what to say, for he could not even begin to grasp the implication of her words. Her mother had prayed for a man who would care for her? *And God answered her request?* He looked at his wife. She was glowing.

"Henry, think of it. We were not brought together by political maneuvering, but by the Creator of the universe Himself!"

The thought was both humbling and thrilling at the same time. Moving into his arms, Rebekah rested her head against his pounding chest. "My mother might not have known how to express love to her children in a demonstrative way," she said, "but it was indeed there."

"It *is* there," he said, "and to think that God would know all of the mistakes we would make…all of our failures and fears…"

"And yet He used them to bring about something beautiful."

He squeezed her a little tighter. How soft she was, how warm. How perfectly they fit together.

"Such forgiveness, such love," Rebekah breathed. "It compels me to offer the same."

He knew what she meant, and he marveled over her faith. "Your father," he said simply.

She looked up at him, her eyes as captivating as the open sky. "I know now part of the reason I couldn't bring myself to trust you was that I harbor resentment toward him."

"That's understandable, darling. And you're not the only one who is angry with him. I am, as well. I'm angry for how he treated you all these years, how he hurt you, how he *still* hurts you." He paused and drew in a weighty breath. "But I know I must forgive him, as well, just as I've had to forgive my own father for the wrongs he has done."

"It's difficult, isn't it?"

"It is, but I know if I don't, I won't be able to be the kind of father to Grace and Kathleen, the kind of husband *to you*, that God wants me to be."

"Forgiveness isn't something we must do on our own."

He smiled at her. "No, it isn't. We have each other, and God is with us. He will help us."

Rebekah nodded contemplatively.

"I should have asked you long before," Henry said, "but will you pray with me?"

Like clouds, nervousness darkened her eyes. He felt a little vulnerable, as well. Aside from at the table for meals, they had never prayed together before, and this time they weren't asking for a blessing over the food. This time they'd be bearing undisclosed, intimate thoughts before each other and God. Henry offered her his hand. When Rebekah laid hers in his and his fingers closed around it, the feeling was unlike anything he had ever felt before.

"Thank You, Lord, for Your forgiveness. Thank You for loving us in spite of our weaknesses and failures. Please give us the ability to trust You. Help us not to be afraid of the future. Give us the grace to forgive."

When he fell silent, Rebekah lifted her own prayer. Her voice was timid but heartfelt. "Thank You for my husband, Lord. Thank You for bringing us together. Help me to be a forgiving person... Help me to forgive my father, so that Henry and I might have a new beginning."

Henry couldn't resist opening his eyes and looking at her.

She was gazing at him. "I love you," she whispered.

They were the most beautiful words he had ever heard, from the most beautiful woman he had ever seen. Oh, how he wanted to kiss her.

"Please…" she whispered.

Henry grinned. He didn't have to be asked twice. Cupping her face, he let his mouth find hers.

Rebekah sat on the study floor, nestled in her husband's arms. Her heart was pounding. Her legs were numb from being folded so long beneath her, but she did not want this moment to end, ever. The sound of footsteps, however, echoed in the hall. Henry drew back as Kathleen ambled into the room.

Rebekah stifled a laugh at the sight of the little girl. Her dress was covered in dirt. So was most of her face and hands.

"Why are you sitting on the floor?" Kathleen asked.

Rebekah could feel the color rise to her cheeks. She didn't know whether to let loose the laugh or look away in embarrassment. She felt so giddy, so light.

"We felt like sitting here," Henry said simply.

"Why?"

"Just because. Haven't you ever felt like doing something *just because*?"

"Yes," Kathleen said, and with a giggle of her own she hit the floor, rolled and landed in a heap before them. Henry pulled her up onto his lap.

Rebekah brushed away some of the dirt from her face. "Did you find any inchworms?" she asked.

"I did." She held up five fingers. "This many."

"I see Aunt Rebekah has taught you mathematics, as well." Henry then chuckled. "You did leave the worms outside, didn't you? Sadie wouldn't appreciate it very much if she found them in your pocket when she washes your dress."

"I put them all inside the lilies so when the flowers close up tonight, the worms will have a good place to sleep."

"Speaking of sleep," Rebekah said. "I believe a bath and a nap are in order."

Kathleen's streaked face twisted with a whine. "Do I have to?"

"If you wish to remain healthy, then yes."

Sadie had apparently been of the same mind, for she appeared in the doorway. "I've drawn water for her," she said.

Henry gave Kathleen an encouraging pat on the leg. "Go on, now."

The girl rolled reluctantly from his lap. Rebekah started to assist, but her legs wouldn't quite cooperate. Trying to stand, she stumbled. Henry caught her squarely in his arms.

"Let Sadie see to her today," he said. "You should rest, as well."

Rebekah had no desire to argue. In one swift movement, Henry lifted her from the floor. She giggled.

"I believe I require only *a little* assistance, sir."

"Perhaps, madam," he said in a most formal tone, "but I should rather offer you much."

Rebekah spent the rest of the afternoon in leisure.

She napped. She reread her mother's letter and did a little sewing for the Freedmen's Bureau, but mostly she thought about the days to come.

On Sunday morning she dressed Kathleen and plaited her hair. Rebekah then donned her nicest day dress and slid a few freshly cut flowers that Henry had brought her from the garden into her short brown curls. Strong enough to descend the stairs on her own power, she joined him in the dining room for breakfast.

"Good morning, ladies," he said, kissing both of them on the cheek. "Don't you each look lovely?"

Worship services that morning consisted of Bible reading in the parlor. Henry read from the book of Romans. Afterward the three of them joined hands in prayer. Rebekah had trouble focusing on his words. She was too busy drinking in the sound of his voice, the feel of his strong but gentle hand as it grasped hers. Knowing one of equal strength and protection held Kathleen's, Rebekah couldn't help but smile.

God had given her not only what she had long dreamed of for herself but also what she had hoped to find for Grace and Kathleen. He had given them a place of safety, a man who thought more of their security than he did his own. God had given them a home full of love.

That night Henry carried a sleeping Kathleen up the staircase. Rebekah tucked the blankets about her after he laid her on her pillow. Dark eyelashes fanned out upon her pale skin. Her pert little pink mouth twitched slightly.

"Have you ever seen anything more beautiful?" Rebekah asked.

"Besides her and her soon-returning baby sister?" he

asked. "Only one thing." The smile that parted Henry's lips told her exactly what he thought that thing was.

Rebekah could feel herself blushing all the way from the roots of her brown hair to the soles of her feet. Taking his hand, she urged him back to the hallway.

"Henry, about Ohio..."

"You don't want to go," he said, but he was still smiling.

"I don't."

Not wanting to wake Kathleen, Rebekah motioned toward her room. "I'm concerned about what effect such a move would have on the children," she said. "Kathleen is only now truly becoming accustomed to this house, and with Grace having been away from us..."

"I've thought of that, as well," he said. "I just want you and the girls to be safe, to be happy."

"I know you do, and I appreciate your willingness to make such a sacrifice. But I want to stay, and I don't think you should give up your position on the city council."

His eyebrow arched. "You don't?"

"Your work is *important*. No one knows what will happen if the conspirators' sentences are carried out. The people of Baltimore need a person they can trust to represent them fairly and justly, especially in times like these. You are an honorable man, Henry, a true public servant. I believe you can make a difference in this city."

Perhaps it was just her imagination, but he seemed to stand a little taller. "Thank you, darling. I want to do so, but more important, I want to make a difference in my own family."

"You already have."

There was a long pause. Rebekah watched as Henry

drew in a contemplative breath. "Are you certain this is what you want?"

"I am," she said. "I am happy. I am loved, and so are our children."

Moving closer, he ran his hand gently through her curls. Rebekah felt her heart quicken.

"I do have one other reason for wanting to remain in Baltimore," she said.

"What's that?"

"The Freedmen's Bureau. You once told me that the council was looking into opportunities to promote education. That volunteers were needed to teach former slaves how to read and write."

Guessing where she was going with this, he smiled. "I think you would be wonderful teacher. You have already proven it with Kathleen."

Her confidence soared. "Truly?"

"Absolutely. I am so proud of you."

Like a bee captivated by a flower, Rebekah moved fully into his arms. *Ours is not to be a loveless marriage... Our union is different.*

She and Henry were bound together as husband and wife, not only by their vows before God but also now by their thoughts, their fears, their dreams, their hearts.

"I love you," Henry said, his breath warm in her ear. Yielding, Rebekah lifted her face to him.

Her husband placed a gentle kiss on her lips. Then, drawing her closer, kissed her longer, more certainly. Her heart was pounding, her hands trembling, but Rebekah let him lead her to a place that, up until this moment, she had only imagined.

Epilogue

September 12, 1865

As the hazy days of summer stretched toward fall, the city of Baltimore slipped slowly back into a slumberous pace. Henry returned to City Hall. The civil unrest expected by many following the execution of Mary Surratt and her fellow conspirators did not arise. Union and rebel soldiers alike made their way back home, some to public celebrations, others to private, but no less joyful, reunions with loved ones. Business shifted from wartime concerns to peacetime prosperity. The people of Maryland began to put the horrors of war behind them.

Theodore Van der Geld mounted his campaign for governor, but without the assistance of his son-in-law. Seeking him out one afternoon following Rebekah's recovery, Henry promised he would pray for the man but told him he would not lend any political support. Henry did not specifically bring his treatment of Rebekah into the conversation, but he was confident he had made his point when he told the man, politely but firmly, "My wife and I wish to maintain contact with you, but please do not visit our home again unless I am present."

Unfortunately, Van der Geld said he did not wish to have any contact with him or his daughter. Susan Van der Geld, however, was a different matter. Following her mother's letter, Rebekah had corresponded with one of her own. Their relationship was growing. The two women had met on several occasions, in the public gardens or in Rebekah's home. Mrs. Van der Geld often brought along her youngest son, Joseph, to play with Kathleen.

When Rebekah was not engaged in family matters, she and the girls could usually be found at the Freedmen's Bureau. Kathleen practiced her letters and numbers alongside a group of former slaves while Rebekah taught them to read and write. Grace bounced and wiggled in her baby carriage as she watched the proceedings.

Every afternoon, Henry hurried home from City Hall to be with his family. Kathleen always met him at the door with a hug and a recounting of the lessons she had learned that day. Today, though, she told a different story. "Dr. Stanton came to visit."

Henry blinked. *Dr. Stanton?* "Are you feeling all right?"

"I'm not sick," she said, and as proof, she quickly scampered off.

Rebekah appeared in the parlor doorway. Henry went to her immediately and kissed her. "Are you well? Kathleen said Dr. Stanton was here."

"I'm perfectly fine," she assured him. "Or, rather, Dr. Stanton says *we* are perfectly fine."

He blinked again. "We?"

Taking his hand, she laid it gently upon her middle. His pulse quickened at once. "Y-you mean?"

She nodded and smiled.

"Oh, darling!" Moving to embrace her, he stopped just short of doing so.

Rebekah laughed heartily. "It's all right, Henry. I won't break."

With a chuckle of his own, he then drew her close, their breath becoming one and the same.

"Do you know how happy I am?" she whispered.

"Do you know how much I love you?"

Rebekah lifted her head and grinned. The kiss she gave him made Henry feel as though he were the richest, most powerful man in the world.

* * * * *

Dear Reader,

Thank you for choosing *The Reluctant Bridegroom*, the fourth story in my Civil War series. I hope you enjoyed Henry and Rebekah's tale.

Recently, my husband and I celebrated our twenty-second wedding anniversary. We couldn't help but reflect on the past. The disagreements and innocent misunderstandings of those early years make for laughable stories now, but back then...oh boy! We've had our share of good times and bad, of blessing and loss. Both of us agreed the secret to our enduring union was an abiding faith in Christ and a good sense of humor.

May you be blessed with both, as well.

By His grace,
Shannon Farrington

COMING NEXT MONTH FROM
Love Inspired® Historical

Available June 7, 2016

PONY EXPRESS HERO
Saddles and Spurs
by Rhonda Gibson

Pony Express rider Jacob Young sets out to search for his birth mother, but instead he discovers his orphaned five-year-old half sister and her pretty guardian, Lilly Johnson. And when he figures out that someone's trying to hurt them, he vows to be their protector.

BRIDE BY ARRANGEMENT
Cowboy Creek
by Karen Kirst

On the run from a dangerous man, widow Grace Longstreet is determined to protect her twin daughters—even if it means pretending she's the mail-order bride Sheriff Noah Burgess's friends secretly arranged for him. But can their blossoming relationship survive her deception?

ONCE MORE A FAMILY
by Lily George

In order to bring his young daughter home, Texas rancher Jack Burnett needs a wife—but he won't marry for love again. And an arranged marriage to penniless socialite Ada Westmore will benefit them both...if she can survive life on the prairie.

A NANNY FOR KEEPS
Boardinghouse Betrothals
by Janet Lee Barton

After widowed Sir Tyler Walker's daughters run off their latest nanny, he hires the schoolteacher next door as a short-term replacement. But when Sir Tyler and his two little girls fall for Georgia Marshall, will the temporary arrangement become permanent?

LIHCNM0516

REQUEST YOUR FREE BOOKS!

2 FREE INSPIRATIONAL NOVELS
PLUS 2 *FREE* MYSTERY GIFTS

Love Inspired HISTORICAL

LIHI5

SPECIAL EXCERPT FROM

Love Inspired HISTORICAL

*A mail-order bride seeks a fresh start for herself and
her twin daughters with a small-town Kansas sheriff—
but will she lose it all when her secret is revealed?*

Read on for a sneak preview of
BRIDE BY ARRANGEMENT,
the exciting conclusion to the series
COWBOY CREEK.

"Make another move, and I'll shoot you where you
stand…" He trailed off, jaw sagging. Had he entered the
wrong house?

"Don't shoot! I can explain! I—I have a letter. From
Will Canfield." A petite dark-haired woman standing on the
other side of his table lifted an envelope in silent entreaty.

At the mention of his friend's name, he slowly lowered
his weapon. But his defensive instincts still surged
through him. When he didn't speak, she gestured limply
to the ornate leather trunks stacked on either side of his
bedroom door. "Mr. Canfield was supposed to meet us at
the station. His porter arrived in his stead… Simon was
his name. He said something about a posse and outlaws."
A delicate shudder shook her frame. "He said you
wouldn't mind if we brought these inside. I do apologize
for invading your home like this, but I had no idea when
you would return, and it is June out there."

Her gaze roamed his face, her light brown eyes
widening ever so slightly as they encountered his scars.
It was like this every time. He braced himself for the

inevitable disgust. Pity. Revulsion. Told himself again it didn't matter.

When her expression reflected nothing more than curiosity, irrational anger flooded him.

"What are you doing in my home?" he snapped. "How do you know Will?"

"I'm Constance Miller. I'm the bride Mr. Canfield sent for."

"Will's already got a wife."

Pink kissed her cheekbones. "Not for him. For you."

His throat closed. He wouldn't have.

"I was summoned to Cowboy Creek to be your bride. Your friend didn't tell you." A sharp crease brought her brows together.

"I'm afraid not." Slipping off his worn Stetson, Noah hooked it on the chair and dipped his head toward the crumpled parchment. "May I?"

Miss Miller didn't appear inclined to approach him, so he laid his gun on the mantel and crossed to the square table. He took the envelope she extended across to him and slipped the letter free. The handwriting was unmistakable. Heat climbed up his neck as he read the description of himself. He stuffed it back inside and tossed it onto the tabletop. "I'm afraid you've come all the way out here for nothing. The trip was a waste, Miss Miller. I am not, nor will I ever be, in the market for a bride."

Don't miss
BRIDE BY ARRANGEMENT
by Karen Kirst, available June 2016 wherever
Love Inspired® Historical books and ebooks are sold.

www.LoveInspired.com

Reading Has Its Rewards

Earn **FREE BOOKS!**

Register at **Harlequin My Rewards** and submit your Harlequin purchases from wherever you shop to earn points for free books and other exclusive rewards.

Plus submit your purchases from now till May 30th for a chance to win a $500 Visa Card*.

Visit **HarlequinMyRewards.com** today

MYR16R1